LIGHT GUARDIAN

BOOK 2 IN THE LIGHT RUNNER SERIES

By Philip Brown

LIGHT GUARDIAN
© 2021 by Philip Brown
All Rights Reserved

ISBN 978-0-9831589-3-6

Caduceus picture by VectorStock

Illustrations by Rita Mirambeau

For my mother,
who opened worlds of imagination

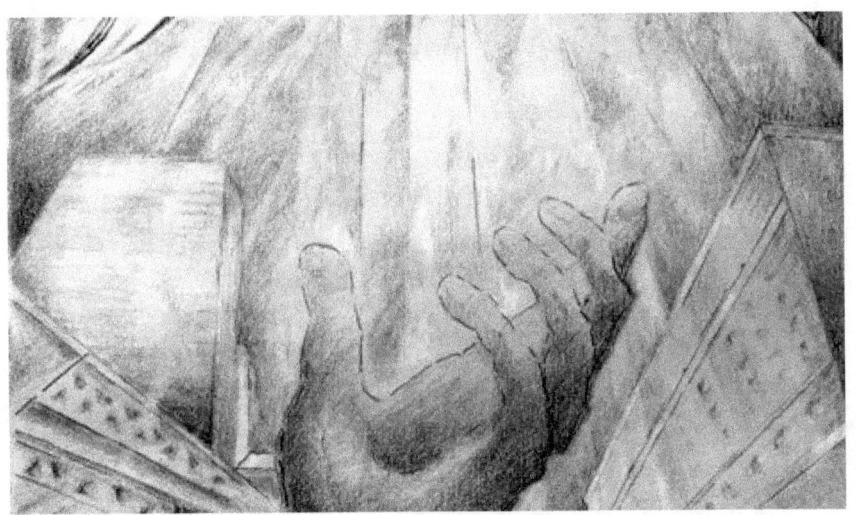

CHAPTER 1

One moment—darkness.

The next—eyes flutter open, cheek pressed against verdant coolness. She stares at the ground, fresh grass trembling with each exhalation. Blades quiver.

Alive.

At least that.

Out of the corner of one eye . . . a picnic table.

Discordant voices break through.

"She opened her eyes. Hey, Dara!"

"Must have been knocked out when she hit the ground."

"Has she still got the armband? . . . Don't see it."

". . . just moved. You okay?"

Dara squints against a blinding light, catches sight of the cliff edge above. On the brink, there'd been some kind of a . . . a struggle.

Her wrist tingles, can't lift her head. Rising sense of panic. Moves her fingers, cries out when a sharp bolt of pain shoots up one arm.

Shuffle and thump of footsteps on the ground next to her. More bright lights. Shouting from all directions.

"Dara!'

"Healer girl! Dara!"

A dog's tongue licks her face. Cold nose, warm breath against her cheek. "Hey, boy." Piercing pain when she reaches up to pet him forces her to gently place her arm back down on the grass.

Someone yanks Linc from her side, and he lets out a distressed whimper.

"It's okay. I've got him." Diego's voice. "The ambulance guys are here. It's okay."

A paramedic grunts, two sets of arms shift Dara onto a gurney and roll it over rough contours of the picnic field toward a red light which slowly strobes through the darkness.

Dad walks beside her, holding her not-numb hand, and she hears Linc's panting as the dog trots alongside.

"Careful," Dad says.

Not sure if he's speaking to her—or someone else.

"Almost to the ambulance," Diego says, then to someone in the pressing crowd: "You're too close. Give her some room."

"Everyone—stay back!" another man commands, then to Dara, "You're gonna be okay, darlin'."

Glimpse of salt-and-pepper beard, two red stripes down a man's shirt. A tall, thin woman in black stands next to him.

The gurney pushes through the crowd, and cell phone cameras flash.

"Wait right there!" The man with red stripes—pair of red suspenders, Dara now sees, taut over large beer belly. "We gotta put her into this SUV here," he says. "She's not goin' in the ambulance."

"She's injured," one of the paramedics says. "Who are you?"

The man in suspenders flashes an ID badge. "Afraid you're gonna have to stand down. I'll take the little sweetheart from here." He muscles forward to stand between the gurney and the ambulance.

"I don't care who you are," the paramedic says. "We've got a job to do, and this patient is ours. Move."

Dara's father lets go of her hand, takes several steps toward the red suspenders. "You heard the man," her dad says, inches from the man's face. "Get out of our way."

Red suspenders steps back to survey the crowd, waves someone over. He reaches down a beefy arm toward Dara. "I *said* she's comin' with us."

"Don't you dare touch her," Dad says, his voice low, menacing.

Linc growls, pulls hard at his restraint.

"Easy, boy!" Diego says, holding the dog back.

A sharp warning bark from Linc, another growl, teeth bared at the man's large belly.

Several black-and-whites, lights flashing, pull up beside the ambulance.

The man steps back, forced aside by the two paramedics who slide the gurney into the ambulance and secure it. Again, Dara catches a glimpse of the slender woman who stands near the red suspenders.

The man turns to Dara's father and speaks softly. "You have no idea what a big mistake you just made. You better watch it. Don't forget, you're still AWOL."

Dad gets in the ambulance beside Dara, neck muscles tight as he looks back at the picnic field. His eyes scan the crowd.

"Where's Diego?" she asks.

"With his dad. They'll follow us."

"And Linc?"

"Diego's got him."

"Let's get this girl to the hospital," a paramedic says, one hand supporting her wrist.

The siren wails, and the tires bounce over the picnic field until they hit asphalt, then the vehicle speeds into the night.

***

Rushed into the emergency room, lifted from gurney onto narrow hospital bed. Privacy curtain whisks. Blur of white coats, footsteps, sharp beeps, rapid hands fussing on her body. Squawk of police radios.

"We've got Johnson in charge of crowd control outside the ER," someone says.

"What day of the week is it?" a white coat asks her.

"No idea."

"How many fingers am I holding up?"

"Three"—squinting—"no . . . two."

"How old are you?"

"I'm"—wasn't her birthday coming up soon?—or maybe she'd missed it, and it had flown right by—"sixteen . . . I think."

"That's a roger," her dad says.

The urgent press of doctors and nurses closes in around the ER bed, and she loses sight of her dad.

"Dad! Stay with me!"

An authoritative voice from the other side of the curtain: "It needs to go . . . I don't care, unless that's a seeing eye dog—no service animals, period."

"Diego?" Dara calls.

"I'll be right outside, Dar." Diego's voice.

Yelling close by. Loud voices, banging against a door.

More rapid footsteps.

The curtain swishes open. A Black man with a thin mustache pushes the bed out of the ER, through double doors, down a corridor. He's dressed in civvies, earpiece attached to a device in his pocket.

"Where's my dad?" Dara asks. "And Diego?"

"Don't know," the man says. "You're being airlifted out of here." Pushes the bed through another set of double doors, increases the pace until he's running down a corridor.

Dara raises her head and a sharp jolt of pain shoots down her arm. Several men in black suits and dark glasses surround the bed, while a doctor wearing light green scrubs rushes in front of the small entourage. Dara drops her head back onto the pillow, and glances to the right where a woman's castanet heels click on the linoleum. The woman keeps pace beside her, carrying an attaché case.

"Where are you taking me?" Dara asks.

The group pushes the hospital bed into an elevator, ascends, wheels through more doors, and through one last set of double doors. They emerge next to a rooftop heliport. A gust of cool air sweeps over Dara in the darkness. The men in suits lift her onto a stretcher and into the waiting helicopter. Only the doctor and the woman with the attaché case board with her.

"Where's my dad?"

No answer.

She tries to swallow, but her mouth is dry. Her chest trembles.

The helicopter takes off, tilts forward, straightens. As heavy rotors whip the air, it clears the roofline, ferrying her—with a wrist she knows must be broken—across a dark, moonless sky.

CHAPTER 2

Groggy, Dara's head rests on soft pillows.

Antiseptic smell.

Dad sits beside the bed.

"Your wrist is broken in several places." Another white lab coat, speaking from near the bed.

Squinting to make out the name above the breast pocket. *Doctor . . . Heavens? . . . Havens.*

"You're just coming out of surgery," the doctor says. "We inserted some hardware. Metal rods, screws . . ." He pauses, looks at her, and lays a hand on the plaster cast as though he wants to bless it. "You're going to be fine, but you'll have a bionic wrist." His voice sounds mildly impressed, perhaps with his own surgery. "Your spine took the brunt of the fall, nothing's broken but we're going to hold you here. Your head took a hit, too, so you've got a concussion. Can't go home yet, need to hold you for, uh, observation."

Dara can't remember exactly where her home is. A street in East Hollywood? Some place with boarded-up windows. No electricity. She'd slept there.

One of her legs lies uncovered, outside the sheets. The knee is gauze-bandaged.

Doctor Havens stares at her arm cast as though he's buried something valuable there and can't bear to take his eyes off it.

"Who—who are you?" Dara rasps, finding it difficult to form the words, her tongue heavy.

"Army doctor. Orthopedic surgeon. I was flown here especially for you— for your, uh, procedure."

"For a broken wrist?"

"Right. A broken wrist. Better not to ask a lot of questions now."

"Why?"

"See, there you go—asking a question. If I tell you too much"—conspiratorial whisper—"I might have to kill you. Like in a James Bond movie. Double-O-Seven. You'll know all the state secrets." Low laugh, a joke. "One thing—no more injuries to that wrist. Next time, you might not be so lucky. You won't be able to heal it there." He turns and leaves the room.

What did the doctor mean? Was he talking about the Jyotisha?

Her dad's hand rests on her forehead. "Broken wrist, concussion, that's not enough reason to hold you. Doesn't make sense."

Dara's wrist throbs, and when she tries to swallow, her throat is dry. "Thirsty," she whispers.

Dad hands her a cup of ice, and she glances at him. "What'd they do?" Dara touches her arm above the orange cast. Under the plaster . . . tingling.

"All I know's they fixed your wrist," her dad says. "You were in surgery for a couple of hours, and they wouldn't let me anywhere near it. Heavy security."

"Where—?" Her tongue is heavy, can't form the words she wants to say.

"A government medical facility," her dad says. "They rushed you here, said it was safer."

That wasn't it at all! Engulfed by a sinking, lost sensation, she finally gets the words out. "Where . . . is it?"

"Somewhere in the Valley." Her dad glances about uneasily.

He still doesn't understand, and her head sinks back onto the pillows.

The room smells of Mr. Clean and fresh paint. Through a window: daylight, gravel-covered rooftop.

Off to one side stands a guy she hasn't noticed before—a large man in white shirt and dark tie. Shoulder holster.

Dara looks at her dad. "Am I gonna be okay?" Her head is clearing.

He nods, smiles. "I think you'll pass muster."

"That man at the park—the one who tried to take over, in suspenders—said something about how you're still AWOL."

"I was kidnapped. That's not desertion."

"But you're free now. Could you be arrested?"

"I'm not deserting *you*, that's the point." Her dad has a three-day beard, handsome face set atop muscular shoulders. Sinewy muscles ripple when he moves his arms. Sandy blond hair grown longer over the past few months, tucked behind his ears. "You're the most important one right now, so don't worry about the Navy—or anything else."

Something wells up inside, and Dara presses back against the tide of anger and confusion that threatens to overwhelm her. She's struck by the silence, punctuated by low voices outside the room. "Who's outside?"

Her dad drops his voice "FBI. Homeland security."

"For me?"

Or an armband she no longer has.

"There was a lot going on at the hospital," Dad continues, "but it seemed like the crowd wasn't the only reason they wanted to get you out of there."

"Where—where's Mercy?" Ice cube clicking against her teeth.

Had Mercy managed to wrest the Jyotisha away—and escape through a crowd of police while viewed by a national TV audience? How would that be possible? It must have been taken by someone else. Police, maybe. Or government dudes in suits.

"We don't know yet. Now . . . someone wants to ask you some questions." Dad pushes his chair back from the bed. "Tried to hold him off as long as I could."

She looks from her dad to the man wearing the shoulder holster. "Who's he?"

8

Dad nods at the man, who introduces himself—"Johnson, FBI"—and moves next to her bed. He has a thick face and close buzz cut, like a Marine.

"It's okay." Her dad locks eyes with hers and gives Dara a slight nod. "They have to do this, promised it wouldn't take long."

The FBI agent sets down a small recording device on the bedside tray and pulls up a chair on the other side, opposite Dad. "I know you've been through hell and back," he says. "But you seem like a strong girl. I've seen kids come through some pretty rough stuff and do okay."

Her wrist itches, as though it's been asleep, the blood flowing again.

Johnson's face is beefy and pock-marked, but his voice is the opposite. Gentle, soothing. He pauses, as though not wanting to rush her into anything. "Mind if I ask a few questions?" He pulls several index cards from a pocket.

"Go." Just get it over with.

He presses a button on the recording device. "How did you come to know this girl—Mercy?"

Dara hesitates. "I didn't really *know* her. I just—found her."

"What do you mean, 'found her'?" the agent asks, narrowing his eyes.

"In the cage—I mean, cave. She's"—Dara can't focus on her own words, and her mind wanders to the scene at the Old Zoo—"related to me." She tries to mentally connect the dots, but the line wavers.

The agent nods, as though this is all common knowledge. "There was a cave, behind the house on Wonderland, we know about that." He looks down at one of the index cards in his hand. "Exactly how was Mercy related to you?"

Dara's mind is knotted in confusion, partly from the anesthesia but also from double meanings of some of the words. *Know. Related.*

"Where's the armband?" she asks. The only thing that really matters now.

Dad opens his mouth to speak, but Johnson motions for him to be silent.

The gesture annoys Dara.

Ignoring her question about the armband, Johnson leans forward in his chair, glances at the recording device. "What can you tell us about Gunarik Miller?" His voice sounds higher, stressed.

"He tried to kill me." She remembers that.

Dara closes her eyes, tries to shut out the scene that plays in her mind: a rusted lion's cage, a struggle, and a broken bottle neck jammed into Gunarik's stomach.

Dad leans over, whispers to the FBI man.

"Okay." Johnson lets out a sigh. "We can talk more later."

Whispers. Gentle whoosh and rustle of a curtain drawn across the window. The light dims. She drifts into unconsciousness.

***

When Dara opens her eyes, Johnson is gone—but there's someone else, a female figure she can't make out, standing at the foot of the bed.

Dara senses the woman has watched her as she slept.

"Dad?" Where is he? "Dad!"

"It's okay." The woman steps closer into Dara's field of vision.

"It's not okay. Where did he go?"

"Your father's right outside." The woman nods toward the door.

"I need him here, with me."

"And what *I* need is to speak with you. This is extremely urgent. Believe me, your father would be right by your side—except that someone with a lot more authority than mine asked him to stand down."

"Who—who are you?" Dara asks, then draws a sharp intake of breath as the recognition hits. "Wait—I've seen you before!" The woman from the helicopter. Castanet heels.

"I'm Rachel."

Late twenties. Blue pantsuit, white scarf, ponytail. She grips a large manila envelope.

"Are you a cop?" Dara asks. "Or FBI?"

"No." Rachel offers a slight smile. "And there's no need to be alarmed." Rachel places the envelope on the hospital tray. She fishes in her pocket, opens a small tin with one hand, and offers Dara a mint. A peace offering.

Dara shakes her head. She shifts the plaster cast on support pillows. Her wrist tingles.

Rachel sets down the tin and, pops a mint into her mouth. She flips open a wallet, flashes a badge. Dara catches a last name: Findley. "I'm with the federal government, and you're in a government hospital." The wallet smacks closed. "You're under protection right now, federal agents are all around the perimeter of the hospital. This wing is totally isolated, all access routes controlled. Several officers are posted outside the door to your room, and your father's right there. No worries, okay?" She shoots Dara a questioning look.

Dara nods, looks closer at Rachel. A memory crashes over her like a wave. "At the house where I was staying, men wearing suits . . . My dad and I saw them go inside the house, and we both—my dog, too—we ran. Were you there—in that house?"

Rachel considers her for a moment before speaking. "They told me you were sharp, even with a concussion. It wasn't what you think, okay? We were moving in to protect you. But . . . yes, we found the house."

"How?"

"We knew you were near a hospital—a fading siren when you did the TV interview from there—with boarded-up windows that showed up on camera. Once we ran down some of the other incidents, we figured you were in Hollywood or mid-Wilshire. Not that hard to find a boarded-up house near a hospital. We tried to get to you first. Might have saved you a lot of grief."

"Why were you looking for me if you're not a cop?"

"Interesting question." Rachel pulls up a chair and sits by the bed, looks at Dara with raised eyebrows. "You had the elem—I mean, the . . . Jy-o-teesha. That's how you pronounce it?"

"That's right. *Had* the Jyotisha."

"In the press, social media, TV, they call it the Lightband. We're going to find it."

Dara's good hand tightens around the bedsheet. "Does Mercy have it?"

"We—we're not sure," Rachel says.

"What do you mean? The whole thing was broadcast on live TV."

"She managed to get away," Rachel says.

"But there were a ton of cops and news helicopters at Griffith Park when it happened." Dara stares at Rachel in disbelief.

"There are underground tunnels," Rachel explains, "once used by zookeepers, and apparently that's how Mercy managed to escape into the surrounding brush. She used the armband as a way of holding people back, defending herself. She's gone, and we're trying to find her before—"

"Before what?" Dara asks, heart pounding.

"Before she causes more damage."

The flash of painful memory again. This time the entire scene plays out in Dara's mind. Vadoma had knelt over Gunarik, her fallen son. At the precipice's brink, a struggle to get the Jyotisha. Mercy managed to wrest the armband away. And then the pain. Diego clutching his stomach, Linc whimpering. Dara on the ground, holding a throbbing knee as blood oozed through her jeans. Mercy must have pushed Dara over the edge of the cliff.

"We need to talk about this." Rachel pulls the manila envelope off the hospital tray and onto her lap. "Griffith Park, I mean. Something happened there—and at least once before."

"Yeah? Really?" Anger surges through her. "Where's Diego?"

"Who?"

"My friend."

Rachel nods. "Of course. The one you healed on YouTube."

As if she didn't know, Dara thinks.

"The hundred-million-views video," Rachel adds.

Diego had been by her side the whole time, and now—gone. She can still feel his lips against hers, that last kiss on the precipice in Griffith Park. "Where. Is. He."

"He's being, uh, questioned," Rachel replies. "Or perhaps 'debriefed' is better."

Dara wonders what that means—_debriefed_—and a chill runs through her. "What about Linc?"

Rachel throws her a questioning look. "You mean—"

"My dog!"

"He'll be given to a rescue outfit. I'm sure he'll be fine."

Dara's good hand grips the sheet tight. She's just skateboarded into a brick wall.

"I know you two were close," Rachel says. "That dog stayed by your side, and I wouldn't be surprised if thousands want to adopt him. Who wouldn't want 'Dara's dog'?"

"What? No!" Dara sits up, swings both legs over the side of the bed. Is this Rachel's idea of reassurance? "You can't give him away!"

"He wasn't yours to begin with," Rachel says. "A stray. You said so yourself, on TV. We're hoping that with all the publicity the rightful owner—"

"You get me Linc—now!" Dara raises her cast.

Rachel scoots her chair back from the bed.

The cast clunks down against Dara's thigh.

Rachel speaks soothingly to Dara. "Don't worry about Linc. All I want is to ask you a few questions."

"You want to know more? Fine. Get me Linc and Diego. I won't talk until they're both here."

Rachel looks at Dara as though assessing her anew, runs a hand over her ponytail, then sighs. "Give me a minute." She pulls a cell phone from her jacket pocket and types. Moments later, she looks up at Dara. "They're going to hold Linc for you, until you can see him."

"What does that mean—and who are 'they'?"

"Your dog's with an experienced police canine handler, and nothing further is going to happen to him."

"Bring him here."

Rachel stares at Dara, nods, types again.

Silence.

Rachel looks up from her phone. "In a couple of hours, Linc will be here."

"What about Diego?"

"We can't do anything while he's being interviewed. They'll let me know as soon as that's done. Now—can we talk?"

"No." Dara's heart races, and her cheeks grow hot. "I told you I want Linc and Diego here right now. Quit stalling."

Rachel purses her lips, gives Dara a hard stare. "Time is running short. For the moment, you're protected, but bad people want what you have—I mean, had—and they're coming for you. You need to let everything—and everyone—else go right now."

Dara returns Rachel's glare. "If what I have to say is so important, you'll do what I want. Linc. Diego. Get them now."

Rachel lets out a deep breath, taps at her iPhone, holds it so the screen faces Dara. "Here."

With her good hand, Dara takes the phone. A message on the screen reads *Connecting*.

A man in a police uniform appears on the screen. He sits in an office with certificates and commendations lining the wall, photo of a German Shepherd visible over his shoulder. Peering closer into his own screen: "Doctor Findley?"

Was Rachel a doctor?

"No, this is Dara." Her heart beats faster. In the tiny image in a corner of the screen: her face, gauze wrapped around her forehead

"Wow, it's you." Pause. "Hey there. I'm Maginty. Mag. You look"— peering at her—"like you've been through stuff. How you doing?"

"Do you have Linc?"

Mag flips the Facetime setting, swivels the screen.

There he is—Linc!—sprawled on the linoleum floor, gnawing on a bone, water bowl set nearby.

"Linc!" Dara screams.

The dog drops the bone and looks toward the screen.

Mag holds it closer to Linc.

Linc stares into the lens.

Dara takes in his eyes, the muzzle, wolf-gray fur. "Linc!" she yells once more, wishes she could reach a hand through the cell phone, dig her fingers into his soft coat.

Mag pulls back for a fuller view.

Linc barks once and rises, steps toward the camera.

The officer flips it back to selfie mode. His badge glints. "Beautiful animal."

"Are you bringing him here, to me?"

"I can be there in a couple of hours." Mag smiles. "Your amazing little demonstration in Griffith Park created a mountain of paperwork on our end, just finishing that up. By the way, what you did . . ." His voice trails off. He reverses the Facetime mode again so Dara can see Linc. "I'm taking good care of him. It's an honor. See you in a couple of hours, okay?"

The connection ends, and Dara hands the phone back to Rachel. A huge weight lifts. Everything might, just might, be okay again, the way it was before . . . before her world crashed. Linc, her dad, Diego. The four of them.

"I'm sorry but I can't do the same with Diego," Rachel says. "On that one, you're just going to have to trust me. Diego is helping us. This is also a kidnapping case—Gunarik held Mercy in that cave, in addition to forcefully imprisoning your dad—and there's a dead body up in Griffith Park."

"Diego had nothing to do with that. That's on me—self-defense."

"We know. But Diego helped to hold back the crowd that surged up there, plus he was with you almost from the beginning. He's not in any trouble. None. As soon as he's done, I'll make sure he's brought here, to your side." She puts a hand on Dara's cast in a gesture of reassurance.

"What happened to Vadoma? She was there, too, at the Old Zoo."

"Gunarik's mother? She's being questioned, too."

"Vadoma was good to me." She remembers the white hair flecked with gray, soft eyes. A Tarot deck. "I hope you're good to her, too." Dara lays her head back on the pillow, tension easing. "You—you're a doctor?" she asks, staring at the ceiling.

"Astrophysicist, with a specialty in metallurgy."

CHAPTER 3

Rachel leans back in her chair, straightens a pant crease above the knee, brushes a hand over the manila envelope. "What do you know about the Lightband?" Casual, no big deal.

"Let's see." Dara tries to gauge where this is going. "It's gold and silver, and floats—at least that's what it did when I first spotted the thing in the swimming pool. And, let me think . . . oh yeah, it heals."

"Any idea where it came from?" Rachel asks.

"Where are the Ural Mountains?"

"Russia." No hesitation in Rachel's answer.

"That's where it came from," Dara says. "A meteorite."

"Have you heard of the Sanskaran?"

"Doesn't mean anything to me."

"They, and you," Rachel says, "appear to have been imprinted with power from this intergalactic metal. We don't know its true origin, other than—like you say—a meteorite."

"Imprinted?"

"Genetically, like DNA. It's in your blood."

"You said 'they'. *They* were imprinted."

"There's you, Mercy, others." Rachel speaks quickly. "Have you heard of someone named Natasha, went by the nickname of Tash"—she opens the manila envelope on her lap, pulls out some papers, and consults notes—"married name would have been Miller. Wife of Ayon, who we know provided you with the, uh, material."

"Never heard of her."

Rachel raises both eyebrows, as though she hasn't expected this answer.

"Is she a Sanska—Sanskaran, too?" Dara asks.

Rachel gives her a blank look and goes back to her notes. "Do you know a girl named Rebecca Steinberg?"

This is turning into an interrogation. "Never heard of her, either."

Rachel shifts in her seat, moves in a little closer. "She—Rebecca Steinberg— was a runaway from Modesto." Her eyes narrow. "You might have known her as Becca."

Another wave of memory. Tinker Bell sleeping bag. Ragged cough in the night. *I'm gonna brag I was healed by a skater girl.*

"Tell me: what happened with Becca?" Rachel's question crackles with underlying tension. Her fingers drum on one knee.

"We were at the far edge of the park, under a tree," Dara replies. "Sometime around midnight, I used the Jyotisha—uh, the Lightband—to heal Becca's terrible cough. Afterwards, I lay on the ground, and before I fell asleep . . . I can still see it so clear in my mind . . . I watched a feather drift down through the moonlight."

"Right. The part about the healing fits with what we got from Rebecca . . . that is, Becca."

"So, that's all you want to know? What's so special about Becca? She's not the only one I used the Lightband on."

"True, there were others," Rachel says. "But that was the *only* healing that took place in a park. That is, up until the Griffith Park Old Zoo incident."

"I don't understand."

Rachel withdraws a picture from the manila envelope, hands it to Dara. "Do you recognize this place?"

Dara raises herself into a sitting position, looks intently at a color photograph of a small neighborhood park. She blinks, and the memory snaps into place. "It's . . . I spent the night there with Diego and Linc . . . and the homeless girl you mentioned. Becca."

Dara hears movement from the corridor outside her room, glimpses a man in a dark suit.

Rachel draws Dara's attention back to the photograph. "It's from Parks and Rec archives." Her voice has grown tight. "It's significant. Do you have any idea why?"

In the photo, palm trees border the park. Concrete benches, stunted trees with dusty leaves, a few bushes, brown grass. Like she's looking at a kid's picture puzzle, trying to spot the hidden animals. How did Rachel have this image? What could possibly be important about it?

"Now this one." Rachel slides another picture from the envelope and hands Dara the same scene. "Notice anything different?" She looks into Dara's face, as if to assess a reaction.

Dara takes a deep breath, wonders if the concussion is making it harder to focus. She sets the two photographs side by side on her lap. "They're watering the grass better?" But there's something there. She sees it now, repositions the newer picture under the light for a better view. "A section of the park looks much greener in the recent picture."

"And?" Rachel asks.

"The trees." Dara drops the earlier picture and stares at the newer one: the verdant leaves are lush, luminous. She picks up the older picture and studies it. Same scene, but . . . withered leaves, emaciated bushes. "Everything's so dried up in this older picture. Like the recent one's been photoshopped."

"The first photograph is file-dated a little over two years ago," Rachel says. "The second, newer photograph was taken a few days ago. Our best estimate is that you were in that park about a month ago, late July, at which time a section of a run-down little Hollywood park was transformed into an instant oasis."

"Oh."

"It was at night, so you couldn't see it at the time, but the trees and bushes next to the spot where that healing of Becca took place became incredibly, impossibly healthy and green. Bursting. That feather you remembered seeing? We believe birds have been affected by the Lightband, too, causing feathers to rapidly molt as new ones grew."

Startled by this new information, Dara closes her eyes, pictures how the Jyotisha had lit the Hollywood darkness—an all-encompassing, three hundred sixty degree immersion of light, wind, and springtime scent. Its rays reached through the night, touching brown grass, dry and mottled leaves, birds—and Becca. "How did—."

"We've been carefully reviewing your use of the Lightband," Rachel continues.

Dara, stunned by this new information, opens her eyes and stares at Rachel.

"We knew about other healings," Rachel says, "from YouTube videos and your TV appearances. But they were all indoors or on streets and alleys with minimal vegetation."

"Becca says she was going to tell everyone she was healed by 'a skater girl'."

"After she came forward," Rachel says, "we found the park."

Dara glances back at the newer photograph.

Rachel stands, faces Dara. "Last night at the Old Zoo, it became crystal clear. You probably couldn't see what happened because—again—it was dark, and things were distorted by the helicopter lights. But the Lightband didn't just heal *people* in that crowd. It also healed the grass, trees, bushes."

With a start, Dara remembers the wind that swept over the picnic field and the precipice, the gusting tree leaves that appeared bright green in the armlet's light.

"There was a barren walnut tree on the hillside," Rachel continues, "that's suddenly producing. And butterflies! They seem to be everywhere around the picnic field. That whole section of Griffith Park's been dying—pollution, drought, neglect. But where you used the Lightband it's completely restored, like a Biblical Eden. I think investigators were well aware that your armband could heal people—not to take anything away from that. But we didn't know about healing . . . everything."

A loud voice squawks from a walkie-talkie in the nearby corridor. Dara jerks her head up. Through the closed window, sounds of other voices, yelling.

"What's happening?" Dara asks.

Rachel checks her phone, concerned look on her face.

Pounding footsteps in the outside hallway.

Dara looks around the white room. "You promised me Diego and Linc. Where are they?"

Rachel taps her screen, scrolls. "Both on the way here right now."

Dara's heart soars.

Rachel holds Dara in an unwavering gaze. "We're running out of time, but there's one more thing you should know. We sent in a covert team to comb an ancient debris field in the Ural Mountains. They managed to recover a small fragment of element 120-X—the main component of the Lightband—buried under peat and soil. No more than a shard, size of a toothpick."

"So?"

"You don't need the Lightband anymore."

"Why not?" She *did* need the Jyotisha. It was hers.

"Your surgeon—Doctor Havens—is with our agency."

"What's the surgeon got to do with—?" Dara stops midsentence as the realization hits.

21

Rachel brushes a thumb over Dara's cast just above her palm.

Stunned, Dara stares at the cast, then back at Rachel.

"It's a safe place to hide it," Rachel says. "We thought since you don't have the armband anymore, it might help the healing process."

"But . . . it's smaller than the Lightband," Dara says. "Maybe it won't work."

"Let's find out. You're one of the few who has the gift." Rachel eyes Dara. "There are a number of cuts on your face, from the fight and fall from the cliff."

"I need a mirror."

Rachel rises, taps the phone camera for a selfie, and holds it in front of Dara.

Dara is taken aback by the image of her own face that fills the screen. The battle at the Old Zoo left one side bruised, eye socket purple. Cuts, small scrapes. A strip of gauze wraps around her forehead.

Rachel sets down the cell and steps back. "Let's see what happens."

Dara passes her hand in front of her face. The cast is heavy, an extra weight she carries.

Nothing.

Rachel watches, motionless.

"Again," Rachel says.

This time, the orange cast quivers, warms against Dara's skin. A glow seeps out from the cast. A bolt of electricity surges through her wrist. Her palm pinks. A breeze ruffles her hair, sweet fragrance of jasmine suffuses the room.

Dara holds her hand in front of her face. Her wrist tingles. She closes her eyes against the blinding light.

CHAPTER 4

Mulu Cave System, Borneo

Three men creep through the dark jungle, guided by an LED flashlight and moonlight. They hike for over an hour, arriving at a shallow cliff covered with dense foliage, the spot marked with a small stack of rocks. One man holds the flashlight while the other two work to push aside thick vines to reveal a cave opening.

The interior opens up onto a luminous, damp landscape of green limestone and icicle stalactites. The walls are covered with cave nectar bats, delicacies that will fetch a good price in the Indonesian markets.

The men step over piles of *guano*, thick with feasting cockroaches.

One of the men unfurls a large nylon mesh net.

***

The next evening, one of the nocturnal hunters allows his wife to prepare a special bat curry dish. After five days, the entire family becomes feverish and has difficulty breathing. Within two weeks, they are all dead. Inside a month, twenty others in the village have also succumbed—virulent fever followed by violent coughing, vomiting, diarrhea, and finally after a few quick days, death.

The village is quarantined, and the military seals off all access roads.

Two workers in biohazard suits arrive and extract several of the netted bats. The bats are placed in secure, locked biohazard containers, then flown to Jakarta.

Still alive, the quarantined bats rest in darkened cages.

***

In dawn's hazy light, the jet lands, taxiing down a remote runway of the Soekarno-Hatta International Airport. The plane bears no markings on the outside, other than a number. Three men disembark. Two wear sport jackets and American flag lapel pins. The third man, overweight and paunchy, has red suspenders visible under a light windbreaker that billows in the jet turbine's wash.

A small delegation of Indonesian health officials meets them. The officials wear brown suits and stern, serious expressions. No handshakes. The sun illuminates a dusty haze.

The group arrives at the Malaysian Institute of Virology and dons white hazmat suits, masks, face shields.

CHAPTER 5

Dara stares into her own face on Rachel's cell phone. Completely . . . healed. She pulls off the gauze wrapped around her head.

A noise outside. The door swings open, and bright, angular light brightens a portion of the room. Someone steps into the light.

Her dad. He sprints toward Dara's bed. "Gotta get you out of here." A muscle twitches on one side of his mouth.

"What—what's going on?" Dara asks.

"The men who were guarding you . . . they took off—some kind of an incident on the outside perimeter. You're in danger."

"What about the other patients?" Dara asks.

"There's just you, no one else."

Dara hears a sound down the hall, elevator doors gliding open. She twists on the bed. "Diego! Linc!"

"There's no time," Dad says. He puts a protective hand on her shoulder, whispers, "Up, Dar!" He slides a hand behind her back, lifting her torso.

"Hurry!" Rachel says, glancing at her phone.

Dara sits, swings her legs over the side of the hospital bed, wobbles to an upright position. She wears blue jeans, t-shirt, socks—the same clothes she's worn since before Griffith Park. She pulls off the sling, tosses it onto the bed. The cast is like carrying a log.

"The freight elevator," Dad says. "Other end of the hall. Let's move."

With Dad holding one of her arms, they step out into the empty corridor. Another set of footsteps, somewhere in the distance.

The polished linoleum floor gleams under bright fluorescent lights.

Dad pulls her down the hall, away from the footsteps.

Rachel punches the elevator button.

Soft crepe soles sound behind them—then halt, as though someone has gone into a room.

The elevator light stops on another floor.

Dad backs up from the elevator door and glances down the hallway. "This way," he says.

They head toward a red exit sign.

"My car," Rachel says. "In the parking lot."

Dad shoulders the door open while still holding Dara's good arm, and they are on the stairs. He holds Dara's hand and guides down one, two flights.

"Wait here." Dad pushes open the ground floor exit door.

Dara leans against the stairwell and listens for anyone coming down the stairs after them, hears Rachel breathing behind her.

After what seems an eternity, her dad returns. "All clear. Let's go."

They hustle out the door, into a darkened parking lot. Somewhere on another side of the building—shouted voices, followed by the sound of gunshots.

"My car's this way." Rachel and her dad rush Dara over grass, asphalt.

Dad shoves her into the rear seat of a small, white SUV.

"Get down," Rachel commands from outside the vehicle.

As Dara lays on the seat on her side, a memory scorches through her. The white van, abduction, legs bound with duct tape as they'd hit a pothole, head banging on the rusted metal floorboard.

The ring tone from a cell phone, outside the open car door, jerks her out of the memory.

"Yeah," Dad says, and pauses. He stands near the open car door, holds the phone up to his ear. "Who the hell are you?" A puzzled note in his voice: "Say that again? . . . Okay, okay, roger that." He ducks his head into the SUV and hands Dara a familiar-looking phone. "Someone asking for you, got your number from Brooke Park."

"My phone—how—"

"I grabbed it from the table in your room as we were leaving."

She remembers now. Brooke, the talk show star, had given her a no-internet burner cell after Dara's last TV appearance. Dara must've kept it in her pocket right up until she got to the emergency room.

"Dara?" A man's voice.

"Who are you?"

"Sebastian Smith." Jamaican accent.

"Now's a pretty bad time."

Sebastian's voice sounds distant, muffled. "Brooke give me your number, thought I might help you."

"What the—how did you know, right now—"

"Listen carefully. You need my help, mon. People are after you."

Sirens in the distance, a sudden yell nearby.

"Oh my God, you can't—" Rachel's voice, outside but close. "Go! Go!"

The SUV's rear door slams shut next to Dara's head. Alone in the SUV, prone on the back seat, she can't see her dad, can't see anyone.

"Get down." Sebastian speaks through the cell phone at her ear. "Are you down?"

"Yeah," Dara whispers.

The blast of a gunshot, shattered window glass, then another shot. The driver's door opens and bangs closed. Peal of rubber, sensation of backwards acceleration. Has Rachel taken the wheel? Or someone else? Dara struggles to see over the back of the headrest in front of her—but can't push high enough to see the driver and lies back down.

"I heard the sound of car taking off," Sebastian says.

She presses the phone tight to her ear.

Silence.

"Tell me, mon. Who is driving you?"

CHAPTER 6

"I've got you, Dar." Her dad in the driver's seat. "Stay down."

Relief sweeps over Dara as she pushes herself into a sitting position. "Dad, thank God it's you." Dara turns to look through the shattered rear window. In the distance, Rachel's body lies on the pavement.

"We had to leave her. No time. Get down."

Dara slouches down in the seat, through the window a rhythm of passing streetlamps. "Where are we going?"

"To get you out of here," Dad says.

In her lap, a faint voice—the cell phone. It's fallen, and she brings it back to her ear.

"Dara, you still there, mon?"

"Yeah."

"I heard him," Sebastian says. "Your fada. The soldier."

She takes a deep breath. "He's Navy."

"On TV, he's called the Missing Soldier," Sebastian says. "I know a safe place, mon, but you have to hurry."

"Dad, listen to this." Dara puts the phone on speaker and sits up, holding the phone so he can hear. "Sebastian, tell my dad."

"I just explained to Dara that—" Sebastian begins.

Dad shouts over the engine noise as he accelerates onto the freeway. "Who the hell are you again? And why should we bother listening to you?"

"I once handled security for media star Brooke Park. She give me Dara's cell number—and now, I'm the only one who can get you out, mon."

"How did you know to call right when all hell broke loose?" Dad asks.

"Brooke had a visit from someone, felt Dara was in danger."

They drive through the Cahuenga Pass, and the call drops. Dara struggles over the seat back and tumbles into the passenger seat next to her father, cast thumping against the center console. Her head throbs.

"Lost call," she says.

"Stay low!" Dad commands.

Dara slumps down.

Dad guns the engine, speeds into the fast lane. "I don't like it." He eyes the cell phone.

"Right now, seems like we gotta take a chance."

He waits a moment, nods once without taking his eyes off the freeway.

Dara taps Sebastian's recent call number and puts it back on speaker.

"Listen to me," Sebastian says. "Ditch that car. You're in a government vehicle, and gotta assume it's bein' tracked. Where you at?"

"101 north," Dad says, "near Vineland."

"Take 170. Get off Sunland. Bernie's Auto Salvage lot, corner San Fernando and Sunland. Park on the street, not in lot. Tell them my name. Someone will take care of you until I get there."

Minutes later, they pull off the freeway and skid to a stop across the street from the junkyard.

Dad helps Dara out of the SUV and they rush across the street into a small customer service area, walls lined with chrome wheel rims.

A sense of unease grips Dara.

A man dashes in from the back, through rows of car parts. "Seb call me five minutes ago," he says. Jamaican accent, like Sebastian. "I'm his cousin. There been nighttime robberies—I sleep here. T'ank gods for that."

The man grabs a crowbar from under the counter, "Come quick." Waving the crowbar. "This way."

Dad seizes Dara's good wrist, holds her back.

"Come fast!" the man yells. "This"—he brandishes the crowbar—"is for car, not to hit you upside heads."

He guides Dara and her father behind some parts shelves, through a back door, and into a junkyard filled with wrecked and rusted cars—hoods bent, doors ajar, seats missing. The lot is surrounded by a metal fence topped with barbed wire, illuminated by overhead security lights.

The man quickens his pace, leading them deeper into the yard.

Dara steps carefully, eyes down to avoid tripping over loose air filters, hoses, and rusted carburetors strewn about.

"Here." Sebastian's cousin jams the crowbar above the rear bumper of a large silver Cadillac with a crumpled front end and no seats. He pops open the trunk. "Get in."

"No way," Dad says. "You could just as easily let us die in there. Or shoot us."

"*Will* happen if you don't get in."

As if in confirmation, screeching tires sound outside, shouts from the street. In the distance, an approaching siren.

Dara squeezes into the back of the trunk, followed by her dad. She lies on her good arm. The lid slams down, and it is dark.

CHAPTER 7

Dara scrunches up in the car trunk facing Dad's back. He's wedged protectively into the narrow space in front of her.

Dara hears their breathing, closes her eyes—darkness seems safer if you bring it on yourself. In the silence and suffocating warmth, she becomes aware of her own hunger. Coupled with the fear, it creates an odd sensation in her stomach.

Outside—footsteps, dog barking, the thwup-thwup of helicopter blades.

***

How long are they going to have to stay like this? They must have been hiding here for at least an hour, maybe more. Dara pulls out her cell phone to check. 5:33. Sunday. The last call to Seb had been at 5:15. Which means they've probably been in the car trunk for all of . . . maybe five minutes.

She holds the phone in front of her, looking for a search icon, messages, Instagram, anything. But then remembers . . . the phone has no internet.

Her eyes close again. She's on the street, running . . . sprinting. Her feet pound the asphalt. It's night, a street she's been on, a place she instinctively knows but doesn't recognize. Next to her old apartment building? Diego holds her hand and runs with her, as Linc lopes along by her side. Her body aches, head throbs from the exertion. She is escaping from something—a fight? Or is she running to *stop* a fight? Either way, her life depends on it.

The trunk lid pops open with a rusty squeak, and Dara awakens with a start, squints against the morning light.

Her dad pushes her back deeper into the trunk, unfolds himself, and steps out. She shields her vision with one hand and sees her dad, knees slightly bent, fists clenched. A man stands before them.

Thin. Long dreadlocks tied back in a thick ponytail, goatee, gold earring. "It's okay, mon," the man says. "I am Sebastian."

"Where are they?" Dad asks.

"Who?"

"The others. The ones who were after us."

"They gone," Sebastian says.

Her dad scans the yard, looks back toward the street, turns to survey the fence. He gestures for Dara to get out of the trunk.

She swings her legs over the bumper, gathers strength, and steps onto the dirt. When she stumbles, her dad's strong arms grab her.

A blue pickup truck is parked next to the open car trunk.

"Get in," Sebastian says, and bangs the truck's rear fender with his hand.

She glances at Sebastian's face. His eyes are bright, reflecting the early morning sunlight, and bore into her.

"We got to move fast," he says.

"I need to know where we're going, Sebastian." Dad pulls Dara back and steps in front to shield her.

"No time," Sebastian replies. "Just get in the back." He lowers the tailgate. "I get you some place safe. And call me Seb."

Dad glances around the junkyard, lowers his voice to Dara. "We can always bail at a stoplight or wherever." He takes Dara's hand, and together they scramble into the truck bed.

"We goin' out back way," Seb says. "Lie down."

Dara and her dad stretch flat on the truck bed.

Seb throws a tarp over them.

The tires crunch over dirt, and the truck lurches to a stop. Voices, the sound of a gate being opened, and then they're moving again.

"How you doing?" her dad asks, speaking over the slick, swishing sound of tires on asphalt.

She can't see him through the folds of the tarp, but reaches over, takes his hand. "Do you know where Seb's taking us, Dad?"

"Like he said, somewhere safe—I trust."

A cell phone's electro-music ringtone jars her, and she tenses, takes out her phone. The glow illuminates the gray tarp over her head. Dara stares at the screen: 'unknown caller.'

"Yeah?" she says.

"It's me. Brooke."

"Why are you—"

"Someone was here," Brooke interrupts, "trying to find out where you'd gone. They've traced your number through my phone. Get rid of that phone. Now."

"Wait—Brooke?"

Silence.

Dara looks at the screen. 'Call ended'. She holds the phone in her hand, feels for the side of the truck bed, and slips the phone over the side. She lets go, hears it bounce off the fender.

After what seems like miles of freeway, the truck tilts slightly to one side as they bend into a curve, turn, slow. It jolts to a stop, engine still running.

Seb lowers the tailgate. "Out, quick." Backlit against a blinding sun. "Get into the front."

Dara and her dad squeeze out from under the tarp. "Why?" Dad asks.

"No sense staying back there, mon," Seb says, nodding at the truck bed. "We're far enough away now."

Dad pauses, appears to be sizing up Seb. Finally, he nods once. "Roger that." He takes Dara's hand, and they clamber into the front seat.

The doors clunk closed.

The pickup truck looks older than her dad, and they sit three across on the worn bench seat, Dara in the middle.

Dara shoots a quick glance at their surroundings. They are next to a park. A woman pushes a jogging stroller as she trots behind it on the sidewalk. She glances over at Dara, but then keeps her eyes focused straight ahead, as though the truck and its occupants—scruffy man, dark-skinned driver, teenage girl—are invisible.

Dara looks back and sees the woman talking into her cell phone, staring after the truck. "You need to go faster," Dara says. "Get us out of here. I think that lady spotted us."

Seb keeps the same slow pace. "Speeding truck, Jamaican driver—big mistake. Then for sure cops be here." He drives onto a side road that parallels the freeway, past a gas station and a McDonald's, and back onto the freeway. A sign says *Palmdale 28 miles.*

"Why are you doing this?" Dad asks. "I mean, I assume you're not going to kill us, or you'd have done that back in the junkyard, right?"

Slow lane. The truck has no air conditioning, windows rolled down. Heat blows in, and Seb's dreadlocks dance in the cross breeze. They have to shout to be heard.

"What is your name?" Seb asks Dara's father.

"Shawn."

"It's like this, Shawn. Brooke called, asked me to do this thing. I seen Dara's story from the TV and radio." He pronounces it like *rah'-deeo.* "Brooke, she also tell me some t'ings about your daughter"—he takes his eyes off the road for a split-second and glances at Dara, who shifts to move closer to her dad—"that there is more to her than meets the eye. Brooke thought I could help, mon."

"I don't have it anymore," Dara says.

Seb shoots her a quick glance, meets her gaze, and looks straight ahead again. "I am here to give you a ride in an old truck, get you to a place where no one can touch you." Hint of a smile in his voice.

"What place is that?" Dad asks.

"It don't have a name, mon. But you can call it the Silver Bullet."

"Nice truck," Dad says.

It's solid, heavy metal, dark blue. The gear shift is a metal rod set into the floor, orange tennis ball split to cover the shift knob. The truck's old, simple dashboard panel is spartan. No GPS. No electronics. Just a speedometer. A wallet-size photo of a woman hangs from the rear view mirror, dancing in the cross breeze from the open windows.

They are going 55 miles an hour. To their left, cars whizz by. Traffic seems light, and Dara remembers that her phone had said it was Sunday. She looks ahead at the freeway signs, trying to figure out where Seb might be taking them.

That's when it happens.

Two cars roar past in the fast lane, a red sedan followed by an SUV.

Seb turns his head and glances at the red car as it passes him.

Through the open windows of Seb's truck, Dara hears a loud bang up ahead, like a backfire. Fifty yards ahead, the red sedan spins out, swerves into the center guardrail, and ricochets back across traffic toward their lane. It is immediately struck by the pursuing car, which in turn sends both vehicles spinning.

It happens in an instant. Dara's heart is in her throat—they are about to drive headlong into the wreckage. She turns to look at Seb as her dad's hand tightens on her arm. Seb takes his foot off the accelerator—Dara senses the truck's loss of momentum—and aims straight into the crumpled, spinning wreckage.

Broken glass showers through the air, smell of burnt rubber. Smoke billows from under the crumpled hood of the still-careening red sedan.

"Dad!" Dara screams.

Seb coasts straight into the crash debris.

Dara's father yells a profanity.

The red sedan just ahead flips and is on its side in mid-air. Seb's only adjustment is a quick flick of the steering wheel to avoid the airborne car as it crashes and rolls upside down into a middle lane. The wreckage seems to flow around and past Seb's truck like an ocean current around a rock.

Dara stares in panic as they sail through untouched. She can see the upside down car's driver looking out, the side of his face pressed up against a white air bag.

She gasps. That face—she's seen it before.

Seb's truck coasts through the debris unscathed, rear tires fishtailing on a fresh oil slick.

Dara looks back. The red sedan erupts in flames.

Dara's heart pounds as she stares at the flaming wreckage. She turns to Seb. "You—you could have gone into the emergency lane—but you didn't. How did you know the car would crash where it did and not hit you?"

"Jus' saw it play out in my head." Seb's eyes are fixed on the freeway ahead. "Like billiard balls, knowing which pockets they'd land in."

Dara sees the reflection of his eyes glancing at the rear view mirror.

"We need to go back," Dad says, his voice tight, urgent. "Maybe it's not too late to pull someone out of the wreckage."

"Need to get you both to safety." Seb doesn't accelerate, but keeps the same steady pace. "I seen that red car speeding toward us in my mirror. It was no accident, Shawn. You heard the gunshot, and then the car lost control."

"Sounded like a twelve-gauge," Dad says.

"That man's face in the crashed car," Dara says. "I recognized him! Agent Johnson from the hospital, the one who questioned me." A wave of panic hits her. "Was he chasing me? Or trying to protect me? How could we have been followed? That lady with the baby stroller, when we stopped—she must have—"

Dad turns to her. "We need to change your appearance."

"Not to worry," Seb says. "We goin' someplace where nobody will see her."

Dara's heart is still pounding, and adrenaline pulses through her.

They drive in silence north out of the Valley past Littlerock and Pearblossom, into the high desert.

Stucco housing developments grow sparser, until only barren hills loom beside them on the freeway. It's like they're leaving civilization behind. Hot, dry air rushes in through the open truck windows, and seems to clear away the fear.

Dara senses the tension easing.

"Who's that in the picture?" Dara's father nods at the photo hanging from the rear view mirror.

"My mudda," Seb replies. He strokes the soul patch on his chin. After those two words . . . silence.

"Didn't mean to pry," Dara's dad says. "It's just—you had a picture. Your mother, okay. I was curious, that's all."

"It's okay, mon." Seb takes a deep breath, brushes back his dreadlocks, and pauses before speaking again. "Was killed."

Dara raises her head to look at Seb.

"I grew up in Kings-tone," Seb explains, keeping his eyes on the freeway. "Jamaica capital. My home was government housing. There were young men we called Yardies, sol' drugs. It was just my mudda and me livin' together, and she tried to guide me in right direction. " He pauses as a big semi thunders past. "She had words with the Yardies," he continues, "to keep them away from me. I came home from school one day and she was gone. A few days later, her body washed up on the beach. I was seventeen and got out of there, made my way to Miami, then Los Angeles."

Dad reaches up and steadies the photograph between two fingers.

"I'm really sorry about your mom," Dara says. Something catches in her throat, and she whispers, "Did they catch her killer?"

Seb shakes his head. "It was hard. I miss her still. I was lost young man for several years."

Dara feels her dad's hand on hers.

"But it did make me strong," Seb says. "Made me value life. Learn to survive on my own. I vowed that I would make world better, help my mudda to clean up the Yard. Came to Southern California, learned martial arts from a master. He taught me certain skills—how to listen, observe, walk without disturbing the air. I learned to fight—and not fight. How knowing leads to confidence. Then started doing personal security work, bodyguard."

"You said you worked for Brooke Park."

He nods. "My first big job. Can never pay her back for opportunity she give me. Got me work for other celebrities, rock stars."

An hour later, they reach the outskirts of Victorville, marked by a gas station with orange pennants flapping in the desert wind and a lone billboard promoting a real estate broker. Sebastian turns down a dirt road that has no name, its entrance marked by a pile of stones next to the main highway. Creosote scrub and Joshua trees dot the brown landscape. They pass scattered RV trailers, bleached white by the sun. Homes are few and far between.

After several minutes of jolting bumps, Dara can make out something in the distance, a bright reflection in the relentless sunlight. When they grow closer, Dara sees that it is an oval-shaped trailer parked at the end of the dirt road.

"Is this where you live?" Dara asks.

Seb pulls the truck to a stop next to the trailer. "Only when I need to plant my feet on the solid earth. Not much changes here, and it is quiet." He gets out of the cab and stands, leaning in the driver's window. He pulls his head back and squints over at the distant hills. "A good place for you and your fada. You will be safe."

Her dad walks over to the trailer, opens the corroded aluminum door, looks inside.

"Does it have electricity?" Dara asks, wondering if there is a TV.

Seb nods up at a set of electrical wires that pass overhead. A single line runs from a breaker to the trailer. "One of the stars I worked for," he says, "gave me this trailer, and I towed it here. I will soon be gone—but these hills, they always be here. Unchanging. It is good to be part of something more permanent than ever-changing streets."

Dara stumbles out of the truck and leans against the hot metal fender. She closes her eyes. Too exhausted to think anymore, she slumps to the ground, leaning against the truck tire. "How long do we have to stay here?" she asks.

"For time bein'," Seb replies.

Dara rises, and the three of them venture inside the chrome trailer. The furnishings consist of a small table with two benches; a stove and mini-fridge; one bed in the front behind a small bathroom; and at the rear of the trailer—in an elevated space next to the ceiling—a second bed. No TV, no computer.

"Food's just the basics at the moment," Seb says. "I'll bring you some groceries later tonight, but will not stay here with you."

"We don't have any money," Dad says.

""Don't worry, mon." Seb smiles. "There is a fun'."

"Fun?"

"Since you went on Brooke's show with your daughter, people been sending money for the both of you. Brooke set up this fun'."

"How much is there?" Dad asks.

"Don't know, mon. But I think on Brooke's show, or maybe the news, it says close to fifty."

"That's not a lot," Dara says, and imagines a few people sending in one-dollar bills.

"Thousand," Seb says. "Fifty. Thousand, mon."

They stare at Seb, and her dad lets out a low whistle. Dara remembers her last appearance on *YOLO with Brooke*, the e-mails that had come in to the TV station: *To Dara—I just saw you on TV with your father . . . Dear Dara, Can you heal my sister?* . . .

And now people were sending money. If that was true, is this desert trailer the best they could get? But maybe Seb's right: the best thing is to lie low where no one can find her.

"I—I don't—" Dad says. "—don't know what to say."

"You don't have to say nothing," Seb says. "Jah provides."

"You mentioned the news," Dad says. "What was—"

Seb interrupts. "You both need rest. The world keeps on turning, never goin' to stop doing that."

After he leaves, Dara clambers up to the elevated bed, at the opposite end of the trailer from her dad's bed, and falls asleep to the labored rhythm of a rooftop air conditioner.

CHAPTER 8

When Dara awakens, the sun is just coming up over the horizon.

Has she really slept sixteen hours?

On the table are two stacks of used clothes—shirts, pants, socks, underwear. One set for her, one for her dad. And folded beneath the clothes is something that catches her eye. She lifts the clothes and pulls out a desert camouflage hoodie. Perfect fit. She goes into the bathroom to check herself in the mirror, and when she pulls up the voluminous hood, her face is practically invisible.

Opening the fridge: milk, juice, eggs. A box of cereal sits on the counter. Dara parts the curtain that separates the bedroom from the rest of the trailer. Her dad is awake, cross-legged, staring out a window next to his bed.

"Did you get some sleep?" she asks.

He shakes his head and looks at her. "Not yet."

"But, Dad—"

"I'll get some now." He stretches out on the bed, closes his eyes, and within moments his breathing becomes deep and even. He'd learned to do that in Iraq, Dara knew—sleep anywhere under any conditions.

After showering, Dara examines her face in the mirror. It's healed, except for a bruise on her throat she must have missed when she healed herself back in the hospital. Let that heal on its own. She puts on fresh jeans and a t-shirt and fixes a large bowl of Grape Nuts, cradling the bowl between her cast and stomach. She steps outside as she slurps cereal. The morning air is still, dry, and the sun beats down on the desert.

It's good to breathe without fear, not looking over her shoulder, no longer in constant protection mode with the Lightband on her arm. For the first time in months, she's free—the way she used to feel before her mother was killed. And how long ago was that? She tries to calculate. Six, seven months? Yet even before that, tension had permeated her home.

Dara gazes into the drab, buff-colored desert, pictures Linc heeling next to her, fetching a stick tossed into the desert. She turns three hundred and sixty degrees, heat already radiating off the Silver Bullet. No one's at her back.

Or beside her.

Is Diego thinking of me right now, she wonders, the same way I'm thinking of him?

He's probably back at his dad's home in Reseda—and doesn't even know where I am.

Nobody knows.

CHAPTER 9

Seb eases his truck into a parking space at the far end of the Market Basket parking lot and turns off the AM transistor radio on the seat next to him. He checks the rear view mirror, pulls out a cell phone, and places it in his lap.

He looks down at the small screen, alert for other cars pulling up next to him, and tugs the multi-colored Rasta cap tight over his ears.

More riots reported, police move in. #Griffith Park #Dara #Jyotisha #Lightband Watch 6:00 News—ABS3
        --ABSNewsLA (@ABS-News3)

Police bring in FBI, other federal agencies, intensity search for #DaraAdengard #Jyotisha #Lightband
        --Newsbreak (@newsbreaker)

Massive police presence overnight, tear gas in #Griffith Park #OldZoo as protestors throw rocks, bottles
--DailyRewind (@DRewind)

#Jyotisha mass delusions, crowd hypnosis discussed in NYT best-selling author's new Kindle pre-release Put Your Faith in Me: The Power of Suggestion
        --GAlbrecht (@GeoffreyAlbrecht)

Seb puts his cell into a pocket, gets out, and walks toward the store, careful to avoid eye contact.

Once inside, he glances at the list Dara and her father have put together, thinking . . . for real, I have to buy this stuff, too? Begins tossing things into the shopping cart, and when he gets to the checkout counter places the Venus razors and feminine hygiene products under a loaf of bread.

He notes the girl's eyes at the cash register, how they flick from razors and Tampons to him. It's almost imperceptible—and for anyone else, might have been—but he'd seen her mentally register the purchase.

After leaving the Market Basket, Seb stops at a home improvement store where he buys the cheapest propane barbeque he can find, plus a pair of heavy-duty angled scissors. From there, he drives to Walmart and purchases another twenty pound propane tank, then to Target where he buys two more. He stops at four different propane fueling stations, has them all filled.

His last stop is at Radio Shack.

CHAPTER 10

"We gonna barbeque?" Dara asks. She helps lift the barbeque and heavy propane tanks from the truck bed. "I'd kill for a good burger."

"It's for you and fada. I don't eat meat." Seb nods at the propane tanks. "In case we lose juice. Survive without electricity—gotta be prepared."

"And I *am* planning on barbequing," Dad says.

"If you needa reach me, Shawn," Seb says, "use this." He holds up a walkie-talkie. "I got one for you, one for me, and two chargers—one for here and the other in my truck. Only for emergencies, because channel is not private."

Dad and Seb set the extra propane tanks outside next to the tow hitch and cover them with a plastic sheet weighted down with rocks.

Dara unpacks groceries, placing them on the narrow kitchen counter: peanut butter, crackers, hot dogs.

"Where do you live?" Dara asks as she walks with Seb to his truck.

Seb flashes her a warm smile. "Apartment near Victorville. Not far."

"How long have you lived there? I thought you worked in L.A. or Hollywood."

"No, mon, now I living there for past month"—he nods toward the dirt road, as though there's an apartment building nestled in the cactus— "close by you and your fada. Brooke wants you protected."

"What are those scissors for?" she asks.

"Need to cut off your cast, mon."

***

Dad barbeques. Hamburgers, chicken, hot dogs. All good.

At first, Seb showed up every other day to bring water, groceries, and supplies. But his visits soon grow more frequent and he stays longer at the trailer.

The cast is gone, and Dara sometimes finds herself gazing at her wrist. One morning after Seb arrives at the Silver Bullet, he grabs a pillowcase from the small bedroom closet. With a black marker, he draws a face on the light blue cloth—strong mouth with lips parted to expose the teeth, heavy eyebrows set above blazing eyes. On the other side of the pillowcase, he sketches long strands of hair, stuffs the pillowcase with old towels, and ties it closed.

"Is that supposed to be Mercy?" Dara asks.

"The news had her picture."

"Am *I* still on the news?" Dara asks. On her journey from the Old Zoo picnic field to the hospital to the high desert, she's had no TV, no computer—and Seb has never offered to let her use his phone.

"It does not matter." Seb shrugs. "You are not pictures on a screen, mon. You are a girl in the desert, here, right now."

She follows Seb out of the trailer and into the shade on one side. While her dad observes a short distance away, Seb holds the stuffed pillowcase in front of his chest. "I will hold 'Mercy'. Kick with your foot."

She strikes at it, off balance, and Seb moves the sack at the last minute. Her foot glances off the side, and she stumbles backwards.

"Again," Seb says.

He makes her practice until her leg aches, but she begins to anticipate where he might move the pillow, and her balance grows steadier.

"Let the force of your leg come from your hip," her dad says.

She learns to kick where Mercy would be—not where she was. Seb teaches her to do the same with her fists, and when she does that . . . energy explodes down her wrist, into her palm. It's invisible, but she knows it's there.

Day after day, she practices.

"Mercy is like a moving shadow," he tells her, inside the Silver Bullet. He holds up the punching pillow. "You need to let go, let her flow past, like shadow of cloud from sky. Passing over, by, through."

She looks at the pillowcase, tries to picture it as a white cloud, seeming solid but wafting through like mist.

"Storm coming," Seb says. "You must get ready. Dis storm not be partial but touch everybody." He turns to look outside, and his dreadlocks glisten in the trailer's artificial light. A gold earring momentarily sparkles.

"How would you know that?" Dara asks. She's puzzled when Seb talks in a way that sounds like it should be significant. His words seem to drift away, lost balloons floating up into the sky. She tries to grasp them, but they're always just out of reach.

"When wind blow certain way," Seb says, "you know storm will be big, mon." He lets out a big, hearty laugh. "You grow up on the island, you learn to listen to the wind."

Dara glances out the window at a clear blue sky.

CHAPTER 11

"Dad?" she asks when Seb has left. "What was Seb talking about when he said a storm's coming?"

Dad's outside, in the process of rigging a narrow hose from an opening underneath the trailer, feeding it up under the sink. A new beard fills in the hollows of his cheeks, and he spends his days tinkering with the Silver Bullet's modest fixtures. He'd cleaned the air conditioner, re-attached one of the stove's electric coils. One time she saw him fiddling with the propane tanks outside by the tow hitch. Seb had purchased a coil of rubber hose, and Dad busied himself with measuring lengths of it, drilling access holes under the two sinks, and running the hose under the Silver Bullet. Dara wasn't sure what it was for, but figured he was making improvements to the water drainage.

"One thing I learned in Iraq"—he puts down a drill to look up at Dara—"is that the enemy doesn't rest—even when you're relaxed and your post might seem boring as hell. That's when the enemy moves, amasses, builds up forces to attack."

"But there's nothing here." She looks out at the surrounding desert. "It's empty."

"The desert is a treacherous place," her dad says. "I drove a construction truck back in Iraq. It might seem like a simple drive through a desert much like the Mojave here, Point A to Point B. Except that the most routine event along the way—a small road crew repairing a pothole—could spell death and disaster. When you're in the battle zone, nothing is routine—especially when you think it is."

"But this isn't a battle zone. It's the middle of nowhere."

"It might feel that way, and I believe you are safe here." He brushes back his hair. Thinner than hers, it hangs halfway down his neck, and his deep-set eyes shine bright as the sun strikes them. "But Seb is right. You might have gotten away—retreated to a base behind enemy lines—but the world keeps on turning, and meanwhile the enemy marshals its forces to find you."

"Why? I don't have the Lightband anymore."

"But you're the one, the girl who healed. It doesn't take a sixth sense to know what's coming. The news was all over it at the Old Zoo. Remember those news choppers? It might be calm here"—he looks around—"but there's a storm coming." He picks up a hose clamp and goes back to work. "It just hasn't arrived at our doorstep yet."

"Dad, do you ever miss the base, what you used to do?"

"Honey, my only reason for living now is you." He puts down his tools, stands, draws her head to his chest, and ruffles her hair.

***

One evening, she's cleaning up the kitchen after dinner. It's unusual, she'd learned, to hear Seb if she didn't see him. But she hears a footstep and turns.

"Finish," he says. "Then come." He turns and walks out the door.

The sun is setting, and the air has begun to lose its intense dry heat. Dad comes out of the trailer, too, and stands with her.

Seb puts down two towels on the sand next to the Silver Bullet, one for her and one for him, and directs her to sit facing him. Dad leans against the side of the trailer.

"What weapons do you have?" he asks.

"I—I don't really have any."

"You were attacked before. How did you defend yourself?"

"I tripped Gunarik and used a broken bottle."

"So you found a weapon." He smiles. "That is good. Anything at hand can be a weapon. And this is a weapon." He bends his arm and shoves his elbow at an imaginary opponent. "Any bone is a weapon. Bones are hard. Yes, they can break, but if used correctly, they are weapons." He reaches out and takes her hand, forming it into a tight fist. "The small bones of your fingers and knuckles can kill a man three times your size." He unfolds her hand. "Your nails are weapons. They can scratch, gouge out an eye."

She looks down at her cracked, dirt-encrusted fingernails.

"Use whatever is available," Seb continues. "If you have nothing else, use your body. The element of surprise is always an advantage. If you can surprise your opponent, you catch him off guard. And for that moment, he is helpless—even if he is much bigger than you."

In one fluid motion, he is on his feet as a heel kicks up and he propels his fist upward, smashing it into an imaginary jaw. It's a violent move, made all the more forceful by the suddenness with which it is executed. Seb spins and his foot broadsides an imagined head. He slices his leg through the air with such force that it seems to Dara it could easily kill a person. His dreadlocks swing and every move is flowing, yet deliberate and choreographed— delivered with overwhelming strength both swift and brutal.

"Get up," he says. "Now, practice with Shawn. He is going to attack you from the front."

Her dad takes a step toward her and Dara backs up.

"That's not the way," says Seb. "You are showing fear. Never show fear to your opponent. They will feast on it."

Her dad takes a step back to resume his position.

"Watch out, Seb!" Dara calls.

Her dad looks over—and that's when Dara springs at him, but her dad casts her off and she hits the ground.

Seb smiles down at her. "Not bad, mon. Except that now you're on the dirt and your fada is still standing."

"I'm military, been in combat zones," Dad says. "Slight advantage there."

They practice into the deepening twilight, she and her dad, while Seb coaches.

***

Another day, in the shade of a Joshua tree, another lesson: "What do you do," Seb asks, "if you're in close combat, fighting an opponent who's only inches away?"

"Just hit him, I guess—or her."

"But that can be hard to do if you're really close," Seb says.

"You can kick."

"That's good—if your legs are free, mon. But maybe you can't kick. In close quarters, you need to do as much damage as you can, as fast as you can. If he is stronger, you use his need to overpower and turn it against. Watch."

Posing her dad as an opponent, Seb shows her in slow motion how to execute a palm punch to the center of the face, followed by an elbow smash. One-two. "Draw him in, closer," Seb says, pulling her dad in by the arm. "Make him aware of his own power, that he is stronger than you, he needs to feel that. Then—" One-two. Palm punch, elbow smash.

Seb makes her practice the same move over and over again: fingers bent, palm upturned, smash out and up, drive with the legs, same arm, elbow. Smash down. One-two, repeat. Step into it. Drive your opponent back.

Seb works with her for the next few days. With her dad as a sparring partner, he shows her how to use elbows and knees against an opponent, flip strength into weakness.

"Important," he says. "Never let down your defense. You are in the ring, mon—the arena— every minute every day and you must always be on guard. Alert, calm. Look ahead. But see everywhere, and feel what is around you t'ree-sixty."

From his cousin's junkyard, Seb brings an axle attached to a set of brake drums. "Weights," he tells Dara.

She groans and lifts. Clean and jerk. Over and over.

She runs when the sun rises and once again in the evening—not along the road, but into the desert, her dad and Seb keeping pace beside her to allay any fear of getting lost.

One morning, they've run for thirty minutes, following the course of a wide gulley—a desert wash carved from flash floods—and turn to head back.

"Look at them hills," Seb says.

She glances over her shoulder to the right.

"See how the sun hits them in the morning," he says.

Dara is breathing hard as their sneakers hit the sand. "So?"

"They reflect back, hold heat in morning, as soon as sun rises. But in the evening, it is opposite. Sun go down over the hills, it become cool. Learn to use geo-graphy to your advantage—wherever you are, here in desert or on streets."

Dara glances again at the hills, and thinks, I don't need a phone here—no Google Maps or GPS. The sun makes life simple. Rhythmic. From east to west.

She spots a desert flower, surprised it's still blooming because it's late summer, and there are no other flowers. It is delicate purple, close to the ground as though afraid to stand tall. She pinches the tiny stem, plucks it, takes it back to the Silver Bullet, and sets it in water. Within a day, it has wilted, the petals flaking off until all that remains is a desiccated stem.

Dara thinks of the pictures Rachel showed her in the hospital, how the Jyotisha restored nature in the park. She holds her hand over the wilted stem, but there is nothing. No light.

Seb startles her from behind.

"I am going to town," he says. "Anything you need?"

She thinks for a moment. "Orange nail polish. It's almost Halloween."

"You think you can bring it back to life?" he asks, nodding at the flower.

"No, I just—"

"I have felt the power you carry in your hand. When you have practiced with me, striking with that hand"—he nods at her right hand, the one with element 120-X in her bone—"I could feel the force."

"It was—," she says. "That is, I mean—when I broke my wrist, I—"

"You never learned to command it—that thing you had, the armband—or your own destiny. You let things happen to you. To it. But you never learned to be in control. To do that, you first have to let go. Surrender. Let the rest of the world flow through you. No resistance."

"I did let go."

"Only with hands. You did not let go with heart. But sometimes wounds must be carried inside"—Seb turns to face her, looks straight into her eyes—"until they heal themselves."

***

Dara grows to love the desert. Rachel had said the Lightband could heal nature. But the desert seems like a place that would never die, would never need healing. It exists outside of time, and Dara loses track of the days. How long has she been here? Weeks? Months?

When she closes her eyes and pays attention from deep inside, Dara can hear the sounds of faint movement, like rustling curtains. When she opens her eyes, there's just the trailer and the sound of the air conditioner. But she can sense a gathering force, things being assembled far away and beyond the horizon.

CHAPTER 12

The unmarked semi pulls into the back of a drab one-story warehouse. The building is one among many similar buildings—gray, windowless, anonymous—that sit next to the L.A. River on the eastern edge of downtown. The sole entrance from the street is through two sets of doors, the first one aluminum mesh and the second re-enforced steel. Nothing is posted on the windowless exterior, no signage that might give a clue as to the building's purpose.

Two men unload the truck's contents—sealed boxes and office furniture—and carry everything into the warehouse. Another truck follows and then another. It takes ten hours to set up an array of desks with computer monitors, secure phone lines, and outside closed circuit TV cameras. Medical equipment is brought in—vital signs monitors, medications, gurneys, hospital beds, protective gear, masks.

A short man wearing a bow tie carries out a series of instructions given by a much larger man with a salt-and-pepper beard and red suspenders.

The larger man opens a folder on his desk, the front of which is stamped *CLASSIFIED TOP SECRET*. Under that are the words *Rodolfo Santee—Caduceus Eyes Only*. And below that is a rubber-stamped symbol: a staff topped by two wings and entwined by a pair of snakes.

After Santee reads the contents—one typed page, an incident report—he looks over at the man in the bow tie. "Hey, Barr, looks like our little sweetheart might be hiding out in the high desert, around Victorville. Apparently, somebody got suspicious regarding purchases a local man was making." Santee looks back down at the page. "Fingernail polish is not part of the usual shopping list for a local desert rat." Santee hooks his thumbs into his suspenders. "And it looks like this same individual purchased an unusual quantity of propane."

"Could mean anything. Maybe the local dude has a daughter at home."

"Here's a full list of his purchases." Santee pulls a paper from the folder and hands it to Barr.

Barr slips on a pair of steel-framed glasses, scans the list.

"Read that," Santee says, "and tell me he's not hidin' a teenage girl. Okay. So where is she? Why all the hush-hush?"

"If . . . *if* it's the Adengard girl"—Barr sets down the list and opens a digital map on his computer screen—"and *if* she's actually in Victorville, we need to put a tracking device on this local guy. It's a pretty big place, plus there are a lot of abandoned mines in the area where she could be hiding. Got a make on the vehicle?"

Santee looks at the folder. "Security footage from the supermarket shows a sixty-four Ford pickup. Surveillance is black-and-white, so don't know the vehicle color. And the video didn't pick up the license number."

"I'll run all the sixty-four Ford pickups," Barr says. "There can't be that many."

"Step on it," Santee says. "As soon as you find that truck, I want a tail put on. Oh yeah. We're finally gonna nail this girl."

Santee leaves to go to the bathroom. The Top Secret folder rests on his desk.

Barr gets up, opens the folder, and snaps a picture.

CHAPTER 13

Dara sits outdoors on the Silver Bullet's doorstep, and Seb hands her dad a pair of scissors.

"You can't look the same no more," Seb says. "Not safe for you."

"But nobody's gonna see me here," she protests.

Clip-clip. Clumps of hair with signature green streaks scatter in the wind, littering the hard sand. Another part of her gone.

When her dad finishes, her hair ends up Peter Pan short, tufted and spiky from the uneven cut of the scissors.

Dad drapes a towel over her shoulders.

"Your fada, he goin' to bleach hair with hydrogen parasite," Seb says.

"What?!"

"Peroxide," her dad clarifies.

"Make you into blondie-girl." Seb hands Dad a brown plastic bottle.

***

Dara, cross-legged on the elevated bunk bed, hunched over, recalls the time when she'd first made her way to Hollywood with the Jyotisha. She checks off a mental inventory of the past. In addition to the precious armlet, she'd had her skateboard, the clothes she wore, her backpack, and Linc. Nothing more. She'd survived.

Right now she counts the things spread out before her:

- three shirts
- two pairs of jeans
- green gym shorts Seb must have picked up at a thrift store—a faded number 52 on the front and a name written in marker on the inside waistband
- underwear—a set she wears and a set to wash

- a friendship bracelet woven from threads of an old beach towel she'd found at an abandoned desert encampment
- socks
- one pair of old black-and-white sneakers, also from a thrift store
- the desert camouflage hoodie

That's it. She piles these meager belongings in front of her. From her perch on the bunk bed, she looks down at the tiny scene in the Silver Bullet—Seb sitting at the small built-in table, her dad under the sink pulling up another length of small hose.

She closes her eyes and does a second inventory. The things that have been taken:

- her mother
- the Jyotisha
- her mother's picture
- a skateboard
- the note from Ayon in which the Jyotisha had been wrapped
- the flannel shirts Brooke gave her
- Linc

She takes a quick breath, and her stomach tenses:

- Diego

***

"You are almost ready," Seb says. He stands facing Dara outside the trailer. "I can see it in your eyes. You look here"—he holds up a finger—"but what you see is far away." He drops his hand. "Something has changed in you."

That night, Dara lies on a blanket just outside the trailer. Under the early autumn stars. she gazes up at countless pinpricks of light which remind her of the spark that first ignited the Jyotisha by the swimming pool. In the configuration of a starry cluster, she thinks she sees her mother's face, glittering down upon Dara. The eyes—circles of stars. And the hair, a cascade of twinkling radiance.

Inside, Dara yearns to see her again.

CHAPTER 14

The next morning, Dara rubs her eyes and stares at the ceiling. After a few moments, she swings her legs over the side of the bunk bed and drops to the floor. The outside door is open, and dry desert air mixes with the scent of coffee.

She finds her dad sitting at the kitchen table next to the stove, empty cereal bowl in front of him. He's flipping through the pages of a motorcycle magazine. "Hey," he says and glances up at her.

"G'morning." Still half-asleep, she casts a glance at the walkie-talkie in its charger on the kitchen counter, grabs a handful of clothes, goes into the bathroom, showers, dresses.

"Scrambled eggs?" her dad offers when she comes back out.

She shakes her head and walks outdoors.

"Happy birthday!" he calls after her.

Seb's truck is gone, but that isn't unusual. He probably won't show up until later in the day. She surveys the barren surroundings. It all seems so desolate now—the nothing landscape, dead hills, scraggly mesquite. All of a sudden, it wells up in her. She's sick of it.

Footsteps sound behind, and she turns.

"Hey, birthday girl," her dad says, "everything okay?"

"Not really, no."

Before she'd found the Jyotisha—or it had found her—her dad had been the Enforcer, and she'd thought of him as a Recruit Division Commander, the Navy's equivalent of a Drill Sergeant.

But that was then.

Although he still seems just as tough—you can take the man out of the Seabees, but you can't take the Seabees out of the man—there'd been a change. She'd gone on TV, broken down in his arms, and his words had stuck—for both of them: *You don't know what you've got until it's taken from you.*

And in her mind now, she sees Diego stepping in front of her to take a bullet—his back turned to her, arms spread wide. The Jyotisha had glowed, bright and radiant above a gunshot wound. *You don't know what you've got—*

"There's no use complaining about it," her dad says, standing next to her outside the Silver Bullet. "You can't go anywhere else now."

"It's not fair. I feel like a prisoner here."

"It's for your own protection."

"I wish I could be in Reseda."

Her dad shoots her a puzzled look.

"Diego. He's probably there." She stares out at the dusty road that leads to the Silver Bullet. "When will it end?" she asks. If there was a specific date, a release point, she might feel . . . less trapped.

"Sometimes," her dad says, "you have to wait out the enemy, until he makes a move."

"You mean Mercy?"

Her dad nods.

"But you said 'he'. 'Until *he* makes a move'."

"You can't go back out there. Things have been happening. You've needed to heal, and not just physically. You lost your mother and almost lost me. That's a lot for anyone to go through."

Dara turns from her dad to look out at the desert, warm sun on her back. "I feel like I lost a part of myself, too," she says, "the girl who used to skateboard, read *manga*—and I don't think I'm ever getting her back."

Her dad puts an arm around her shoulder, and she leans into him.

***

Late afternoon. Seb shows up with groceries. Her dad steps outside and Dara hears their voices before Seb comes in carrying two paper grocery bags.

"Did you bring us more toilet paper?" Dara asks. She peers into one of the bags. "I can hardly wait to eat more Grape Nuts."

"What's up with you?" Seb asks.

"Just a little sick of this game," she replies. "No offense to your Silver Bullet." She looks at her dad, who follows Seb carrying another bag.

"It's not a game," her dad says. He wears a backwards baseball cap, and with his long hair, beard, and sinewy build looks like he just got off work on a construction crew.

"I brought you something," Seb says, and heads back out to the truck. He returns with both hands behind his back, smiles, and brings out one hand, which grips an In 'n' Out take-out bag. He brings his other hand from behind his back—a chocolate shake.

Seb starts humming the opening bars of "Happy Birthday," and Dad joins in as he and Seb burst into the song's words.

She smiles as she takes the first sip of the best chocolate shake she's ever tasted. While Seb eats just the fries, Dara bites into the Double-Double, savoring the perfect mixture of toasted bun, grilled beef patties, and melted cheddar. She eats half of it and lifts the top bun to drizzle a packet of ketchup over the cheese. She devours the rest of the burger before attacking the animal fries. They're the best things she's tasted for weeks and, as she eats in silence, recalls a time many weeks ago.

She'd sat next to Diego at the Crossroads Youth Shelter as he chomped down on a burger. The metal chair had squeaked, and she can still see the yellow cinder block walls. *Diego.* Clear black eyes, golden skin. And much later: his kiss, the way his face had perfectly aligned with hers. The softness of his lips had been a total surprise, and she ached with longing to feel his arms around her once again.

***

A short time later after eating, they sit at the small kitchen table, its surface strewn with fast food wrappers. The ceiling air conditioner strains to cool the air.

Her dad reaches down to the floor, pulls up a paper supermarket bag, and places it in front of her.

"What's this?" she asks. Excitement rises in her chest, and she reaches into the bag to withdraw a box wrapped in Snoopy gift paper. Her hands shake as she fumbles with the ribbon and tears off the paper.

Inside the box is a pair of high top sneakers—black canvas, white rubber.

Before she can say anything, Seb brushes back his dreadlocks and hands her a shallow, narrow box. Shiny, black, laminated. Inlaid on the lid is an iridescent abalone shell in the shape of a flower.

She opens the box, and inside lie three feathers. Red, yellow, and green.

"You could wear them in your hair," Seb says, "but I strung them on a leather cord."

Dara loops the three feathers over her head, and lets them fall around her neck, below her throat. Outside, it's twilight, and she admires her reflection in the window. The feathers, dangling against her camouflage hoodie, appear as splotches of bright color.

"They are special feathers," Seb says. "From Jamaican legend. Story was that island had lost all color and girl must find a rare bird, pull three feathers, and return with them. When she does this, all the colors of the island come back bright and strong."

"I love these," Dara says. She watches herself stroke their silky softness, brushes a hand over her blonde, almost white, hair.

"Remember whenever you touch those feathers," Seb says, "you can let go, like a feather in the wind. Just say, 'Feathers fly. Feathers fall. Be like the wind and let them go'. "

Dara repeats the words in her head, caresses the soft, silky feathers.

As she looks out the Silver Bullet's window, something moves against the desert landscape—a small coyote. She squints, trying to make it out through the waning light. It runs free in the desert wind, and is soon lost in the distance.

"How much longer do I have to hide?" she asks.

"Things are happening out there," her dad says. "You just need to hole up here a little longer."

"*What*'s happened?" Like she's pressing at a door to get in, but someone on the other side keeps ramming it back.

"You must let things pass over and through now," Seb says, "like the wind."

"Our home has been Seb's Silver Bullet," her dad says, lowering his voice. "But you—and me—right now, we have no home. If anything happens to me, you go on the run and you stay on the run. You understand?"

"I don't want to do that anymore," she says.

"Survival is at ground level," Dad says. "If someone comes after us—I'm not saying that's gonna happen—but just in case it ever does, you keep as low to the ground as possible. When I was in Iraq, that's one of the first things they taught us. And don't run back here to the Silver Bullet if there's trouble because this is not your home. I can always take care of myself, and so don't you ever worry about me. I'm used to the desert and can survive here. But your best hope would be to get out. Roger that?"

She nods and looks at her dad, then at Seb. "Thanks for my birthday," she whispers. "I thought—"

"What, you thought we'd forgot?" her dad says. "Oh, there's one more thing." He gets up and fiddles with something on the counter. He returns to the table and places a chocolate cupcake with silver sprinkles in front of Dara.

"I forgot to buy matches and them little candles," Seb says.

"But you can still make a wish," her dad says. "Happy seventeenth birthday."

She closes her eyes, thinks for a minute, opens them, and blows out an imaginary candle.

CHAPTER 15

The following day, Seb drives down Pearblossom Highway. Early morning , and the Friday traffic rush to Vegas has already begun. Seb glances once more in his rear view mirror. Black SUV. It's been there for the past ten miles, pulled over when he stopped at a McDonald's, but then resumed tailing him. When he slows, the SUV slows. When he speeds up, it keeps pace.

Seb pulls into a gas station, plastic pennants flapping in a hot, dry wind. He pays cash—always cash—but senses the eyes of the station attendant on him the whole time he gasses up.

When he gets back in the truck, he checks his rear view mirror. The SUV is nowhere to be seen, and he eases the truck forward before he spots the SUV pulling into view on the road a short distance behind him. Seb stops the truck next to a pair of water and air hoses near the gas pumps and gets out, crouches down next to the tires. He busies himself letting air out of the tires, putting an equal amount back in while he surveys the landscape. The SUV has once again melted into the landscape, invisible.

When he gets back inside the truck cab, his phone dings. A text from a number he doesn't recognize.

Sebby, this is Brooke. I'm using the hairdresser's phone . . . mine is being monitored. They're threatening to arrest me . . . not sure how much longer I'll even be here . . . take extra care of Dara. One of the feds Santee according to his ID was here, asked lots of questions. Be careful stay safe.

Seb goes back inside the gas station's mini-store and purchases a Zippo cigarette lighter. Once ignited, it will stay lit as long as necessary.

"Pack of smokes?" the attendant asks. She wears a witch's hat.

"Wins-tone. Is today Halloween?"

"Tomorrow."

Back in the truck, he sets the cigarette lighter and Winston cigarettes on the bench seat and pulls out his cell phone again. He checks Twitter, top trends. Variations of *Dara Adengard, Jyotisha,* and *Lightband* are near the top, as they have been for weeks. But there are others, too.

> Demonstrations block Sunset Blvd. overnight, protests mount, looting, arrests made. #Lightband #Dara Adengard bit.ly/76YT4989
> --FeedBuzz (@Feedbuzz)

> #ExpectAMiracle #EAM group meetings lead to more arrests. Police: large group gatherings a public safety threat. Watch Good Morning USA live.
> --GoodMorningUSA (@GMUSA)

> #Comic-Con #Jyotisha flex-band, fits any size arm. Just $29.99. Booth 807. Retweet for 10% discount. View on Etsy bit.ly/98JK043
> --HeroicJourneyJewelry (@HJJewelry)

> #IWasThere #Jyotisha #GriffithPark #Lightband #WasHealed2
> --BethanyBethany (@Bethbeth)

> If #Dara father #MissingSoldier is ever found, I wanna see him on #DWTS sexiest eyes everrrr!!!!
> DarlingDar (@darleeeeeene)

Seb scrolls through several other trending news tweets, then stops.

> H2ND #batvirus spreads from Indonesia into Thailand, Singapore. Concerns raised. #Quarantine bit.ly/8762UOP65
> --DailyNewsFeed (@DNFeed)

And finally, this:

> Check out the new single by #Kiara
> #TheLightband streaming now on Spotify.
> --OlioRecords (@ORMusic)

Seb slips the phone back into his pocket and eases the truck back onto the main road. The SUV is still there, a safe distance behind. Its windows are tinted, and he can't see the driver. He reaches into the glove compartment, pulls out the walkie-talkie, and turns it on.

CHAPTER 16

Dara awakens, steps down from the bunk bed. She glances toward her dad's bedroom, and hears the sounds of a walkie-talkie coming from outside.

"Dad?"

No answer.

She steps out into the desert air.

Dad has removed the plastic sheet covering the propane tanks, and is attaching plastic hoses to the nozzles. The walkie-talkie lies on its side in the dirt next to him.

"What are you doing?" she asks.

"Preparing."

"What does that mean?" She tries to steady her voice.

He brushes back his hair, takes a deep breath. "The storm might be about to hit our doorstep." He speaks fast, sweating, eyes red-rimmed. Dara knows he must have been up all night, vigilant.

"And so . . . the propane tanks?"

He doesn't answer but scoots on his back under the trailer and pulls down on a length of hose, giving it more play.

"I thought that was for water drainage," she says.

"Been preparing the whole time," he replies. "Quick, hold this." He pokes out a hand and gives her the hose while he slides out from under the trailer. He stands, grabs the hose, pulls it, and draws it back to the propane tanks, attaching it to another nozzle.

Her heart pounds, and she scans the horizon. The sun has risen over the barren, brown hills, and the air is cool and dry. The cacti's dark silhouettes, eerie stillness. A world that's been struck into silence.

She turns to look back at the trailer. A carved pumpkin guards the Silver Bullet's door, and a few yards away something skitters in the dirt. In the distance, the faint chirrup of a bird.

Her dad looks into the distance, and Dara follows his gaze.

A dust cloud moves toward them down the desert road, the sound of an approaching engine.

Her dad dashes back to the propane tanks clustered against the tow hitch. She sees him turn the handles.

Seb's blue truck emerges from the dust, racing at full speed. It grows closer, and moments later pulls up next to her, motor still running.

"Get in!" Seb yells out the window. "We have to go!"

Her dad sprints toward her, the muscles in his neck taut.

She hesitates.

"There is no time," Seb says. "Now! Come!"

"Dad!" she calls.

Seb flings the driver's door open and jumps out. He points back at the road.

Another large dust cloud races toward them. Dara freezes. It's a black SUV, speeding nearer, sunlight glinting off its paint. She sees a flash from the window, followed by a muffled pop, and something strikes the dirt near Dara.

"Dara!" Seb yells. "Run!"

Another pop.

Seb collapses to the ground, and what looks like a square, silver cigarette lighter rolls out of his hand.

Dara takes a step toward him.

Dad grabs her, throws her on the ground behind the truck, and dives after her. His body thuds onto the ground next to the front tire.

Dara lies there as a bullet whines past them. Her dad reaches up and yanks open the passenger door.

"Get in!" he says.

Dara catches a quick glimpse of Seb's motionless body as she leaps into the front seat. She stares at his legs—distressed denim, ragged hems—visible through the driver's door. His Rasta cap lies on the ground.

Another gunshot sound, and a bullet dings into the truck.

The truck's engine is running, keys in the ignition. Her dad crawls over her into the driver's seat, jams the floor shift with one hand, and hits the accelerator. The truck jerks forward.

"Seb!" she yells, looking back at the body sprawled in the dirt. The black SUV stops near his body, and two men get out, sprinting into the trailer.

"Keep down!" her dad says. "They think you're in the trailer."

Dad careens past the Silver Bullet and stops the truck several hundred feet away. Dara looks back.

Seb struggles to stand, a small flame in his hand. He limps toward the door of the Silver Bullet.

Seconds later, the Silver Bullet explodes with a deafening roar. Sand and metal fragments shower the truck as it's rocked from the blast.

"Let's get out of here," her dad says.

"We can't leave Seb!"

"We can't save him," her dad says. "He can only save himself now." He steers the truck into the desert.

Dara looks back, sees flames and smoke. She is shocked to see a black SUV—the same or a second one?— emerge from the smoke, racing past the burning trailer in pursuit of Dara and her dad. Was there someone else, one who'd survived the blast?

"Shut that damn door!" her dad yells.

In the rush to escape, she hasn't closed the passenger door. Dara stretches, but it swings just out of reach.

The door lurches and sways on its hinges as her dad veers to avoid hitting a mesquite bush. Dara reaches out one arm toward the swinging door and fights to maintain her balance, holding onto the door frame with her other hand.

Her dad yanks the wheel hard to the left, and the sudden maneuver causes Dara to lose her grip on the door frame. In desperation, she claws at the air, trying to grasp the open door.

She sails through the air, thrown from the truck as it continues to race ahead. She lands on the hard ground and rolls several times, ending up at the bottom of a rutted desert wash.

Although bruised and jolted, she's able to raise her head and catch a glimpse of the roof of Seb's blue truck rushing ahead. The SUV speeds after it, close enough to hear its tires crunch over the sandy grit.

Dad's trying to lead them away from me, she thinks. Tossed from the side of the truck and away from the pursuing SUV, her side hurts. She prays she hasn't been spotted and shudders with the sudden realization: she's been abandoned in the middle of the desert.

She throws her camo hoodie over her head and lies with her legs tucked under so the beige camouflage provides as much concealment as possible. There could be others after me, too, she thinks.

When she can't hear any vehicles, she lifts her head. No sign of the truck or SUV. Her shoulder throbs and she's scraped her leg, but other than that seems to be okay. She's wearing green gym shorts, hoodie, new birthday sneakers. The three feathers around her neck are dusty but intact.

Behind her, dark smoke billows from the trailer. Sounds of approaching sirens. Ahead and to the right, the vast open desert. To her left the brown, sun-beaten hills.

She doesn't dare head back to the remains of the Silver Bullet. Another route leads where her dad was heading, into the desert flatness. That's no good, either.

In the distance are the barren hills, baked in the morning sun. If her dad is caught, they'll discover she's no longer with him—and come back to look for her. She needs to move.

She wonders who it was that found them, and sets off in the direction of the hills. Without water, she'll have to find shade and somehow survive until the sun sets. Then she'll look for lights to find her way back to civilization. How far away is that? Two miles? Three?

She remembers Seb's words. If she can just survive until late in the day, make the desert landscape work to her advantage. She knows how unforgiving the desert can be, but if she could just make it through the daylight hours, she has a chance.

After Dara walks a short distance, she spots a Joshua tree grove. Spartan cacti, bare branches tipped with bouquets of bright green, palm-like spears. She uses their rough, corklike bark to saw a length of string from her hood string, stretches the hoodie between two trees, and secures it to the branches. It makes enough shade for her to sit in, but the ground has already heated. She removes her new sneakers, turns them upside down. Seat cushion.

In the distance, more sirens.

Stunned, she tries to absorb what's happened. Her dad, in an effort to save her, had continued on without her. And what happened to Seb after he caused his own Silver Bullet to explode? It's like she's surfaced in the middle of the vast ocean only to discover that the ship has gone. It's just her and the glistening mirages.

CHAPTER 17

Nineteen year-old Mercy—a slender girl of nineteen with thick, dark hair—stands on the edge of the boardwalk, next to a food cart that sells empanadas and smoothies. She wears a white, tasseled hemp blouse over loose tapestry pants, and frequently brings her hand up to a leather pouch hanging from her neck. A worn, bulging backpack rests near her feet, and by her side stands a young man with short dreadlocks.

She looks down the coast and in the distance sees Miranda Park, connected to the land by a short jetty. Mercy stares at the passing crowd of tourists, street people, and hustlers selling CD's. A young girl skips past holding her father's hand, and the memory once again sweeps over Mercy.

She'd been so young when they came to kill her.

Eleven years old. The day had started on a note of happy anticipation. She'd lugged a small fishing pole in one hand, a yellow beach pail in the other. A crown from Burger King sat on her head, and she followed her father, Ayon, who was young and muscular. He walked with a purposeful, forward-leaning stride and carried a tackle box in one hand, a long fishing pole in the other. They walked past the boardwalk and along the concrete jetty connecting the shore to a manmade island converted into a public park.

Mercy bounced after her father, trying to catch up with him or maybe escape some invisible thing that nipped at her heels. She glanced back to check on her mother, Tash, who followed wearing a long black cloak. She was tall, thin, and had a lean face. Mercy caught a glimpse of her mother looking back over her shoulder, as though she'd forgotten something.

They reached the island park, its perimeter constructed of large boulders, the interior an idyllic landscape of grass, palm trees, and picnic tables. On one side of the park was a paddleboat and kayak rental. Birds perched on the rocks at water's edge, and butterflies danced in the sweet-smelling air next to roses and wildflowers. A man sold hot dogs from an aluminum cart.

Ayon placed his fishing tackle box on a large boulder. "We'll catch some dinner," he said.

Tucked inside a space beneath the angled trays of the tackle box, Mercy caught sight of the small, silver-handled pistol her father often carried.

With a quick thrust-twist of the fishing knife into the herring, Ayon sliced off a small piece and baited her hook. He baited his own and cast his line into the water while Mercy did the same.

He looked at her, concern in his eyes, and reached a hand to rough her hair.

Tash had brought a folding beach chair and sat under the shade of a nearby palm tree. Alongside Mercy, her father reeled in kelp, fixed the bait, and recast his line.

Mercy looked over at him and positioned her pole just like her father's.

A pelican swooped, skimming the surface of the ocean.

As the minutes ticked by, Mercy grew impatient and propped her pole against a boulder while she skipped over some rocks. Her father looked over his shoulder and pulled the tackle box closer. When Mercy returned to her fishing pole, Ayon jerked his own rod to make the bait move, and Mercy copied him.

She felt a slight tug and pulled. Another tug.

"Papa!"

He took over the pole for her, and five minutes later a foot-long jacksmelt lay on the rock.

"We'll pan fry this tonight," her father said.

Some other children and adults came over to stare at what the girl had hooked. Mercy was proud of her catch.

Facing the small crowd of onlookers, Ayon shifted uneasily next to Mercy and put a hand on her shoulder.

Tash's beach chair was empty.

At that moment, a pelican dove straight down in a plummeting freefall. At the last minute, the bird spread his wings, hovered, and grabbed the fish with his large beak. Dismayed, Mercy watched the bird flap into the sky, jacksmelt clamped in its beak so that only the fish's head and tail were visible. The pelican, wings beating, headed out over the water.

Mercy ran, stumbling over the boulders, arms outstretched as though she could reach into the sky and snatch the fish out of the bird's beak.

"Mercy!" Ayon yelled behind her. "Stop!"

But Mercy, hopping over boulders close to the water, continued to chase the bird. The pelican soared higher and banked toward land. It tilted its head up and the fish slipped into the bird's hanging throat pouch.

Mercy found herself partway down an embankment where the rocks formed a miniature cove hiding her from view. The cove faced the wide-open sea, and here the waves crashed with explosive force against the rocks.

"Hello, Mercy." A deep voice behind her.

She spun around to face a man who stood only a few feet away. Intent on the stolen jacksmelt, she hadn't heard him. Wraparound sunglasses, basketball shorts. A multi-colored serpent tattoo wound around his leg, two red snake eyes staring back at her from his shin. In the man's hand, a long knife.

Jolted by fear, Mercy retreated a step and looked past the man's shoulder, hoping to see her father at the top of the embankment. But there were only green palm fronds against a blue sky. She took another step back, tripped over a boulder, and fell sprawling onto the rocks.

The man advanced on her, knife blade glinting in the sunlight.

A bird lighted near them and cawed.

She screamed.

"I make you be quiet," the man said. His words carried a foreign accent. "I do this for Shandor. Wipe clean the blood." He brought the knife down with sudden force, and she jerked her head aside just before the blade sparked against a rock next to her ear.

She scrambled backwards, pushing with her palms, scooting over the rocks, and let out another scream.

A shot rang out, and a fine spray of rock dust hit Mercy on the cheek.

No, not dust.

It was warm . . . wet mist. She brought a hand to her cheek.

Blood.

The man was no longer moving to stab her, but instead limped around in a 180° swivel.

Mercy followed his slow pivot.

Ayon stood below the top of the embankment, concealed from the rest of the park, a gun in his hand.

Blood trickled down the back of the man's leg, tiny crimson rivulets caressing the tattooed serpent's coils.

"Jyotisha armband!" the man yelled. His head was turned toward Ayon. "Must never be hers." He pointed back at Mercy, his wounded leg struggling for purchase on the rock.

Mercy's head whirled, and she labored to her feet.

Ayon stepped down closer on the rocks, raised the gun, and fired again. The bullet ricocheted off a stone, the sound lost in the crash of a wave colliding with the rocks.

Dazed, Mercy looked up at the dazzling sun, and in the blinding heat, the sun became confused in her mind with the armband called a Jyotisha. She grew dizzy and could almost see an outstretched hand holding the monstrous light in the sky, radiant heat penetrating her skin, deep . . . deep within.

Her mother appeared next to her. Where had she come from? Was she here all along?

Although Tash stood close, her voice sounded far away. "Marko, you didn't kill her?" But another crashing wave sounded, so maybe those weren't her mother's words at all. They could have been something quite different.

The world spun, dissolved, her knees buckled, and eleven year-old Mercy collapsed onto the rocks.

When Mercy came to, her head pulsed and throbbed. Her father was by her side, holding her head in his hands, the gun tucked into his belt.

"He's gone," Ayon said. "You'll be okay." He helped her to get up and walk up the rocks onto level grass.

Tash lingered behind on the rocks.

A man who wore a white shirt and blue latex gloves checked Mercy for injuries. "The blood on your cheek is scatter spray from the gunman's leg wound. But you cut your head when you fell." He applied a gauze bandage.

A police officer took a report. He had a small notepad and gave Mercy a green lollipop. "Did you know the man?" he asked her.

"No."

"Ever seen him before?"

"Uh-uh." The lollipop was lime, and she rolled it in her mouth, the sour sweetness mingling with the shock of her experience.

"You say you heard something?" the officer asked. He was polite, and Mercy thought he must have kids. He looked like a dad.

"It sounded like 'Marko, you didn't kill her.'" As she repeated the words, they confused and chilled her—but more than the words, she was bothered by something else, a tone she'd detected in her mother's voice that seemed to suggest . . . disappointment.

"And who said that?"

"My mom."

"Don't listen to her," Tash said. "She's just a kid. I was so terrified and yelled, 'Don't kill her'. I have no idea what his name was."

Mercy overheard a police officer use the word "unstable" when referring to the suspect. "Suspect homeless. Went on a rampage with a knife. Check hospital ER's, see if they've got anyone with a bullet wound to the thigh." Turning to Ayon. "Sir, we're going to need to see a registration for that gun."

But nothing came of it. No one turned up in the ER, no one came forward. There were no witnesses other than Mercy and her parents. Ayon had fired a gun to defend his family, and the story appeared in the news for a couple of days—but it was quickly forgotten.

***

"Beef or chicken?" A voice pulls her out of the memory.

"What?"

"What kind empanada you like?"

"Oh, no, I—I don't want any." Mercy backs away from the sidewalk cart, stares once more down the coast to Miranda Park, the connecting jetty now lost in sea mist.

CHAPTER 18

Dara listens for vehicles, hears nothing, but sees flashing red lights in the distance near the Silver Bullet's smoldering wreckage. The sun blazes across the desert sky. After a couple of hours, her mouth is dry, throat parched, but she can't chance moving. Better to remain immobile. Conserve body water.

A lizard suns itself a few feet in front of her, out of the shade.

Sweat trickles down her forehead and into her eyes.

When at last the sun begins to set, Dara feels dizzy and her head hurts. She wants to fall asleep, but makes herself stand and walk back in the direction of the dirt road that leads between Seb's trailer and the main highway. She's careful not to get anywhere near the Silver Bullet. The hills parallel the dirt road. Under a salmon sunset, she can make out flashing emergency lights.

It grows dark. She follows twinkling lights from other trailers, listens for the sound of cars that could lead her to the highway.

CHAPTER 19

"Goddammit!" Santee has just read the incoming secure fax—six pages— and whacks the papers down on his desk.

"What's going on?" Barr gets up and walks over, picks up the pages.

"Things just went haywire, that's what's going on."

Barr glances at the pages and nods. "Yeah, I guess you could say that. So somebody tipped off the local press?"

"Just about this dude—" Santee rifles through the pages and pulls out one, shows it to Barr. A surveillance photo, taken in a supermarket parking lot: a man walking to his car.

"What kind of hat is that?" Barr asks.

"It's an oversized beanie cap. Rasta wear."

"Huh?"

"He's probably from the Caribbean. Jamaica, maybe. Fortunately, though, we heard about it before they sent a reporter to check things out, but it caused us to speed up the timetable. We moved in, tracked the Adengard girl back to a trailer where she'd been living with her dad and this reincarnation of Bob Marley. The trailer had no phone, no TV—almost totally off the grid, except for one electric wire. Bob Marley got shot, but Dara escaped with her father—you know, the Missing Soldier of TV fame. The trailer was torched, and we lost two of our operatives."

"What happened to Bob Marley?" Barr nods at the surveillance photo.

"Disappeared, but we're calling him dead, still searching the wreckage. Cover story about a meth lab that got blown up, feds were raiding it, killed in the explosion. We've secured the perimeter."

"So you think this Bob Marley dude blew up the trailer, willing to die— just to protect her?"

"That's pretty much it."

"One less retard in the gene pool, I guess—assuming he didn't make it. Why would anyone want to take a risk like that to protect a fugitive?" Barr straightens his bow tie and shakes his head. "So what happens now?"

"We find our little darlin'. That's what happens. She can't have got too far."

"We know she doesn't have the armband, though," Barr says.

"But if we get her," Santee says, "we've got half the equation. We just need to get the other half—and the 120-X."

"You could use the Adengard girl," Barr suggests, "to lead you to the 120-X. You know that's where she'll try to go."

Santee waves a dismissive hand. "She doesn't know where it is, either. And so far, we don't know where *she* is, so how could we put surveillance on her?"

"Don't forget about the dog," Barr says. "That could make things easier for us."

"They're not together." Santee leans back in his chair, thinking.

"But maybe they will be. It was part of the contingency plan."

"Don't hold your breath," Santee says. "For now, we just gotta focus all our energies on findin' our missing desert munchkin. I need every available agent to get out there—now."

CHAPTER 20

Dara stumbles onto the main road. Cars whizz past. Semis thunder by, backdrafts blowing her clothes.

A police car races—lights flashing, no siren. She crouches behind a bush, takes in the faint odor of creosote.

Unable to walk further, Dara rests on a low sign—*Homes from the low 200's*, green arrow pointing in the direction of a housing development built into the desert landscape up ahead. A car slows, pulls up next to her, and she jumps. It's an older, light brown sedan, well-kept despite its age. Inside, someone leans over and cranks down the passenger window.

"Everything okay?" A woman's voice. Dara catches a glimpse of white hair.

Dara turns away, keeps her head down, and gets up to resume walking, stumbles.

"Give you a lift?" the woman calls as the car keeps pace.

Dara takes a step toward the car, pulls the torn hoodie low on her brow, and bends down to see inside. She hangs onto the window sill to steady her balance. The driver is an older woman, heavy-set, look of concern on her face. In the backseat, toddler strapped to a car seat. No other passengers.

"Girl like you shouldn't be out here at night," the woman says. "Maybe you ain't heard what happened."

"What?" Dara says.

"It was just on the news. Meth heads blew up a trailer just as the Feds was servin' a warrant." She nods at her dashboard. "Just heard it on the radio. One of the druggies is still on the loose. That's why you shouldn't be walking out here by yourself."

Dara catches a quick breath. "I'm just going into"—what's the name of the town?—"to Victorville," she says.

"Ain't far," the woman says. "Hop in."

Dara opens the passenger door, but before she gets in notices a flag clamped to the metal frame above the driver's window. Dara hadn't seen it at first because the car is stopped and in the still night air, the flag hangs limp, a tattered piece of black cloth.

"Thanks," Dara says. She keeps her face averted, tugs the hoodie to make sure it hides her eyes. Her fingers tremble as she fastens the seatbelt. Head pounds, skin feels cold, and she has difficulty swallowing.

"You can call me Ginny. I'm takin' my grandson back home to his daddy, I watch this baby most afternoons." She eases the car back onto the road, looks over at Dara. "You're shaking, hon. And looks like you cut your leg. What happened to you?"

Dara crosses her arms, holding them tight so they won't tremble. "I'm just real thirsty." She hears the sound of her own voice—cracked, parched—finds it hard to speak through the dryness.

"Look in the back seat there. I think I got a water bottle."

Dara undoes her seatbelt, turns around, and leans over the seat back. The toddler is asleep and his quick, even breaths make a wheezing sound. Dara moves aside a floppy cloth hat, under which is a bottle of water. But she's also seen something else, tossed on the floor—a pair of aluminum forearm crutches.

Dara guzzles the whole bottle, and the warm liquid flows down through her throat, into her stomach. The hoodie falls back on her head.

"Good Lord," Ginny says. "You was thirsty."

The black flag whips above the driver's window.

Dara pulls the hoodie back over her brow. The water revives her. "Sports team?" Dara asks.

Ginny eyes Dara. "Is that how you hurt yourself? Playin' a game?"

"I meant the flag. Is it for a team?"

Ginny lets out a sigh and laughs. "Where you been, hon? Under a rock?"

"I just thought—"

"The healing girl. Dara. Don't' tell me you ain't never heard of her." Ginny takes her eyes off the road just long enough to cast another quick glance at Dara.

Dara grips the empty water bottle and looks down at her lap.

"She's gone," Ginny says. "Disappeared. The police won't say where she is. Nobody'll say. But you can bet somebody knows."

Dara hears the flag whipping in the wind. "So then that flag is—"

"It flies until Dara comes back."

"Why's it . . . black?"

"Because she lit the darkness. Maybe you can't see it, but the flag's got her armband printed on it. That's how we know."

"Know what?"

"That there's hope in the night." Ginny laughs again. "Really? You don't know none of this?"

"I—I did hear some things, now that you mention it."

"She'll come back. She has to. Alex there"—she nods toward the back seat—"he's got a problem in his lungs, and the doctors can't do nothin'. He needs that—what did they call it?—that bracelet thing." She pats one of her own legs. "We all do."

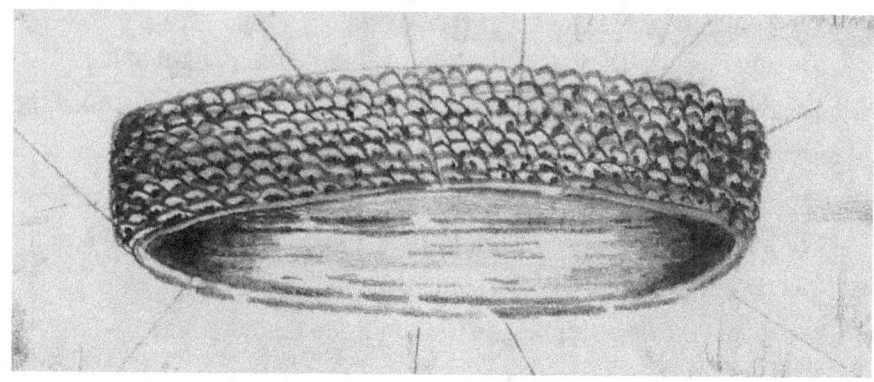

CHAPTER 21

Mercy in her sleeping bag on a grassy hillock near a rusted hot dog stand, stares into the sky. A shirtless young man sits next to her, beating a soft rhythm on a handheld buffalo drum. The area where they lounge is part of a deteriorated island park, connected to the land by a jetty.

Drought appears to have taken its toll: the area where they sit has turned brown. The palm tree has died, fronds hanging crisp and sere. Waves lap against the nearby rocks, and on the small beach, a surfer with a boogie board steps to avoid a dead sea lion washed up with the waves.

Every so often, Mercy raises a hand to her neck, caressing a leather pouch the size of a large coin purse. She sheds her sleeping bag. A snake tat spirals around her ankle, and above it another tattoo, a name in red cursive. *Ayon.*

Next to Mercy, the shirtless boy sets down his buffalo drum and puts a hand around Mercy's ankle, caressing it, his thumb stroking Ayon's name. His thumb presses into her ankle bone. "Cop," he says.

"I see him, Jasper," she whispers.

Mercy and Jasper edge away from the approaching police officer. The reflexive movement is almost imperceptible, giving the appearance of a random rearrangement for individual comfort. The subtle shifting of a leg, a morning yoga stretch.

The cop steps up to face them. "You need to move along."

"We're going," Jasper mutters. He stands and tucks the buffalo drum under one arm.

Mercy, however, remains seated with her head down, shielded by Jasper. One hand goes to the leather pouch around her neck. She opens the soft flap, feels the cool metal bands begin to warm, catches the odor of salty air and tar. A slight breeze kicks up, ruffling the dead palm fronds.

The police officer winces as though a nerve has pinched his back. A passing jogger stops to recover from a sudden spasm of coughing.

Mercy thinks better of it, closes the pouch, and drops her hand.

The jogger pulls a water bottle from a belt clip, takes a swig, and resumes his run around the park. His pace has slowed, however, and he seems bothered by an irritating stitch in his side.

The cop's handheld radio squawks. He turns his attention to something else and strides away.

Mercy and Jasper both rise, and Jasper—short blonde-ish dreads, baggy shorts—wraps an Indian blanket about his shoulders and heads alone down the jetty, away from the island park.

Mercy is cloaked in a heavy black shawl. She shuffles down the jetty and walks a short distance to the boardwalk, before stopping to wait for Jasper under the green glow of a medical marijuana sign.

"Here." Jasper returns and hands Mercy a foil package.

Inside is a stuffed grape leaf, which she wolfs down, pausing to spit out a piece of stem. She crumples the foil into a ball, and tosses it to the side. It makes an unpleasant, tinny sound, and the wind blows it skittering down the boardwalk.

Jasper, the same height as Mercy, puts an arm around her, pulls her close. "You need to be more careful," he says. "That cop—what if he saw the armband?"

"He didn't." She puts a hand to the side of her head. "If my father was alive—"

"What would he do?" Jasper asks.

"He told me he once healed his brother, Gunarik, when they were boys," Mercy's head throbs, and she leans back against the wall.

"What, like the healer girl?" Jasper steps back, mimics someone holding the Lightband above a crowd. "Why does it cause pain when you use it? Shouldn't you be able to heal, too?"

"My father told me," Mercy says, "that the tree branch is shaped by the water which feeds it, why he and my Uncle Gunarik were so different. When Gunarik held the Lightband in front of me at my *bunica*'s party, he poisoned me."

"Poisoned?" Jasper knows the story, but lets her tell it once more.

"Cast a spell. My father says Gunarik transmitted a vibration deep within me, so that if I ever used it, it would hurt people." She pauses, remembering. "It started with a bug."

Jasper gives her a puzzled look.

Mercy lowers her voice, as though speaking to herself. "Someone else has been found."

"Who?"

"I was remembering my father's words, when he told me that. *Someone else has been found.* Meaning Dara. Then I was abducted—and Dara killed my father." Mercy bites off the last words and stares straight ahead, a steely look in her eyes. She brings a hand to the neck pouch and turns to look at Jasper. "I'm glad we found each other. You know who I am, and yet you still love me."

The touch of his fingerless cloth glove, salt mist-damp on her lips.

"Just you and me," Jasper says. He lowers his hand from her lips and draws Mercy's shawl about her shoulders, over her head. "Let me see the Lightband."

His breath warms her face. Mercy lifts the pouch from her neck and opens its leather flap. Inside, something glitters, lighting both their faces as they peer down at it.

"Just . . . be careful," Jasper says. He glances around to make sure there are no passers-by, spots only a homeless man some distance away. He pulls Mercy's shawl to screen them, and Mercy draws out the Lightband, holds it between two fingers. It glows with a faint light.

Jasper holds out a hand and touches the braided metal armlet. "So warm," he whispers. The Lightband flickers brighter. A pink and white aurora licks around the metal bands, and a slight breeze ruffles the shawl.

Jasper flinches as though he's been bitten, then through gritted teeth: "That pain feels good, takes away . . . other hurting."

Mercy lowers the Lightband, cupping it between her palms so that it glows through the pink skin like a Chinese lantern. "Yes," she says, "pain to ease the pain. I know about that, too."

"You could do so much more than kill Dara." Sweat has broken out on Jasper's brow. "Although that would be a step. You have the Lightband now. Think what you could do with this."

Mercy brushes the armband, and its light dims. She nestles it back in the pouch, secures the flap, and loops it back around her neck, tucking it under her shirt.

Jasper's shoulders slump, and the tension drains from his face.

Mercy drops the shawl from her head and kisses him, whispers in his ear, "I can't do this without you. I need to find her. Dara killed my father, and I need to make sure she never again holds what is"—she looks hard into Jasper's eyes—"mine."

Jasper strokes her hair. "There are others—not just Dara—seeking the Lightband. The whole world wants your precious jewelry. Everywhere you turn—the news, cops, Reddit crowdsourcing—"

"I have to stay here," Mercy says, "where I can't be found." She blinks back the throbbing ache in her head. "At least, not yet. I need to be invisible, blend like a grain of sand on the beach, part of the tide, so that Dara won't see me coming—and neither will anyone else."

Jasper cups her chin in his hand and turns her face toward his. "The boy," he whispers. "I have found him for you."

Mercy draws back the shawl. "The boy?"

"Dara's boyfriend. Or ex. I've been waiting for just the right moment to tell you."

Mercy remembers him—the one who came for Dara in Gunarik's cave. He'd tried to shield Dara on the precipice at the abandoned zoo. He had a dog.

"Diego Mendez," Jasper says. "He was on TV. After Griffith Park and the Old Zoo, everyone wanted to talk to that little star. Then he dropped out of sight and the news media seems to have forgotten about him."

"He's not the one I want to kill," Mercy says.

"But Dara will try to find him," Jasper says. "Or he will find her—so you must go where he goes."

"And?"

"You tried to kill her already and failed. You know she'll come back. And when she does, you need to be ready." Jasper takes her hand.

"But Diego will recognize me," Mercy says. "He saw me before, at the Old Zoo."

"He doesn't have to see *you*," Jasper says. "Let me reach out to Diego Mendez, befriend him. And let Diego lead the way—to Dara."

***

After Jasper leaves, Mercy sits on the grass near the boardwalk and stares at the ocean. As though being pulled by the incoming tide, the memory washes over her.

Soon after the trauma of the knife attack on the rocks, there'd been a party—and for the first time, she'd seen Gunarik. It was held in a large backyard with a white gazebo. Inside the gazebo was a table, upon which had been set a pink-frosted sheet cake with "Happy Birthday, Vadoma" in purple letters, a Tarot card—the Moon—set into the frosting.

Tash knelt next to her and whispered, "Your Uncle Gunarik will be here soon."

The closeness of her mother's breath awakened in eleven year-old Mercy a sudden fear of the man who'd tried to stab her, and Mercy shivered. "What does he look like?"

"Shh." Tash had put a finger to her daughter's lips. "You must ask him a question."

"What?"

"Asks him if you can see . . . the arm bracelet. He won't show it to you, but watch his eyes, see where he looks."

Mercy imagined Gunarik as a majestic figure, dressed in a flowing purple tunic, towering over everyone as he tossed a golden armband into the air, caught it in the palm of his hand.

The birthday candles were lit, and they were about to sing "Happy Birthday" when there was a knock at the door, so loud it could be heard from the backyard. A terrible fear engulfed Mercy. She was certain that the man on the other side of the door would be Marko, and that he would be holding a knife.

Ayon went inside to open the door, and everyone stopped singing. A man came into the backyard, walking with the aid of a gold-tipped cane, and on one leg he wore a funny shoe. It had a sole that was much thicker than the shoe on his other foot, and it caused him to walk unevenly, as though one foot was on a curb, the other on the street.

Gunarik was not the tall, imposing figure Mercy had imagined, but leaned forward as he walked, which diminished his height. He wore an expensive shirt and jewelry, and under one arm carried a box wrapped in red paper, secured with silver ribbon. Mercy surveyed him from a distance, but couldn't see an armband. His long, dark hair swung, keeping time with his uneven steps, and once or twice it fell back to reveal a scar running the length of one cheek.

Vadoma sat in the gazebo, in front of her a cake with burning candles. Her eyes were on her son Gunarik, and she waved one hand loosely over the candles as if that gesture might extinguish the tiny flames.

Tash got up, leaned over the table, and blew out the candles for Vadoma. Mercy wondered if either Vadoma or her mother had made a wish.

Gunarik surveyed the room and limped up to the table where he stood facing Vadoma. "Hello, mother," he said.

"Son." She spoke the word softly, and glanced at Ayon.

Vadoma and Gunarik spoke quietly and, because Gunarik's back was to Mercy, all she could see of the conversation was what was written on Vadoma's face. Mercy could not read all the feelings that flickered over Vadoma's visage but her eyes looked sad.

Gunarik thrust his gift down in front of Vadoma and stepped back from the table.

Mercy was aware that the backyard had become quiet, and everyone was watching the scene. Only the sound of tearing paper filled the silence.

Vadoma lifted the box lid and gasped as she lifted out what at first appeared to be a blanket. Vadoma stood and held it up—a knee-length patchwork sweater, stitched from lengths of fawn and sepia-colored cloth. It looked like late autumn leaves with a pointed elf hood and wide hem at the bottom.

The guests were hushed, and something in Vadoma's eye glittered in a shaft of sunlight.

"How—how did you get this?" Vadoma asked, her voice gripped by emotion. "I have not worn since you were child."

"Now you have a part of the past," Gunarik said, "and maybe if you wear that you will be forced to remember what you did to me." He looked around the room. "Since I am not welcome here, I shall leave."

All eyes were on Gunarik as he made his way back to the house, cane clicking on the cement patio.

Tash prodded Mercy with one hand and whispered, "Go, ask him. Watch his eyes very carefully, see where he looks."

Mercy sensed danger because this moment seemed connected to another moment. Marko had tried to kill her because of this—because of Gunarik and an armband. But Mercy thought if she could just do this one thing—ask her uncle a question—the danger might be removed. She took a deep breath, ran to Gunarik, and caught him just before he reached the house. She glanced back to see her mother, and was surprised to find all eyes were on her, Mercy.

Gunarik, too, stared down at her.

Mercy, taken aback, remembered her mother's directions, and peered at Gunarik's eyes—but realized she hadn't asked him anything yet. Instead of cunning and secrecy, though, she saw sadness in his eyes, and wondered if that was always there or had just appeared. Mercy's mouth was dry and she struggled to form the word. "Uncle?" Her hands shook.

Gunarik gave her an inquiring look.

"I'm Mercy, and I want to ask you something." She tugged his sleeve to pull him down closer. She tried to remember her mother's words. Blood pounded in her ears, and her head throbbed. "Can you show me the arm bracelet?"

"You don't yet realize what you are asking for." Gunarik paused, studying her. "But . . . here." He rolled up his sleeve, and with one hand worked something down from his upper arm—an armband, woven of gold and silver braids that sparkled in the sunlight.

A slight vibration began at her fingertips, an electric current that went up her arm and into her chest. Did it come from the bracelet just a few feet away?

Gunarik held up the armband, raising it above his head. He closed his eyes, and the Jyotisha began to glow and crackle as though it was on fire. He opened his eyes and moved the armband closer to Mercy, holding it directly over her.

Mercy smelled something thick, dark, and glutinous that reminded her of wet tar. A wind rustled her hair. She winced and put a hand to her brow, to the wound she'd sustained a few days earlier when she'd fallen back onto the rocks.

"No!" her father yelled.

Mercy looked around and saw others shift uncomfortably, as though possessed of some thought or memory they didn't want. Tash had grown pale and hugged herself.

Mercy's brow pounded. She stepped back from Gunarik and removed her hand from her forehead: blood.

The light from the armband faded and Gunarik threaded it back over his hand, up his arm, and then lowered his sleeve. He rested his cane against his side and reached both hands down toward her.

She stepped closer, hoping he would offer the armband to her. Her fingers tingled, and she yearned to hold it.

Gunarik looked down at her, as though trying to gauge something. "You already feel it, don't you?" he asked.

She didn't know what to say. *Yes, she could feel it.*

Gunarik placed both hands around her head, clasping it tight. "Mercy," he said, and paused as though tasting the sound of her name for a moment. "You must take care of that wound. And may you find the meaning in your name. You will need it."

When he let go, she saw that there was blood on one of his palms.

He grasped his cane, limped to the door, and left.

Mercy turned to see her mother, a stricken look on her face. And there was her father, mouth drawn tight with rage as he glared after his brother. She noticed others, too. Blood trickled down the side of a woman's face, and a young man pressed a hand to his jaw. Mercy's face burned with shame. She'd failed her mother, caused her father's anger.

When the guests were gone, Mercy sat on the cool grass playing with her Tamagotchi. She reran the scene with Gunarik in her mind, the sensation that had tingled in her fingers—and tucked behind the curtain of her thoughts: *Marko, you didn't kill her?*

An arm touched her shoulder, and she looked up. Vadoma.

"Come, you must sit with me." Vadoma's dark hair, streaked with gray, was long and full, and her eyes were red.

Heart still pounding with fear and trepidation, Mercy sat on her *Bunica* Vadoma's lap. She'd seen the bracelet now, knew what it could do. Mercy sensed the cushion of her grandmother's thighs and swayed slightly on the softness as Vadoma sang in a voice that sounded like it was trying hard not to cry.

Hush-a-bye, baby, I am rocking you.

The seahorses dance with the fish,
The foals are in the waves.
We'll sail the sea in a teacup dish—

Her grandmother's voice was soft and mournful, but at the same time guttural, the word *seahorses* swallowed into the throat before being spit back on the tongue.

—and live in ocean caves.
Hush-a-bye baby, I am rocking you
to sleep by the waters blue.

***

Later—days? weeks?— June bug upside down on the kitchen floor. Helpless and vulnerable, tiny legs wiggling. A sheet of paper, glass jar. Scoop up the bug, take it back outside, set it right. But then, as she carried the jar . . . something in Mercy's hand tingled, a sudden jab of nerve pain.

She poured out the dead bug.

It was never more than that—a quick little shot of pain, and only when she touched a small wound, brought her hand to another's sore, a bruise. Or when she sensed fear and weakness, as with the helpless bug.

There was a boy Mercy liked who'd ignored her at school. He sat next to her in art class, and she noticed that the knuckles of his hand were scratched. Mercy asked him what happened. A conversation starter. She ran a flirty hand through her hair.

"Hurt it in soccer," he told her, then quickly turned away like she was bad news, muttering, "Weirdo."

"Let me see it." Made her voice sound sweet. Before he had a chance to react, she reached for his hand and let one finger brush the red knuckles.

He winced—"Damn!"—and quickly withdrew his hand, shook out the pain.

There'd been something in her touch, the feel of it, that couldn't be explained by static electricity or a quirk of the nerve endings. It had seemed to travel from inside her chest into her fingers, and she could sense its embryonic power.

***

The evening fog rolls over the water, touches the sand, and drifts further, shrouding the boardwalk. Metal grates rasp closed, shuttering t-shirt and reggae music shops. The tourists are gone, along with street performers juggling chainsaws. Tattooed denizens of the night stride the boardwalk, and longboarders slalom down the walkway. At the outdoor Six-Pack gym, a lone man wearing shorts lifts weights, while nearby comes the sound of a basketball being dribbled, pounded, swished through a chain metal net.

Mercy puts away her memories and slinks through the vaporous twilight.

CHAPTER 22

"You can drop me here," Dara says.

Ginny eases the car into the Coco's parking lot and pulls up to the front entrance. She glances at Dara. "You meetin' somebody?"

"Yeah. Thanks for the ride and the water."

"Mmm." Ginny purses her lips, as though trying to piece something together. She nods at Dara. "Well, you take care now."

Dara takes a quick look back at Alex and thinks about holding a hand over his chest, his tiny lungs, healing them—is the fragment of the Lightband she carries powerful enough to do that? But Ginny would see, and Dara can't let that happen. Not now.

She opens the car door, steps out, and backs away.

"Watch out for yourself," Ginny calls. "It ain't so safe out here."

"Thanks for the ride," Dara calls back.

The toddler begins to cry.

Ginny, with great effort, twists and stretches over the front seat to pick up a teething ring. "Right here, little one," she says, short of breath as she hands the teether to the child.

Ginny speaks to the child—"Hush now, baby"—smooths his hair, strokes a tiny cheek. She cocks her head to look out the passenger window at Dara, but it's too dark for Dara to see the expression on her face. Ginny turns her attention back to the steering wheel and puts the car in gear. The red tail lights glows, receding out of the parking lot, black flag fluttering in the breeze.

Dara continues to stand there for several moments before she notices that her lip is trembling.

She keeps her head down and walks into Coco's. "I'm meeting somebody," she mumbles to the hostess and rushes past, scanning for the restrooms.

They're in the back, past a well-lit bar area with several TV's. She steps into the restroom and cups her hands to drink from the faucet—the water she'd poured down her throat in Ginny's car hasn't come close to quenching her thirst. The automatic faucet keeps shutting off, the water coming in fitful spurts. She holds her hands in desperation under the spout, waiting for each burst of water, and gulps mouthful after mouthful of cool liquid. At last, she splashes water on her face, dries it with a paper towel, moistens another towel. She dabs at her leg to remove the dried blood.

She holds her hand over the cut, sliding it up and down her calf. Her fingers begin to tremble, glow, and her hand and leg both become warm. Light shoots from her palm, and when the glow subsides, she lifts her hand. The abrasion is gone and only a streak of new, pink skin remains.

She stares at her own hand, turning it over as though she's never seen it before. It looks . . . normal. An ordinary hand.

Her face in the mirror, and she does a double take: short blonde hair, skin tanned by weeks in the desert sun. Dark circles under her eyes. Seb's feathers dangle, fluttering in a slight current from the overhead air conditioner.

Dara steps out of the restroom and into the too-bright lights of the bar area. A server passes by carrying a plate of creamy mashed potatoes and meatloaf ladled with gravy. It's been a full day since she's eaten, and the tantalizing aromas overwhelm her.

Her attention is drawn to the TV mounted above the bar. Dara's hands clench into fists and her jaw tenses. *Taped Earlier*, the graphic reads. The sound is muted, but a breaking news chyron runs across the bottom of the screen.

Hunger pangs momentarily forgotten, Dara's attention is now fixed on the TV.

An aerial view of the burned-out Silver Bullet in the desert.

Drug bust leads to explosion, deaths, the chyron reads. *Suspects flee scene. Two federal agents, one suspect killed in drug lab explosion. Police conduct manhunt, search for suspect pickup truck.*

A picture flashes on the screen. *Sebastian Smith. Age: 42.*

Dara lets out a quick breath and unclenches her jaw.

Police seek information regarding teenager in getaway vehicle. Wearing hooded sweatshirt, military-style camouflage. Call 911, do not approach.

They don't show her picture. Do they know who that teenager is? Dara wonders. And they'd said "a drug bust." But there hadn't been any drugs. Seb didn't even smoke. Were they lying about Seb's death?

She continues to stare at the TV, and the screen image switches to a picture of a place she recognizes. A parking lot near the merry-go-round, where she'd accessed a fire road to the Old Zoo. The TV shows a surging crowd held back by police. Yellow tape cordons off the hillside behind.

Police break up demonstration, the news scroll reads. *Bottles thrown, numerous arrests.*

A young man is shown being handcuffed, loaded into a police van. He wears a black armband emblazoned with a golden Lightband. Behind him, a group appears to be shouting at the police and the TV camera.

Dara ducks back into the restroom and carefully removes the feather necklace. She pulls the hooded sweat jacket over her head, and slips the feathers back on. In the mirror, she sees three soft quills —red, yellow, green—dangling against the white t-shirt. She turns the camouflage jacket inside out and bundles it under her arm.

She makes her way through the parking lot to the back of Coco's, behind the kitchen, where she finds a pair of half-empty dumpsters in a penned enclosure. She squeezes in through an opening in a heavy metal gate, hoists herself up to the top of one of the dumpsters, flips open the lid, and reaches down to drag up a black trash bag.

An image flashes through her mind. Months ago, she'd scrambled up another dumpster. It had been the night she first ran with the Jyotisha, and two men had chased her. She'd hidden in an alley dumpster—but back then, it had been a struggle to clamber up the side.

But this time—one smooth movement and she'd boosted herself to the top.

She rips open the trash bag and stuffs the hoodie inside. In the bag, she sees a half-eaten sandwich—bread, roast beef, lettuce.

"Hey, *mi amiga.*" A voice from behind.

Startled, she drops the bag into the dumpster, pushes off, and jumps to the ground. She turns to face a burly, unshaven man wearing a stained white apron.

"You should no have done that."

She swallows hard. "I just thought I'd—" Her voice is hoarse. She wants to run, but he's blocking the gate.

"*No comida aqui.*" He gestures toward the dumpsters and mimes eating with his hands, a look of concern in his eyes. "You wait. I bring *plato.*"

He turns and disappears into the back of the coffee shop. She debates whether to wait or to run, but feels light-headed. Besides, he'd said something about bringing a *plato*—of food?

The man reappears with a take-out bag and a plastic cup of water. "Here," he says. "Eat. Keep out from—" He pauses, searching for the word. "—*problemas.*" He hands her the bag and water, wipes his hands on the food-stained apron.

"Thank you," she says. "I mean, really, thanks."

Seated behind a big rig at the edge of the parking lot, she uses a plastic fork. The meatloaf tastes like something her mother used to make, and Dara savors every mouthful. The baked potato is still hot, wrapped in tinfoil, dripping with butter. Last is a slice of chocolate cream pie. She keeps each bite in her mouth until it dissolves, lets it glide sweet and rich down her throat.

CHAPTER 23

The desert wind picks up, gusting over the asphalt, and a tumbleweed rolls across the parking lot. The plate of meatloaf has steadied her, and the aftertaste of chocolate cream pie is still fresh in her mouth. Dara stands and stares out into the night as the wind whips over her.

Should she stay and find her dad? How can she search an entire desert? If her dad had indeed escaped, he'd survive. He was a Seabee. And he'd been in Iraq. As long as he wasn't captured, he'd be okay.

On the TV news, they'd known about the truck and a teenage girl. But they claimed Seb's trailer was a drug lab, and Dara knew that was a lie. She couldn't trust any of it.

Right now, she needed to get further away—but where?

Another unanswered question: Who is after her? Who'd been driving the black SUV?

A bird fights against the wind to land nearby and pecks at crumbs in the parking lot. Dara feels a twinge of anxiety and runs a finger over one of the feathers dangling from her neck.

Ayon had once told her she couldn't run from her destiny. *It is here,* he'd said, *right where you are.* Was destiny something you could never shake, like a toothache, an inflamed nerve that keeps on throbbing?

Is it still here, right where she sits in this parking lot?

She thinks of her mother's eyes, the way they'd looked down upon Dara from the starry clusters that shone in the desert's brilliant night sky.

"You're keeping some late hours."

She jumps. Absorbed by the intensity of her own thoughts, she hasn't heard the man come up beside her next to the truck.

Thin. Blue jeans, an old corduroy jacket, and a brown trucker's cap. *RJ's Ribs* logo. Tufts of white hair peek from beneath the cap. "You work here?" He smiles.

The man's smile reminds her of Diego's. She glances back at Coco's and shakes her head.

"So you're just passin' through." It's a statement, and it seems like he knows she's on a journey.

"More or less."

"I got a feelin' it's more and not less." He smiles again, steps closer to peer at her face. "I had a grand-daughter looked a lot like you. Same kinda deep-set eyes." He pulls out a wallet and shows Dara a school picture of a teenage girl. "She died in a car accident couple of years ago. But she gives me strength on the roads every single day."

"I'm sorry," Dara whispers.

The hand holding the picture is pale and delicate.

"My name's Art, by the way." He tucks the picture back in his wallet. "And this is my rig." He pats the slatted gray side of the big freight container. "You know what I got in there?" He nods at the truck and smiles at her. A Diego smile.

She shakes her head.

He laughs. "Candy. Can you believe it? On this run, I'm carryin' a load of candy." He chuckles. "Sometimes, I been sneaking a little for myself." He eyes Dara.

Art could be her grandpa, and she likes his smile, the *RJ's Ribs* hat. The thought of a plate of barbeque ribs makes her hungry all over again.

Art looks at her as though he's considering something. "Give you a lift?" he asks, but there's a hesitation in his words like he isn't quite sure about her. "Where you headed?"

"I'm going back"—she stops, thinks of her dad, of Seb—"home."

"Where might that be?"

You and I—her dad had told her—*right now, we have no home. If anything happens to me, you go on the run and you stay on the run.* "I—my dad—"

The man shifts his feet, glances about. "Is he here?"

"I don't know where he is. That's—see—"

"Maybe I can give you a lift back home, to your daddy?"

Was this Destiny—*here, right where you are*—offering her a ride?

She considers for a moment. And then it comes to her. She knows exactly where she needs to go.

***

Inside, the truck is lit with a lime green glow from the dashboard console. The ride is gentle, and she sits on a cushiony bench seat. Lulled by the chatter of muted voices on the AM radio, Dara lays her head back, closes her eyes.

"You ever listen to this guy?" Art asks.

She opens her eyes. "Who?"

"Of course you wouldn't. *Late Nights with The Peter File.*"

Dara shakes her head. "Never heard of him."

"I listen to him a lot," Art says, "when I'm driving at night. That's when all the wackos is coming to life." He chuckles. "It's a riot, but some of the stuff sounds true. Who's to say?"

Dara looks down and sees Art's hand splayed palm down between the two of them in the middle of the seat.

"And then there's the bracelet," one of the voices on the radio is saying.

Art reaches forward and turns up the volume, returns his hand to the seat.

"It's an armband." A second voice. "Go back and watch the video."

Dara snaps to attention, turns her head toward the darkened window, sees her reflected image. No more hoodie. Could Art possibly recognize her? She brushes a hand over her hair, and in the reflection catches a glimpse of Art glancing over at her.

"Whatever," one of the voices is saying. "Before they took her away—"

The truck enters a short tunnel and the voices turn to static.

Art's hand moves closer to Dara's leg. She edges away.

"I don't know." The radio resumes as the truck emerges from the tunnel. "But you can bet they're checking out that thing, figuring out how it works. It's somehow connected to genetic manipulation. Has to be. If you can tamper with genes, you've got total control over people."

Art's finger touches the side of her thigh. She jerks away, crosses her legs, and stares straight ahead. White lines whizz by in the headlights' steady glare.

"He came once and walked among us and we crucified him."

"Now surely you don't' mean to suggest that this girl is the Second Coming. That's just—"

"She's sure got some believers," the caller says. "I tell you that. You've heard of the EAM?"

"Wackos," Art says. He switches off the volume and glances at Dara. He withdraws his hand and rubs it on his blue jeans. "I like your feathers. How many you got there?" He reaches an arm toward her, his hand fumbling for her chest and the feathers.

She pulls back, pressing into the seat. "They're a gift." Her voice shakes. "For my birthday."

He drops his hand into his lap and appraises her. "How old are you?"

Was he looking for younger or older? She needed to be the opposite. "I'm twenty."

He frowns. "I figured you for sixteen, maybe eighteen tops."

The truck slows.

"Why—h-how come you're getting off the freeway?"

"Gotta stop. Nature calls. You know how that goes."

Dara's heart pounds. She grips the door handle.

The truck lumbers to the end of the freeway exit.

She fumbles with her seatbelt, unbuckles it, and pushes on the door handle. Nothing happens.

Art laughs to himself, slowly navigates the turn, and drives several blocks down a darkened street to an empty gas station. The station is closed, unlit. The truck turns into the entrance, chugs to a stop next to a water hose. The air brakes hiss.

"I—I think these restrooms are closed," Dara says.

"I'm just gonna go out back here." Art shuts off the truck lights, but keeps the engine running. "Why don'tcha come with me."

Frantic, Dara pushes on her door handle again. It still won't open.

"Oh," Art says. "Forgot to tell you. That handle don't work. You gotta get out over here." He pats his lap.

"You go first," Dara says. Her voice trembles. "I'll follow you."

"You're not gettin' it," Art says. His tone is flat and he swallows hard. "Come here." He scoots nearer, grabs for her shirt.

Dara puts a hand around Art's forearm, partly to halt his advance—but in that moment there is something else she understands. The panic stops, and Dara hears Seb's voice in her head: *He believes he's stronger. Leverage his need to overpower.*

She holds Art's arm, feels the corduroy jacket. Gentle. Tender. *Guide your opponent where you want him to go.*

"That's more like it," Art says.

She pulls him in closer.

He bends toward her.

That's when she tightens her grip around his forearm—and with all her strength wrenches it behind his back, pushing it up so hard she hears his shoulder pop.

Art lets out a scream and, pulled off-balance, topples toward her.

She rockets her other palm into his face, and light explodes from her hand. There's a crunching sound as the open palm connects, and then she brings her elbow down onto his nose. *One-two.*

With both hands, she flings his head back. Blood flicks over the dashboard and her white t-shirt.

"Umf—"

She's on her knees on the seat, one of her hands around the back of his neck.

He gurgles.

She slams his face down onto the dashboard, and he makes a muffled sound, followed by blood-congested nose breathing.

She shoves him aside and reaches for a button—the one with a lock icon—on the driver's arm rest, clicks it, flings open the passenger door, and tumbles out.

Dara runs down the street, away from the gas station, and stops to catch her breath. Still gasping for air, she finds herself next to a feed store, and looks down at herself—gym shorts, sneakers, and a blood-spattered white t-shirt. The frontage road seems barren, deserted, but from nearby comes the occasional muted whoosh of a vehicle on the freeway.

There's a chill in the late night air.

After several minutes, she hears the rumble of Art's semi as it pulls out, heading back toward the interstate.

Behind the feed store, Dara finds several empty burlap sacks. She piles them to make a thin mattress next to a stack of wooden pallets, pulls other cloth pieces over her, and slips into a restless asleep.

CHAPTER 24

Dara awakens with a start and jerks her leg. Something had touched her thigh. Like a finger.

But it's only a small rock beneath the thin cloth sacks. She must have rolled over on it. She rubs her leg and looks up at the pale blue sky. Where is she?

She flexes her hand. It hurts, and the memory comes back in a rush: Art's fingers fumbling near her chest, her hand crunching into his face.

She hears noises inside the feed store, and looks over at the small receiving dock where she'd grabbed the empty gunny sacks. The back door slides open and a man steps out. Compact and stocky, he wears a checkered flannel shirt.

"What the hell you doin' here?" he asks. "You homeless gotta stay up in the hills, and don't be using this lot for a motel."

Dara stands, steps back.

"Well, damn," the man says, "ain't you the young one. What's that on your shirt?"

She brings a hand to the three feathers.

"No, I mean that—"

Dara glances down at her shirt—dried blood droplets. "Somebody—a truck driver—tried to—." She glances back toward the freeway.

The man in the flannel shirt tromps down a set of stairs from the loading dock. "You okay?" he asks. "You want I should call a ambulance?" His teeth are crooked, discolored, beard stained with nicotine.

She'd misjudged the good intentions of the man who brought her food—and she'd been wrong about Art. She can't afford to keep being wrong. Trust. Or not trust. She takes another step back. "No need to call the cops—I mean, the police," she says. "He didn't hurt me. Old dude. And you should be asking *him* if he's okay—not me."

"That's blood," the man says, staring at her shirt.

"I guess he could still drive—somehow. I'm sure he made it home, or to a hospital."

The man smiles and nods at her. "Tough little cookie," he says. "C'm here. I'll get you a shirt to wear."

She holds back.

"Hell, I'll just toss it to you. Wait a sec."

He disappears up the steps and into the rear of the loading dock, returning moments later with an oversize flannel shirt similar to the one he wears. Red and green plaid, a lumberjack's shirt. He tosses it from the platform, and it sails through the air, landing by Dara's feet. She puts it on, buttons it. It reeks of cigarette smoke and hangs on her like a robe. The feathers nestle underneath, next to her t-shirt.

"What place is this?" Dara calls.

"Joy's Feed and Mercantile. I'm her son. Joy's, that is."

"No, I mean where am I? I'm trying to get to Reseda."

"You're in Pacton. And if you don't know where that is, well then—you're just lucky." He chuckles. "Go around the front. I don't know whose home you're running from or what's so special about Reseda, but there's a couple of geldings my mother's gotta haul in a horse trailer to the pony rides out by Hansen Dam. I'll try to get you outta Pacton. Although why you'd want to leave this beautiful spot beats the hell out of me."

CHAPTER 25

"I gotta drop you here," Joy says. She pulls the horse trailer into a Home Depot parking lot, eases down on the brake. She wears scuffed cowboy boots. "I ain't too sure, but I think you're only a few miles from Reseda." She shrugs. "Sorry. I gotta get these nags to where they're supposed to go."

"Thanks for the lift," Dara says. She watches the trailer pull out, two horsetails hanging out the back, and walks from the parking lot to the street. At the stop light, she notices another car flying a black flag—like the one on Ginny's car.

Clusters of high school kids stroll down the sidewalk. It must be a weekday, a new school year already. One of the kids wears a *Scream* mask, while another is dressed in a Spiderman costume.

Diego's two years older than she, and had told her about wanting to become a computer repair tech. Maybe he's taking classes—somewhere.

She walks a little further and stops to rest on a low cement ledge in front of a YumYum Donut shop. With only a general location to go on—Reseda— finding Diego seems next to impossible. And Diego can't bring back the Lightband, can't find her dad. I'm a ghost, she thinks, hanging between two worlds—the past and some future that isn't clear.

Three teenagers wearing backpacks saunter into the donut shop. One has a skateboard, and she thinks of her old deck, her mom's picture. She catches a quick glimpse of something on the skater boy's backpack—a black and gold cloth patch—before he disappears into the donut shop.

There's an autumn crispness in the air, and Dara stares off into the distance of traffic, billboards, and strip malls. Was it only yesterday that she'd hidden in the desert?

She lowers her head and looks at the cement walkway in front of the donut shop, littered with crumbs and a couple of small, empty bags.

She squints through the donut shop window at the boy inside, the one with a skateboard. He walks out of the donut shop and glances at her as he walks past. His hair is blonde, shaggy, hangs down over his brow.

She catches his eye and he stops. "Nice feathers," he says. "Let me guess. Pocahontas?"

"Oh." She raises a hand to brush the feather necklace, which hangs over the lumberjack shirt. "Halloween. Yeah."

He drops his skateboard and sweeps back a lock of blonde hair to reveal a surfer's reckless, catch-the-wave confidence. "Check it out," he says, munching on a bite of cinnamon roll. He pulls out a cell phone, taps it, and shows her a picture of a mask, white with red slash marks. "This is what I'm gonna wear tonight."

She manages a laugh. "You'll be very frightening."

"Here." He breaks off a piece of a cinnamon roll and hands it to her.

She debates a moment before she lets him drop the piece into her open hand. "Thanks," she says. "Do I really look that desperate?"

He smiles. "Actually, yeah. Are you waiting for somebody?"

She shakes her head, swallows the bite of cinnamon roll, and shifts uncomfortably on the low cement wall as she considers him: blue-eyed surfer boy with floppy blond locks and a puka shell necklace. Her chest warms as the smell of sugar and fried batter wafts out from the shop.

"Do you have a name?" he asks. "So that I can call you something besides The Girl With Three Feathers who Ate Part of My Cinnamon Roll."

Dara laughs but avoids his eyes. She'd used an alias once before, at the Crossroads Shelter. "Chloe," she says, and glances at his eyes. The pleasant warmth in her chest expands into her throat.

"Chloe." He says the word slow and then swallows, like her name is a sweet pill. "And my name's Tyler. You go to Monroe? Haven't seen you before."

"Just visiting." She stands, places one foot on Tyler's skateboard, and rolls it back and forth. The concrete walkway is rough, pitted.

"Right," Tyler says. "The Valley donut shop tour."

"I'm trying to find a friend, actually."

"Can't help you there." He breaks off another piece of cinnamon roll and hands it to her. "Although . . . maybe I can. What's her name?"

"He's a guy."

"Oh." Voice edged in disappointment.

"He's in"—she swallows a bite—"Reseda."

"You know that's where you are, right? In Reseda."

"Yeah?" She looks around. "I thought it was some other—" A thought strikes her. "Where's a library? I need to use a computer."

"Don't be in such a hurry all of a sudden. What's your friend's name? If he goes to Monroe, I might know him."

"I don't think he goes there anymore."

"I can give you a lesson," Tyler says.

"Huh?"

"Skateboard lesson. Right here, won't even charge you." He glances at Dara, who still stands with one foot on his board. "It's all about balance."

Dara eyes the landscape of sun-bleached sidewalks. "Is that right?" With the back of her hand, she wipes sugar glaze from her lips, places both feet on the deck, and pushes off.

Partway down the sidewalk, she bends her knees and goes airborne into a frontside 180 ollie before skating back to Tyler. She pops the board up and hands it back to him.

"Whoa!" he says. "She might be lost, but she can skateboard—and do tricks. I guess maybe you don't need no lesson." He sets the deck upside down on the retaining wall, gives her an admiring nod, then turns to basketball swish the empty donut bag into the trash.

Dara stares at the cloth skateboard patches on Tyler's backpack: *Thrasher, Obey, Vans Off the Wall.* But there's one that grips her attention. On a black background, a golden crown forms a circular 3-D word. *BELIEVE.* "What's that on your backpack?" she asks.

"What?" He turns around to face her.

"That . . . that 'Believe' thing."

"Where you been hiding, Chloe?"

It was the same thing Ginny had asked her. *Where you been, hon? Under a rock?*

"It's for my sister," he says, "so maybe she'll get well someday." Tyler hands her a last piece of cinnamon roll. "Chemo ain't working. She needs to be healed."

Her face grows warm and she looks away from Tyler. "Healed? How do you mean?" she asks, mouthful of cinnamon roll.

"That healer chick. My sister, Mia, is like obsessed. She spends half her life watching Dara videos. I figure those are all in the past and not worth obsessing over, but if we could find Dara and that armband"—he gives a backwards nod of the head toward his backpack—"it might save Mia's life. Gotta believe that."

Dara swallows the cinnamon roll and puts her hands under her thighs to stop them from trembling. "That—that's too bad about your sister."

Tyler's eyes study her. "You look so freakin' familiar," he says.

She looks away, stares at a billboard advertising an airline and thinks of the Lightband, how it had flown from her hands before it exploded with light over the crowd at the Old Zoo.

"Are you feeling okay?" Tyler asks. "You're shivering."

"I'm fine." She turns up the collars of the flannel shirt to hide the lower part of her face.

Tyler taps the screen of his cell phone. "I got my sister's picture right here." He hands the phone to Dara.

In the sun's glare, Dara squints to make out the picture. The girl's maybe ten, pale, with long blonde hair. Her head lies on a pillow, teddy bear nestled against one cheek.

"Just before she started chemo," Tyler says. "Before her hair fell out."

"I'm sorry." A feeling of helplessness sweeps over Dara.

"That's why she's in the EAM, why I got that patch on my backpack. I just want to—"

A black military assault vehicle rumbles by, the word POLICE in white block letters.

Tyler shifts around so his back is to the donut shop.

"What exactly does EAM stand for?" She's heard the initials before, on the radio in Art's truck.

"Expect A Miracle. They got meetings, secret meet-ups, it's all on social media. Gotta be careful, keepin' it all on the down-low because we don't know what they done with her. But if we can find Dara and get the bracelet back, maybe . . . maybe my sister can get healed." He stares past Dara, and his eyes shine with a newfound intensity. "Right now, we need a miracle—and that miracle is a missing bracelet."

Black flags. 'Believe' patches. EAM. Dara wonders what else has changed since she's been gone. If Tyler only knew who's right here in front of him— scuffed up from survival in the desert and two days of being on the run, teeth not brushed, no deodorant or make-up, and most of all no Lightband, no miracle—what would he believe then?

Dara takes a deep breath, exhales. "That sounds pretty insane." She runs a hand through her hair. Look lame. Be a dumbass. "Right now, I just need to get to my friend, Diego—"

Tyler jerks his head up. "Wait—what did you say his name was?"

She wishes she could take it back, but she'd already said it.

Tyler pauses, stares at her "You're kidding. Not *the* Diego? Is that—does he by any chance have a sister?"

Dara blinks in surprise. Was that a lucky guess? Could Tyler just be leading her on? She remembers Diego's story of his younger sister, abused by their stepdad.

"That's—" Her heart leaps. "Do you actually know him? Diego?"

"Not really, but Mia knows his sister—wow, that's who you're looking for? Diego? Dude's famous. We've all seen the video where Dara healed him. Seven billion views or something crazy like that. But Diego won't talk about it. Tells the press to leave him alone—and he ain't polite about it, either. Refuses to come to the EAM meetings, too, according to my sister—even though they're are all about the girl he lost, Dara."

"So maybe . . . they know each other?" Dara asks. "Your sister and Diego's sister? I need to find out if it's my Diego—I mean, the one I'm looking for." Dara looks down to conceal her growing excitement. Diego had been at Crossroads, too—that's where they'd met—and might remember the fake name Dara had used. If he heard that "Chloe" was looking for him, would he make the connection? "Where's the, uh, the—the EAM meeting?" she asks. "Could I meet your sister? Maybe she can help connect me—"

"Wait, you're not a cop, are you? Or a reporter?" Tyler appraises her. "Well, obviously not. But you just show up out of nowhere and want to meet the dude who used to be Dara's boyfriend?"

Used to be . . . She looks away, feels Tyler scrutinizing her.

"It's curious," he says. "Your wanting to find him. How do you know Diego, anyway?"

"We go way back, and that's why I thought maybe I could . . . find him."

"And you somehow knew he was in Reseda?"

"He told me he was gonna move here when—when we used to know each other." Dara's voice tightens.

"I'm gonna take a chance and tell you something, but you better be straight with me." Tyler's bright eyes laser into her. "Diego's kid sister comes to the EAM meet-ups."

Dara runs a hand over the feather necklace, looks down at her flannel shirt, and back at Tyler. Unnerved by the piercing force of his gaze, she stands and moves away from the cement wall where she's been sitting.

"Oh. My. God." Tyler takes a step after her. "You're her, aren't you?" he whispers.

"Who?"

"I told you to be straight with me. I've seen enough pictures, videos. You dyed your hair, cut it, but it's you."

"You gotta be kidding. Why would I—I mean she—"

"You're looking for Diego, and—do you have it? The bracelet?"

"No. Why would I—"

"Your voice. Mia's replayed those TV interviews enough times. I've seen them, too." He stares at her, the recognition sinking in. "And those dark eyes. You're no blonde."

"That's crazy. You're"—She manages a quick laugh—"you're sadly mistaken."

"Like hell I am. Listen, you gotta heal Mia."

"I'm not Dara, but even—even if I were, that would be impossible. To heal your sister, I mean."

"Oh my God, this is unbelievable," Tyler says, a smile playing about his lips. "The whole world's looking for you."

Two other boys come out of the donut shop and stand by Tyler.

"Hey," Tyler tells them, "can't you see I'm talking to someone here? I'll catch up with you later."

Dara looks at Tyler for a moment. thinks of his sister Mia, teddy bear nestled by her cheek. "And so what if . . . if I am . . . her, Dara?"

"So what!? I need you to heal my sister." Tyler takes a step closer. "I won't go to the press or the cops, won't tell nobody. I just need that one thing."

She thinks for a moment. The pretense is gone—but she needs to make sure Tyler is going to stay on her side. "I don't have the Lightband anymore," she says, "but if the chemo doesn't work and you ever want your sister to get better, then . . . you can't tell anyone about me." She's about to add something regarding the power in her hand, but has no way of knowing if there will be a chance to use that with Mia. The main thing is to find Diego.

"The police are looking for you," Tyler says.

"I don't have the armband, honest."

Tyler stares at Dara and lowers his voice. "You're trying to join up with Diego to get it back, aren't you?"

Dara looks away.

"I'll take that as a yes. I can find some way to get Diego to the meeting, if that's what it'll take for you to get the bracelet so you can heal Mia. Come to the EAM. It's tonight." Tyler drops his backpack to the ground, opens it, rips a page from a notebook, and writes down an address. "Don't give this to anyone. You'll need a pass-phrase to get in."

"What is it?"

"Guard the light."

"Okay."

"If I recognized you," Tyler says, "it means others can, too. But it's Halloween, and people will be wearing costumes. You need a mask."

He pulls something from a pocket of the notebook and hands it to her. A black half-mask designed to cover the eyes, forehead, and top of the nose, sprinkled with silver glitter, narrow slits for the eyes. "A little project our teacher gave us," he says, "for *Romeo and Juliet*. Put it on and keep it on."

CHAPTER 26

Hey Diego, ad said ok to text u. Found link to the Craigslist ad from your fb. Is the Harley still for sale?

Yeah, Jasper. I'm selling it for my dad. U interested?

Very. Can I come see it? Where u at?

The Valley. Reseda. U?

Near Miranda Park. Can I see the bike today? I got cash.

CHAPTER 27

The SUV chasing Shawn Adengard is gone. In the pickup truck's rear view mirror—desert hills, Joshua trees, mesquite, sand and rocks. Got to ditch Seb's truck. Probably not much time before they pick up his trail again.

He pulls the vehicle into a culvert under an abandoned railroad spur, loosens the radiator drain plug, fills a plastic gallon jug he finds lying in the truck bed. The water's rusty, no green coolant— rust'll settle to the bottom. Working fast, Shawn pierces the old vinyl seat fabric with a car key, rips it off. Grabs a first aid kit from the glove compartment, Seb's two-way radio.

He straightens the backwards baseball cap so the bill shades his face.

Mission now: simple. Find a place where he can replenish water—and hide. The hills seem close, but desert expanses are deceptive. In the far distance, high voltage transmission lines proceed up into the hills, and Shawn figures they must come from a power substation. He trudges until he can no longer see the truck or the railroad tracks, then settles down in the shade of a Joshua tree to wait for sunset. He drinks measured sips from the plastic jug.

Dara. She'd been tossed from the truck. Part accident, part intention. In retrospect, it was the safest thing for her. At the time, Shawn had no way of knowing if he'd escape from the black SUV, but at least he'd been able to lead it away from Dara. He trusted her skills—and Seb's training. If Dara could evade whoever was after her, she'd be okay. If he and Dara had stuck together, survival would have been difficult, if not impossible. Splitting up was the best option.

When cooling twilight descends, he sets out on foot, following the power lines in the moonlight. By dawn, he's within sight of the power substation next to an empty backroad. Ignoring the *Danger—High Voltage* signs, he scales the fence and drinks from an outdoor hose faucet next to a concrete shed, refills the plastic gallon bottle.

Shawn finds an abandoned mine shaft some distance from the substation. He checks it for scorpions and snakes, then hunkers down for the night, using the strips of vinyl seat covering for a blanket. The next day, he returns to the power station and replenishes his water supply. He pries open a door to the square concrete shed. Inside are control panels—but also crackers, a bag of sunflower seeds, stale Doritos.

Over the next few days, he survives on that and edible desert plants— agave, prickly pear, chia sage. He uses a car key to strip the cacti and tests it by rubbing some of the pulp on his skin. If it doesn't redden the skin, it's okay.

In the abandoned mine, he has time to think—of Dara and Julia. The way Julia had looked the last time he'd ever seen her, walking toward the car behind the apartment building. His one regret, aside from letting her make the PX run the evening she'd been killed, was that he'd been deployed overseas when Dara was born, although that was out of his control. Shawn had taken paternity leave, but the Navy delayed it because he was in a combat zone. By the time he got back to the States, Dara was already six weeks old.

At the entrance to the mine shaft, he turns on the two-way Motorola and finds the channel broadcasting NOAA weather reports and alerts, a standard safety feature on all two-way radios. He's worried about running down the battery, but listens. Clear skies. One hundred ten degrees daytime high, seventy-nine at night. After about ninety minutes, he's about to turn the radio off when he hears it—a series of three warning beeps, followed by a static-filled interruption: "Child Amber Alert, Call 911. Blue Ford pickup truck. California License PDK196." The message repeats three times. He turns off the radio.

The next day, Shawn finds an FM radio station by pressing and holding the search button on the Motorola —but the broadcast's in Spanish. He listens anyway until he catches the name "Dara Adengard" and the words *camioncito azul*, followed by *padre detenido*. Blue truck . . . father arrested. That much Spanish he could figure out.

If they're claiming he's been arrested, chances are they're broadcasting something similar on TV and spreading fake Twitter stories. They could leverage his "capture"—and get Dara scared enough to turn herself in.

Shawn realizes he has to get the message to her himself. If she's still out there, it's essential that she stay on the run, and she's got to hear it from him. Also, he thought, Dara can't put herself at risk by looking for me. She has to know I'm okay.

There's only one way to do that.

He sleeps in the concrete control station of the power plant and waits for someone to show up.

CHAPTER 28

Dara stares at the flag, a golden bracelet emblazoned on black cloth. It hangs from a tree limb in the front yard. Twilight. She walks across a brown lawn to the narrow, two-story home's front door and adjusts her *Romeo and Juliet* half-mask. The doorbell doesn't work, and Dara's uncertain knock is answered by a young woman wearing Minnie Mouse ears and a paint-spattered apron. "Wait here a sec," she says. "Gotta get the candy." She turns around and starts to walk away.

"I'm not here for candy," Dara blurts after her. "It's—I mean—guard the light. That's what he said."

Minnie Mouse comes back to the door. "Who said?"

"Tyler. He gave me this." She waves the paper on which Tyler scribbled the address. Dara rushes out the words. "Told me I should come here—some kind of, uh, meeting."

"Then you're"—the woman puzzles for a moment—"Chloe?" She offers an apologetic smile. "When Tyler texted me, he said I'd recognize you by the feathers, but he didn't tell me you'd be wearing a mask—and I didn't see the feathers at first."

Dara glances past the woman to scan the well-lit interior, big picture windows and blonde wood. An easel and drop cloth sit in one corner of the main room.

"Don't just stand there. Come in." Still smiling, as though trying to make up for dismissing 'Chloe' as a trick-or-treater. "I'm Sidney. And yes, we are guarding the light."

Dara takes a tentative step inside, hears the low volume thump of hip-hop music, the gurgle of a miniature fountain mounted on a table near the door. "I hope I'm not too early," Dara says. "Tyler didn't exactly tell me when."

"People will start arriving soon—but it's fine. Maybe you can hand out candy—although we don't get that many trick-or-treaters here."

"I can come back later if you want."

A delicious smell permeates the house. Fresh baked bread or muffins. Dara's mouth waters.

"Tyler texted that you're trying to find your friend," Sidney says. "Jenny's brother, the famous Diego. And how is it that you know him?" She closes the front door behind her and regards Dara.

"We go back a ways," Dara says. It's the first time she's heard the name of Diego's sister—Jenny. At one time, Diego had opened up to Dara about what happened to his sister, but he'd never mentioned her name.

"Diego never comes here, but you'll probably be able to talk to Jenny. You're about the same size as me and look like you could use a"—she steps back and appraises Dara—"a change of clothes, at least."

***

The shower feels good and washes away some of Dara's concerns. The water pours over her head and shoulders. Warm, steamy. She washes her hair with thick, scented shampoo, lifts up her face, lets the sudsy water run down her shoulders and back.

Sidney's set out fresh clothes in the bathroom. Blue jeans, sleeveless black top.

Dara dresses and steps out of the bathroom.

An idea strikes her and she smiles. How long has it been since she's used make-up? And how great it would be to fool Diego, have him totally not recognize her—make-up, mask, blonde hair. "Is it okay if I use some of your make-up?" she calls.

"Sure."

Dara sits at the small vanity in Sidney's bedroom. It's begun to grow dark, and she switches on a small table lamp. After she works on her hands, she holds them up to admire fresh-painted, glittery, ruby nails. Lamplight sparkles off the shiny varnish. It wouldn't have been her first color choice— that would have been teal— but it's all Sidney has. Dara remembers how she'd looked when Brooke's TV make-up artist did her hair, applied blush and eye liner. That was the last time she'd worn make-up. But back then her fingernails still carried the worn remnants of some school girl, silvery polish. And the make-up she'd worn on TV had been subtle. Light pink, soft blush.

This time, there's no TV camera. Dara scans the vanity for eye shadow and lipstick.

After she's done, Dara looks at herself in the mirror and is startled to see someone else staring back at her—a total stranger, a woman she doesn't recognize. Her eyes widen.

She's been so intent on applying detail to lips, eyes, and fingernails, she hasn't seen the whole picture. But now, with her blonde hair, blood red lipstick, lip gloss, dark mascara, and feathers hanging in front of the black shirt, she is . . . stunned.

She stands and steps back. The stranger in the mirror looks strong, tall— she'd grown over the past few months—and striking. Weeks of working out in the desert have toned and tanned her body. The first TV interview with Brooke might have once captured a guileless, French-braided naïf, the face of an innocent teen runaway. But now, as the lamplight casts her face in soft shadows, the mirror reveals a young woman gazing back with eyes that seem to have grown hard and guarded. She tightens Seb's leather cord so the three feathers—red, yellow, green—dangle against her skin, just below the throat.

She reaches up, encircles an upper arm with her fingers and red-glazed nails. She bends her arm at the elbow and feels the sinewy muscular bicep. *Wear it on your arm—here.* Ayon's voice sounds in her head, and she once again sees his bloody hand encircle his own bicep. *Its rays will help to protect you. Its power was passed to you.*

She catches a glimpse of a quick movement behind her, a motion in the mirror.

Dara spins around. It's Sidney.

"Oh my God!" Sidney says.

Dara grabs for the half-mask she'd set down on the vanity and slips it over her head. "I'm sorry," Dara says. "Maybe I shouldn't have used your nail polish. But you were so nice, and I just thought—"

"It's not that. It's just that you're—you look"—Sidney takes a deep breath and shakes her head once like she's trying to clear it—"amazing. I had no idea. I mean, sorry, but that old Pendleton and baggy gym shorts you were wearing didn't—" She takes a step toward Dara, as though to get a closer look. "What exactly is your relationship with Diego, the YouTube hero you're so intent on seeing?"

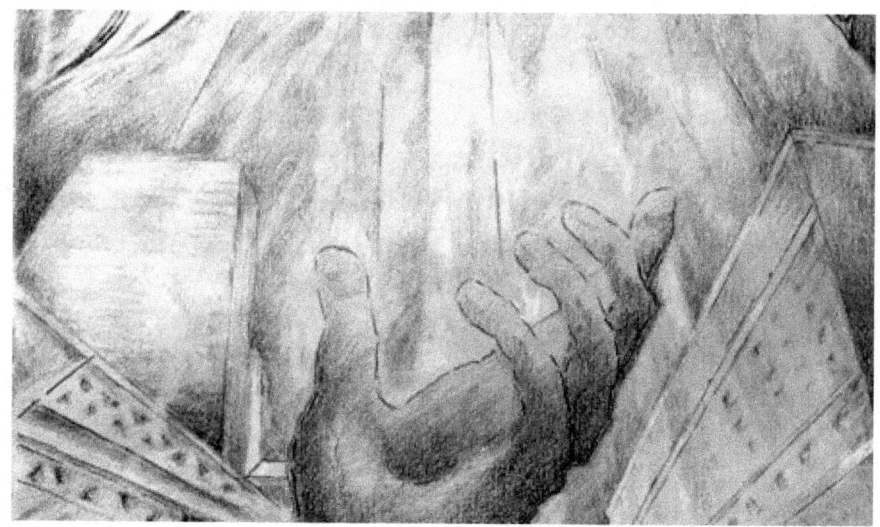

CHAPTER 29

It's grown dark outside, and the room swells with people.

At first glance, the scene appears to be a normal, although somewhat subdued, gathering of friends and acquaintances, some costumed and some not. As Dara surveys the room, however, she notices that several people appear weak or ill. A boy who limps, a woman in a wheel chair. An older man coughs, while a listless girl clutches a box of Kleenex. Others with no visible disability hang quietly near the perimeters. But in many of their eyes, Dara recognizes the same bright look of hope she's observed in Tyler and Sidney.

She feels uneasy. These people have come because of her—and now here she is. Different name. Different look. No healing arm bracelet—but still the same person. The one they wait for. The one with, unbeknownst to any of them . . . a strange, powerful metal implanted in her wrist. Unlike the Jyotisha, no one can take that away. Her secret—hidden, unseen.

At the same time, she wants to come clean, tell these people to forget their expectations. The girl who once held magic in her hand is gone. But if she does that—

"Welcome home." A woman with a wide, too-friendly smile steps in front of Dara and gives her a big hug. "It's going to be okay now. Expect a miracle." She holds Dara by the shoulders and appraises her from head to toe, as though trying to figure out where Dara might be broken. She nods like she's just seen the x-ray, releases Dara, and moves on.

Three young people sit on the couch, huddled over a computer tablet. Others linger around Sidney's painting on the easel: a hand, palm raised, suspended over a cityscape at night. Beams of light rain down on the hand from an unseen source that bursts from above. The hand, desperate and beseeching, stretches toward the radiant heavens. There are a dozen other completed paintings leaning against a wall, all variations on the same theme. A hand, bathed in light, reaches up from the darkness.

The paintings' subject matter makes Dara think of her mother, and she seeks the feathers that dangle around her neck, strokes their downy silkiness.

Sidney is in the kitchen, uncorking a bottle of wine, heating up pepperoni pizza. "Dara's fave," she says.

Dara spots Tyler wearing the white face mask with red slash marks. When he sees her, he lifts the mask, rests it on the top of his head. Underneath the mask: puka shell necklace, sunburnt nose.

He does a mock double-take and sidesteps several people to get close. "From run-away to runway," he says. "Almost didn't recognize you. The mask looks good, too."

She smiles, runs a hand through her hair, fluffs it.

He takes her other hand in both of his. "I'm glad you came," he says. His fingers are cool, and she imagines him in the ocean, paddling down the crest of a wave.

"This place okay?' he asks. A press of her hand.

"Yeah, Sidney's been great." She pulls away and glances around, hoping for Diego.

"Over here," Tyler says.

Dara's heart beats faster, but Tyler instead leads her to a young girl who sits, legs pulled up under her in an overstuffed chair in the corner.

"Chloe, Mia."

Mia, several years younger than her brother, holds the same teddy bear Dara had seen in the photo. She wears a long yellow nightgown, pink knit cap pulled down low over her brow. There are dark chemo circles under sunken eyes, and she offers a wan smile.

Dara feels the tug of a helpless longing. "Hope you get better," she says, and once again reaches a hand to encircle the smooth skin of her own upper arm. Dara's hand tingles and she longs to heal Tyler's sister, but there is no way to do that in this press of people. She drops her hand back down and turns to Tyler. "Diego's sister—Jenny? Is she here, too?"

Tyler stands on tiptoes and looks about. "That might be her over there," he says.

A girl dressed in a Red Riding Hood cape stands with lowered head, leaning back against a wall, and fingers a pendant that hangs from her neck.

Dara sidles through the small crowd until she stands facing her. "Jenny?"

Jenny raises her face, framed by the red hood, and regards Dara with dark eyes that seem to plead for retreat even as they meet the outside world. Fifteen, maybe sixteen. Long dark hair with blonde streaks, angelic face. The pendant, which Jenny keeps massaging between thumb and forefinger, is a golden heart. Dara recalls Diego's pained words: *My stepdad was—was doing stuff*... Jenny's scars are invisible, but Dara knows they must still be there. At least she's safe now, back with her brother and real dad.

"Hello, Jenny," Dara says. "I know your brother. My name's Chloe."

A hint of a smile crosses Jenny's face. "So you're—Chloe. I texted him."

"And?"

Jenny pulls a phone out of her back pocket, taps it a couple of times, and holds it up so Dara can read the texts.

Hey bro, a girl named Chloe's going to be at the EAM tonite. According to a friend, she knows u.

Wha???!!!!

Yeah

U sure, Jen? U know I don't like those EAM meet-ups, but if it's Chloe ... Chloe??!!

Dara's hand shakes as she hands the phone back to Jenny.

Jenny smiles. "Sounds like he knows you," she says. "Hey, I like your mask."

"So he doesn't like this Expect A Miracle thing—" She catches herself before adding the word *either*. It's not the people in the room who bother her. They're driven by simple hope. It's the fixation on her, Dara, and the light in their eyes. Like a wall. You either stayed on the outside, separate— or got pulled over to the other side, the inside, the light-in-the-eyes side. "He ever say anything about Dara?" she asks.

"You're aware he knew her, then?" Jenny draws out the words, a note of amazement in her voice. "My brother knew Dara."

"Yeah, that's what I heard."

"They hung out together. I mean, Dara healed him—my own brother." For the first time, Jenny grows more animated and sheds some of her protective inhibition. "He doesn't like to talk about it, though. Some reporters tried to get him to say stuff, but he refused. Won't even talk to *me* about it."

"Did he send any more texts?" Dara asks. "About Chloe, I mean?" She casts a yearning look at the smartphone in the palm of Jenny's hand. "Will he be here?"

"He was planning on it, for sure. Earlier this afternoon, though, he met up with someone who wanted to buy Dad's Harley. He left to go meet the dude, and I haven't heard from him since. He knows where I am, though." She glances at her cell phone." I can shoot him a text right now."

Dara's heart throbs with anticipation.

"Hmm," Jenny says, staring at the screen of her smartphone. "That's weird."

"What?"

"He says he's still with the Harley buyer. How long does it take to sell a bike?"

Gripped by a sense of foreboding, Dara remembers another text message in another time and place. Her dad's cell phone, but not her dad.

"Pizza." Someone thrusts a tray in front of her. Small, bite-sized pizza squares.

"*Not* my fave," Dara says, "but since you're here." She piles five pizza squares onto a napkin, removes the pepperoni slices, and gobbles each piece.

Some of the older adults are drinking wine.

Philip Brown

"How about some music while we wait for the video to get set up?" someone announces, "You all know the song."

A murmur of anticipation sweeps through the room as someone dims the lights. Dara looks over and sees Jenny texting on her phone.

Sidney says something to an Echo Dot on the table, then: "Alexa, volume eight."

The first piano notes are wistful, followed by a woman's voice—strong, pure, unmistakable. Although the song is new to Dara, the singer is instantly recognizable. Kiara. She sings with restrained power, and Dara taps a foot as the percussive beat kicks in.

Sidney opens the door to hand out candy, and Dara glances expectantly, hoping to see Diego enter.

Jenny steps away from the wall and holds up her cell phone, screen turned toward the music.

Is she recording? Dara wonders. But she notices that others also hold phones aloft—and on every cell phone screen is a picture of the Lightband. The small, glowing screens in the darkened room are like digital rectangles of hope, a geometry of faith. We're here, they seem to say. We still believe.

Dara strains to make out Kiara's words:

I'd soar above the world,

far above the sting.

Mingled with the tender lyrics is the thought of Diego pressing his lips to hers on the precipice at the Old Zoo. She closes her eyes and listens to a bridge of solitary saxophone notes—lonely, seeking solace.

She hears the front door. Her eyes fly open and her heart skips a beat. But she blinks in disappointment when she sees a young man with a scruffy beard and short dreadlocks at the entrance. Tanned, he wears baggy shorts, a faded brown shirt, and flip-flops. His eyes scan the room.

Was Diego ever going to come?

Cell phones are still held in the air as Kiara's voice sings pure and clear:

I'd fly toward your everything,
rest my feathered head,
let you hold the Lightband
above my bent-wing wound.

Stunned, Dara reaches for the wall in the dim light, takes a step, and leans against it. Did she hear the lyrics right?

"Are you okay, Chloe? You look like you've seen a ghost." Jenny lowers her cell phone. On the screen, the Lightband shines against a night sky.

"I'm—can I get some water?" The idea that the Jyotisha has made its way into a song by Kiara, plus its image on so many cell phones, makes her dizzy.

"I'll get it." The voice comes from beside her. Dara slowly turns. It's the dreadlocked young man who'd entered a few moments earlier. Up close, he smells of salt water and patchouli oil.

Before Dara can respond, he fetches a Styrofoam cup.

"For you," he says. "Because you're so damn beautiful."

Dara takes the cup, glances down. Purple liquid. Not water. But her throat is dry, and she's overcome with exhaustion. The long escape from the desert. The chance meeting with Tyler. Sidney. So tired of making choices.

Dara hesitates, holds the cup below her nose, and sniffs. It smells of sweet berries.

"Don't worry . . . Chloe." He pauses, looks at her. "It's only fruit juice." Tight grin.

"And you are?"

"Jasper. Drink."

CHAPTER 30

She stares at the cup, thinks for a moment. "I'm good." Hands the cup back without drinking.

Jasper holds up both hands in a gesture of refusal. "I insist. You need something. Please, I'd hate to see a lovely girl like you pass out. Then I'd really have to rescue you."

Thirsty, dizzy, still overwhelmed by the song's lyrics, Dara swirls the liquid. Kiara had just sung about the Lightband like it was common knowledge. In response, the EAM group had raised their cell phones with images of the Lightband, as though it was some kind of sacred artifact, a modern-day holy grail waved in time to the music.

She downs the sweet, syrupy contents in three swift gulps.

The gold and silver armband displayed on Jenny's cell phone looks so real that Dara can almost feel the warmth of its coiled bands. As she surveys the room, she clenches and opens her empty hand. A queasiness starts in her stomach, and her face is hot.

She'd come to this house because of Diego—and the possibility that Diego might be here. But he wasn't.

Instead of Diego, there are people with an unsettling light in their eyes. In need of comfort, they'd turned for hope—a miracle—to a radiant armband that was gone. It had disappeared, leaving behind a picture on a cell phone, a lyric in a song, and a black flag fluttering from a tree limb.

A strong need to escape grips Dara. The room has become stifling, and the walls seem to be closing in on her. Her fingers dig into the empty cup.

. . . . hold the Lightband above my bent-wing wound.

Expect . . . a miracle.

Dara wavers on her feet, leans into Jenny. Her stomach churns. The Styrofoam cup drops from her hand. "I feel sick," she says. "Is there some place I—I can lie down?" In her mouth the aftertaste of fruit juice, sweet grape mixed with a faint trace of bitterness.

"The couch?" Jenny suggests, concern written on her face.

The other boy, the one with short dreadlocks who'd given her the fruit juice—she can't remember his name—puts an arm around her. The smell of patchouli oil: yes, now it comes to her.

Jasper.

She takes a step away from him, staggers, light-headed.

Jasper follows, wraps his arms around her from behind. His lips against her ear, warm breath on her neck. "Hello, Dara," he whispers.

She freezes. Too fatigued to resist, too weak to pretend, she turns and steps back. Her eyes try to center on him. "How—how do you know—?"

"You're the only one without a cell," he murmurs, "without a picture of the Lightband. Because you've held the real deal, haven't you?" He stares at her with dark soulful eyes, bottomless wells into which she tumbles. "What's this?" He moves closer, fingers the three feathers against her bare neck. "You think you can fly now?"

She wobbles, starts to fall.

Jasper steps beside her, braces her about the waist." Outside, where you can breathe. Come."

She's dizzy, faint.

With his arm wrapped around her, Jasper walks Dara toward the front door. "Just a little farther." His voice strains with the effort of supporting her.

She lifts her head and glimpses people watching her.

"Too much to drink," Jasper says.

Several people step aside to let them pass. Someone snickers.

Dara squirms, but Jasper's hand digs into her side.

"Too tired," she mumbles. "Don't. Hurting." The room starts to spin. Her knees fold.

Jasper places his free hand under her armpit and hauls her onto the porch.

She has trouble forming the words she wants to say: "Who—" It comes out like, "Uh."

Dragged across the brown lawn, she collapses onto the curb next to a motorcycle where she vomits into the gutter. Although still weak and disoriented, the cool, the evening air steadies her. Her temples throb as Jasper tears off her *Romeo and Juliet* mask and tugs a helmet over her head.

"Get up."

A sharp knee in her back sends her tumbling off the curb. But she manages to stand, swaying to her feet.

Jasper grabs her wrist and pulls her toward the motorcycle.

She stumbles and falls over the seat, her helmeted head striking the gas tank.

Jasper jerks her shirt collar from behind. It chokes her throat like a dog leash, forcing her back. Jasper shoves her so that she sits straddling the motorcycle seat. He mounts the bike in front and yanks her arms around his waist.

A red elastic tie-down strap is in his hand, and her own hands are quickly bound, secured in front of his stomach. There's a loud rumbling as Jasper starts the engine. A quiver of fear courses through her. Has the motorcycle started moving already?

Someone steps in front of the motorcycle. Backlit by a streetlamp, Dara can't tell who it is. All she can see is a pair of black leather gloves that reach for the handlebars, as though to block the motorcycle's forward motion.

Who else could possibly be after her? Dara yanks her arms in a feeble attempt to loosen the elastic strap, but can't free her hands.

"Back off!" Jasper yells to the leather gloves. "It's mine now!" He revs the engine into a harsh roar.

A male voice says something in response.

Dara can't hear the words through the crash helmet and the sound of the engine. But that other voice. Somebody she'd just met at the party? Tyler? No, Tyler has blonde hair. This guy's hair is . . . black.

Tousled black hair. Black leather jacket. A thick silver chain hangs from his neck.

The leather-gloved hands rock the bike back and forth in a violent shaking as though attempting to dislodge her and Jasper. The engine's been shut off. The motorcycle tips, and she puts one foot down to keep upright.

The motorcycle is too heavy, though, and it tumbles over. Dara's crash helmet strikes the asphalt with a sound like a hard-boiled egg being cracked. Jasper loosens the strap from Dara's wrists, but her leg remains pinned beneath the bike and she can't dislodge it.

Jasper pulls himself free, and there are sounds of a struggle. Grunting. Fists on flesh. A body hits the ground near her.

The bike is lifted off her legs; a hand pulls her up. She straddles the motorcycle seat again, but this time her hands aren't tied and it isn't Jasper who sits in front of her. She struggles to lift her arms, to hold on to a leather jacket.

Dara's head sways, nods. As her head tilts back, she looks up and sees faint, pinprick stars glittering in a black sky. *I'd soar above the world, far above the sting* . . . The motorcycle is moving, rush of wind. Her head begins to clear. It's as if they are racing to catch one of those stars.

I'd fly toward your everything, rest my feathered head . . .

She leans her face into the black jacket, takes in the smell of leather mixed with another, more familiar scent. From his hair? He isn't wearing a crash helmet, and she raises a hand to stroke the back of his head.

Yes. She whispers his name.

As the Harley thunders down the darkened street, Dara summons all her remaining strength to wrap her arms tighter around Diego.

CHAPTER 31

Dara digs her fingers into the pockets of Diego's jacket and closes her eyes. The bike tilts and she instinctively leans the other way, feels the engine's roar as it accelerates out of the turn. Her head throbs, lips tingle, arms like big, downy pillows.

She slips into semi-consciousness, and when she comes to finds herself leaning into Diego's back, arms limp but hands still secure in his pockets. They're headed downhill, and soon Dara—looking past Diego's shoulder— can make out the moonlit ocean up ahead. It looks like a void at the end of the earth. As they draw closer, white waves crest in the light of a full moon.

They turn down PCH. The motorcycle slows and Diego banks, navigating a sharp turn onto a dirt road. The motorcycle bounces and jerks until Diego stops close to the water. He shuts off the engine, boots the kickstand, and helps Dara off. He turns back to the bike, pulls out a piece of paper lodged next to the gas tank, glances at it, and stuffs it into his pocket.

Dara sits on the sand and tries to take off her crash helmet, fumbling with the strap to release it. Her fingers are clumsy and can't get a grip.

"It's already unfastened, dumbass," Diego says. "Here." He gently lifts the helmet off her head and stands looking down at her. "What's wrong with you?"

She falls back against a clump of high beach grass. "Juice." She knows there's more to say, but her tongue is heavy, numb. "Made me . . . sick."

Diego helps her to stand, wraps an arm around her shoulders to keep her upright, and walks her a few steps to a nearby picnic table.

She turns to look at the ocean, but the vastness makes her dizzy. Diego supports her as she sits on the bench. Behind them, a car whizzes past on the Coast Highway.

"He drugged me," she says over the sound of a crashing wave. "Jasper."

"Probably told you it was juice, right?"

She can still taste the bitterness.

Dara gets up and stumbles over to a water faucet that comes out of the ground. She turns it on, drinks, rinses out her mouth, and goes back to sit beside him.

"You should have known better," Diego says. "All that time on the streets and you let some guy hand you a roofie?" He takes off his moto jacket and drapes it around her shoulders. Underneath, he wears a long-sleeved black shirt.

"Where are we?" The words sound thick, disconnected from her own voice.

"Near Zuma," Diego says. "A little north of Malibu. I've come here a few times." He sits down next to her, his legs straddling the picnic table bench, a concerned look in his eyes. "Look at you now. Beautiful blonde." He smiles, strokes her short hair. "What's up with the feathers?"

"Birthday present . . . Seb." She looks at Diego and leans back, supporting herself with her elbows on the table.

A look of confusion crosses Diego's face. "What's Seb?"

"Dude . . . owned the desert trailer . . . been hiding. My dad . . . we got separated."

Diego drove the bike all this way without a helmet, and his hair, which had always been slicked-back, has grown into loose, wind-blown curls. As the moonlight reflects off his face, he seems to have grown even more handsome.

Dara's head begins to clear in the cool Pacific air. "I was trying . . . to find you. What happened to Linc? Did they give him away?" Engulfed once again with the sensation that things are spiraling out of control.

"Linc's okay," Diego says. "But you'll have to wait."

She breathes a sigh of relief. "I want so bad to—"

Diego puts a gloved finger to her lips, leans over and kisses her. His lips are soft, yielding. He pulls back to look at her. "Remember the last time?" he whispers.

She nods. Her lips tingle, but she isn't sure if it's from the kiss, the drug— or both. The last time: Griffith Park. Just before the radiant, letting-go moment, she'd kissed Diego—hard, a kiss of desperation, an end-of-the-world kiss.

Not like this. Not soft.

He pulls back to look at her. "Right now, we need to get you out of harm's way. Jasper was about to take you some place where he could finish the job—and probably kill you. He contacted me, said he wanted to buy this bike." Diego nods at the motorcycle, and Dara notices for the first time that it's deep purple with an orange flame running along the side of the gas tank. "Belongs to Pops, and I was just selling it for him. That's how Jasper found me."

"Jasper bought it?"

Diego shakes his head. "A setup. He jacked it." He stands and turns away, looking out at the moonlit water. "He took it for a test drive while I rode on the passenger seat. Pulled into an alley, forced me off the bike, had a knife, grabbed my cell when I tried to call nine-one-one. He checked texts, saw the ones from my sister Jenny about 'Chloe', so he put two and two together. When he said your real name—Dara—I realized it was more than an armed bike-jacking."

"Thank god you're okay."

Diego sits back down, and she takes his hand.

The sky has begun to lighten.

"Jasper took off with the bike," Diego says. "I managed to get a ride, made my way to the EAM house—just in time, as it turned out. I'd dropped Jenny at that place before, so knew where it was."

"That thing was insane. Like, if they only knew I was there."

"It's all gone crazy," Diego says. "The military cordoned off Griffith Park, from the Old Zoo to the picnic field, and made it a no-fly zone. News helicopters, drones, nothing can get close. There are other things happening, too—lawns out by the beach have turned brown overnight, wetlands gone suddenly dry. The whole world's looking for you. You've heard of Weibo?"

"Way-what?"

"The Chinese Twitter," Diego says. "They're obsessed with you, call you Light-healing-girl. At least, that's how it gets translated."

"Seb told me that a storm was coming."

"I hate to tell you"—Diego's eyes lock with her own—"but it's already here."

As if to punctuate his words, a wave crashes onto a nearby rock, sending up foamy spray against the gunmetal dawn.

"There've been riots, too," Diego says, "when people tried to get into the Old Zoo and the picnic field right next to it. Maybe they thought they could pull in some left-over healing energy. Scammers claim to have the actual Lightband, charging money for a minute of its power. The cops are patrolling, searching for any sign of you."

"But I don't have it anymore." Images flash through her mind: the black-and-white SWAT truck that had cruised past the donut shop, Tyler turning to hide the logo on his backpack. Then at the EAM, there was the unsettling light in people's eyes, the cell phones held aloft like celestial receivers. A surge of anger courses through Dara. "The Jyotisha was given to me, my destiny, my blood. I don't fully understand why I'm supposed to have it, but I do know one thing—it's mine."

As she stares out at the sea, an osprey soars low over the nearby rocks, its magnificent, wide wings banking away toward the dim horizon.

"Maybe this'll help." Diego fumbles in a pocket, and pulls out a piece of paper. "When I parked the bike a few minutes ago, I found this wedged between the seat and the gas tank. It must have gotten torn from Jasper during the struggle." He hands Dara a ripped piece of paper, part of a receipt from Miranda Mini-Mart.

"That doesn't tell us much," Dara says.

"One of the texts Jasper sent me said something about Miranda Park. It might be a place we need to go, if you want to find Mercy." Diego pockets the scrap.

Dara shivers and pulls the motorcycle jacket tighter. "First, I think I need to find Vadoma. She's the link between the two sides of my family, the two branches of the tree. She'll have answers." The poison has almost worn off, her head mostly cleared, and there is renewed strength in her limbs.

"But you don't know where Vadoma is," Diego says.

"If I could somehow get in touch with Brooke," Dara says, "she might be able to find out where Vadoma's gone. Brooke's got connections."

"I heard she's in trouble," Diego says.

Dara's chest tightens. "Brooke? Oh my God, no. What happened?"

"They wanted to arrest her, something about a shield law."

"What's that?"

"Not sure, but they wanted to put her in jail over it."

Diego stands, removes his gloves, and drapes them over the gas tank. When he turns, his face is tense, voice urgent. "We need to get out of here."

"On the run again, a mouse wheel, just like before."

"But this time, you need to run *to* something instead of away."

She stares out at the pewter sea, takes a deep breath, turns to face Diego. "Right now, I've got nothing, except you—and this." She holds up a hand.

"What do you mean?"

"I've got a piece of it here—in my wrist."

Diego stares at her. "The—the armband? But then, where—"

"Not from the armband, a piece of metal from the meteorite, it's got the same power." She explains the story of how it was implanted and the narrow escape from the government hospital.

Diego takes her hand, intertwines Dara's fingers with his own, strokes her wrist with his other hand. She leans into him, feels his breath on her hair.

"Here's what you need to do," Diego says. "Find Vadoma, who might be able to guide you to Mercy. When you get Mercy, take back the Lightband."

"She blames me for her father's death," Dara says. "Mercy will kill me before she lets me take it."

"Then you need to kill her first."

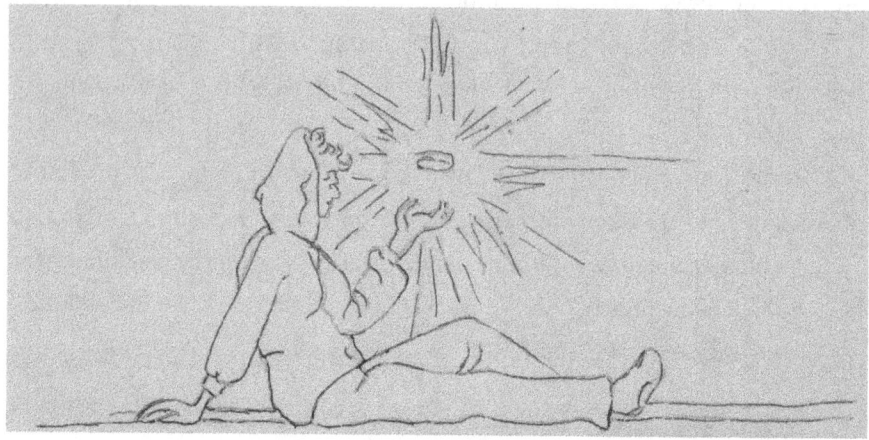

CHAPTER 32

Sunlight flashes over the apartments just beyond the boardwalk, and the ocean has grown lighter. Mercy lies in a sleeping bag on the expanse of lawn between the boardwalk and the beach. She rolls over and glances at a garbage truck in an alley that faces the boardwalk. The truck grinds as it hoists a dumpster on robotic arms, flipping it upside down. The dumpster shakes violently on the two arms and retches its contents into the truck.

In a world that hungers for the Lightband, Mercy thinks, it's important to be invisible, soundless. Maybe Dara—who'd also carried it through darkened streets, kept low, out of sight—had once felt like this, too.

Mercy's head pulsates.

She looks around. Where is Jasper? He should have returned by now—with Dara.

Mercy shakes her head and pulls back the hood of her sleeping bag. The sun warms her, and she experiences a growing sense of excitement. She caresses the Lightband through the pouch.

Down the boardwalk, past the shuttered reggae shops and Fashion Factory, she sees him. Short dreadlocks and board shorts. He is alone, and as Jasper draws closer, she senses the meaning of his blackened eye, the quick shake of his head as their eyes meet. The blood rises to her cheeks. She sits up in the sleeping bag, and it falls away from her chest like skin sloughed off by a snake.

"Dara got away." Jasper hangs his head and kneels next to her.

"What?" Bite the rage. Hold it in. She puts a hand on Jasper's arm. "It's okay, Jass, my love."

"I thought you'd be angry."

One hand seeks the Lightband, snug in its pouch. "What happened?" Her voice trembles with suppressed rage.

Jasper explains how he'd met with Diego and discovered text messages about Chloe—"total faker, I knew right away who it was"—on the cell phone. "I told you Diego would lead us to Dara," he says, "and I was right. I swear to you, if I have another chance, she ain't getting away. I've still got this." He pulls out the switchblade. "Used it to jack the bike, next time it's for Dara."

Mercy stands and sheds the rest of the sleeping bag. She rolls up the bag, secures it with a bungee cord, and looks out toward the still-misted sea. "I need to find her," she whispers.

"We'll find her again. *I'll* find her for you."

"Not Dara. Someone else." Her father was dead, and Dara still alive. And at the old Griffith Park Zoo, it had been her grandmother who came too late. Her *bunica*. Mercy looks at Jasper, at his bruised eye, and makes a decision. "Come, let me show you something. Here, on the side by the ocean." She takes Jasper's hand and leads him behind the skateboard park, bathed in golden morning light.

A lone skateboarder zips on whishing polyurethane wheels over the smooth, banked walls.

Mercy's hand finds Jasper's, caresses his fingers with her own while she fumbles with the pouch that hangs from her neck. She squeezes his hand, and a fragment of a lullaby repeats in her mind.

The seahorses dance with the fish,

The foals are in the waves.

The water stretches to the distant horizon, suffused in a delicate, ghostly vapor.

She will hurt Jasper for failing. She holds the Lightband in her hand, raises it for him to see. It begins to glow.

She looks through the oval bands framing Jasper's face. Jasper smiles back at her, leans in as though to kiss her through the armband.

"You cut your cheek," she says, tracing the scratch.

Jasper winces.

The armband makes a crackling sound. In the air is the smell of asphalt, as though from a new-laid road. Mercy thinks of her father, of Gunarik, and of another girl who strove to wield the Lightband.

Jasper lets out a startled shriek of pain.

The skateboarder pops the board into his hands, pauses, and raises his head to listen.

We'll sail the sea in a teacup dish—

Patchwork sweater . . . a soft cushiony thigh.

And Marko—the knife blade.

A gunshot.

Blood splattered on the rocks.

Mercy's fingers tingle with electrical current, and her dead father is a ghost who beckons her forward.

The Lightband continues to glow, and its vibrations become violent shudders in her hand. Her head throbs like it's being torn in two, as though her actual mind is being cleaved.

The ocean breeze whips up, gusts away the smell of asphalt, and in its place is the scent of sweet wildflowers.

On Jasper's cheek, the cut has healed.

Trembling, Mercy lowers the Lightband and clings to Jasper as the rest of the verse spins out in her mind:

—and live in ocean caves.

Hush-a-bye baby, I am rocking you

to sleep by the waters blue.

CHAPTER 33

It's mid-morning when Dara and Diego arrive at the worn tract home. The air is still and silent except for the screech of a crow pecking for seeds. A pair of motorcycles, parts strewn about nearby, are parked in the dirt yard.

"Careful, we gotta hide this thing." Diego strains to push the bike behind a splintered gate.

The back patio is concrete and weeds, black Weber grill, tattered billiard table.

"My dad's at work right now," Diego says, fumbling in his pocket for a key to the side door. "And Jenny's at school."

Something bangs against the door from inside, followed by frenzied scratching, more thumping. A desperate whine.

When the door opens, Dara is almost knocked over by a blur of gray fur. Linc leaps on her, wet kisses covering her face. "You *did* find him!" she screams. The last time she'd hugged Linc had been on the precipice that overlooked the healing ground at the Old Zoo, where she'd held him against the whirlwind of the Jyotisha's ascent.

"I missed you so much, boy." She squeezes him, brushes his ears with her fingers, digs both hands into his fur.

Diego kneels beside her, and it's like parts of her that had been taken are now restored.

"How'd you get him back?" she asks.

"Turns out that before you found him," Diego replies, "Linc'd been a fire station mascot. Not a search-and-rescue, just their pet. A hills fire got out of control, and things got kind of hairy. The fire crew lost Linc, and that's when *you* found him."

"He had a big wound on his hindquarters," Dara says.

"It was in the news. Here." Diego rummages through some newspapers on the kitchen table and hands Dara a news clipping.

"Healing Girl's Dog Turns Out to be Firefighters' Best Friend." As Dara reads the article, she pats Linc and kneels down to hug him. She recalls how he'd lain in pain, whimpering next to the sidewalk trash can the night she ran for her life from the Buena Gardens—and how his fur had smelled of smoke. "How'd he end up here, with you?" she asks.

"The fire station had a special welcome home ceremony for Linc—they had a different name for him, I forget what—and when I heard about it, of course I showed up." Diego draws frayed drapes across the sliding glass door, lowers a bamboo curtain over a front window. "I was kinda famous, so when they saw how attached Linc was to me, they let me take him back—on condition that I bring him to visit there once in a while."

She hugs Linc once more, presses her cheek against his side. "I'm so glad to see you, boy."

"We should probably try to get some sleep," Diego says. He tosses her a sleeping bag and switches on the TV.

Dara unfurls the sleeping bag on the floor and is about to lie down when her attention is arrested by something on the TV screen. She freezes.

It's her dad.

CHAPTER 34

Unshaven and pale, dark circles under his eyes, face bruised, Dara's father sits at a wooden table in a barren room. The walls are white, and he wears an orange tunic.

"Dara, I hope you can hear me. I'm okay—but you need to stop running. Please, turn yourself in. Come . . . back . . . home." He says the words carefully. "You will be protected, I promise."

Dara's hands grow cold.

Her own pictures flash on the screen, side-by-side screen grabs from two videos that had catapulted her into fame—healing Diego and then the man in the underground parking garage. Nothing like how she looked now.

"Not good," Diego says. "Sounds like your dad's working with the cops to bring you in."

"Can you rewind it?"

Dara watches the replay: *Come . . . back . . . home.*

In her mind, she also hears her father's words at her seventeenth birthday in the desert: *Right now, we have no home. If anything happens to me, you go on the run and you stay on the run. You understand?*

Dara turns to Diego. "He's not with the cops. He's with me."

"How do you know that?"

"Trust me, I know."

She sleeps in the sleeping bag on the floor, Linc curled up by her side. Vivid dreams stream through her head—a girl on a high wire, barefoot, without a net . . . stumbling, grabbing onto thin air . . .falling, desperately clawing at empty space, rush of wind, helpless tumbling through clouds . . .

Her eyes flutter open.

Diego sits next to her on the floor and strokes her hair.

Over the past months, apart from Diego, something has blossomed in her heart for him. It's happened so slowly, she doesn't even recognize it at first, a special flower that withstands storm after storm.

She reaches out her hand, and he takes it, gently stroking her palm with his thumb.

With his other hand, he touches her brow . . . her cheek ... a finger caresses her lips.

She kisses his finger. "I need you with me," she says. "I can't do this alone." She draws in a sudden breath, surprised by something new—a sleeve tat on Diego's right arm.

Dara raises herself on one elbow to rain kisses on the dark tattoo. In the thicket of black ink, she sees the word. Her name.

***

She showers while Diego heats up leftover pasta.

Some unresolved tension hanging in the air, they make a couple of phone calls. Diego contacts his dad, and Dara gets in touch with Brooke.

"Are you okay?" Dara asks Brooke. "I heard you—you might get arrested."

"They wanted me to tell where you were, a location." Brooke pauses, and Dara assumes Seb must have shared that information with her. "Don't worry," Brooke continues, "I'd never betray a confidence. The network's got the best lawyers. I'm still here, and since you went on my show, the ratings are through the roof. The studio wants me on the air, not behind bars."

After an initial expression of shock at hearing Dara's brief explanation of recent events—including Seb—Brooke manages to recover her customary poise. "Call me back in a half hour," she says. "I'll see if I can find what you need."

When Dara calls back, Brooke has Vadoma's address. "I want to get you back on my show," she says. "The world's waiting to see you again."

"I don't look the same now," Dara replies, "and if I go on your show, people will start to recognize me. I've got to stay low, under the radar. Once I have the Lightband again, you'll be one of the first to know."

"So—it's gone." Brooke's voice registers surprise. "And you're trying to find it. Why is that so important now, to get it back? Considering all that's happened to you, I'd think you might be glad to get rid of it."

"The Jyotisha's on a path of destruction—and I need to stop it."

"I don't know where you are right now," Brooke says, "but if you're near a TV—"

"I know. My dad—I saw it last night."

"He wants you to come home," Brooke says, "to stop running."

"I know that's what he said—but it's not what he meant."

"Okay." A mix of puzzlement and doubt in Brooke's voice.

"Do you know where he is?" Dara asks.

"He's in protective custody. At least, that's how they're spinning it. But I don't know exactly where." Brooke pauses before lowering her voice. "They're after you."

"Who?"

"Special ops, somehow connected to the CIA. Run by a guy named Santee. They won't stop until they find you—and the armband. When they do, I wouldn't want to be in your shoes."

"I've gotta go," Dara says.

"You take care," Brooke says. "Be in touch. Okay?"

When Dara hangs up, she turns to Diego. "We need to leave."

"I'm ready," Diego says. "Been ready for weeks." He goes into the rear of the house and returns with two backpacks. One is already filled, and he unzips the top to show Dara protein bars, trail mix, flashlight, gloves, heavy socks, toiletries, bungee cords, rope. "Jasper got my cell," he says, "so that's one thing we don't have. But phones are traceable, so we're better off without it."

"Why'd you have all this?" Dara asks, nodding at the backpacks.

"I knew you'd be back. And I also knew that when you got here, the world would be after you. We'll need to survive. This is a start."

Deep breath. Focus. "Thanks."

"Take some of Jenny's clothes." Diego gestures to another bedroom. "She's about your size, and if she'd known who you were really are—*the* Dara—she'd have given you everything she owns."

In Jenny's bedroom, the Red Riding Hood cape is draped over the end of the bed. Dara scrambles to change out of the pants and black top. She slips into a pair of ripped blue jeans and a t-shirt that says "Wolf" with a faded aerial view of a river, puts on the feather necklace and an orange and black Harley-Davidson baseball cap. Last, she throws on a black hooded sweatshirt.

Diego disappears into the back of the house, returning moments later with a wad of bills which he stuffs into his pocket. "Pops said to take it."

"Your dad was cool about your leaving?" she asks,

"He was there with me at the Old Zoo," Diego says, "and he knows what it means." He glances toward the window. "Let's go."

Diego clips Linc to a leash and the three of them set off on foot before hopping a bus into Hollywood.

"Service dog," Dara tells the bus driver in response to his irritated look.

With Linc lying under the bus seat and the bright interior lights overhead, Dara sits several seats behind Diego. With one hand, she clasps her wrist, presses, feels for bone, hard metal. Her blood pulses.

The bus rumbles up Barham and barrels down onto Highland.

CHAPTER 35

Dara walks ahead along the sidewalk on Hollywood Boulevard, Diego and Linc following half a block behind. A cold afternoon breeze gusts dead leaves and fast food wrappers up against street gutters. They pass a wax museum, souvenir shops displaying t-shirts and faux Oscar statuettes.

Three days ago, she'd been in Sebastian's desert trailer. Now, with Diego in his black leather moto jacket—hair grown into luxurious dark curls—and Linc straining at the leash, it seems unreal to be back in civilization.

Dara feels like people are watching her, keeps her head down, looking at the Walk of Fame's sidewalk procession of salmon-colored stars. Whenever she lifts her eyes . . . nothing. Except for the sight of a small black pennant affixed to the window frame of a passing pickup truck.

"Hold it." A man's voice behind them.

Dara spins around.

White shirt, bow tie, Angels baseball hat, camera with a big zoom lens. He wears steel-framed eyeglasses. "Take your picture?" he says. "Nice souvenir." He looks friendly and has a high-pitched voice. He holds up the camera and . . . click.

"No thanks," Diego says.

Lowering the camera. "Nothing like a picture—worth a thousand words, you know." He laughs.

He has a salesman's easy manner, and reminds Dara of a late-night commercial.

The man looks down at Linc. "Nice dog," he says. "Mind if I pet him?" He ruffles Linc's ears, strokes the back of his head, and reaches his fingers under and behind one of Linc's ears. Linc lets out a low growl, and the man quickly withdraws his hand.

"Let's get moving," Diego says as he pulls Linc's leash.

Dara looks back and sees the man studying her before he turns and walks away. "Linc did not like that man," she says.

"Just being protective," Diego says. "Good boy, Linc." He quickly tousles the fur behind the dog's ears.

Dara stops, turns to Diego. "You know what? Aren't we near that park where we slept on the grass and I healed Becca? I need to check something out."

They make their way several blocks to the small park on Franklin. Patchy brown grass, metal benches, trees with wilted leaves and dead branches.

"Looks just the same," Diego says.

They trudge over to the corner of the park where they'd slept several months ago. "No, it's not the same at all," Dara says. "Look."

There's evidence of an investigation—yellow caution tape tied to a tree, excavation of a square plot that's been staked off and dug up.

Around the immediate area, tree limbs spring fresh, and although it's autumn there are already buds on the new growth. Moss and lichen cover the bases of the trunks. The grass is green and sprouts a multitude of daisies.

But there's something else, too. Sap oozes from the tree bark in long amber driblets, as though the lifeblood will not be contained. And as she looks more closely at the daisies, Dara notices they are sifted with so much golden pollen, the petals sag under weight of the fairy dust. It's nature coming apart at the seams.

"So incredibly green," Dara says, admiring the grass. "But twenty yards away from here"—she glances at the rest of the park—"it's brown."

"This is crazy," Diego says.

"Look," Dara says. She sinks to her knees, runs one palm over the grass, and shows Diego: her skin is stained green. "All I did was brush my hand over it. There's so much chlorophyll, it's like juice."

CHAPTER 36

Vadoma's apartment building—across the street from the Hollywood Forever Cemetery—turns out to be a large, pink two-story box. It looks baked into the landscape, a square of strawberry cake between two houses.

A police SWAT truck cruises by while a helicopter circles somewhere in the distance. Sirens race down Santa Monica Boulevard.

Diego tugs the hoodie tighter over his head.

Dara averts her face from the street and checks the apartment number written on the palm of her hand. They duck onto a shadowed flagstone walkway next to the apartment building, and she tugs Linc. There are just two apartments on each floor.

A sudden movement on the second floor landing startles Dara, and Linc breaks into a frenzied bark.

They step behind some bushes as a screen door bangs shut and a man races down the stairs, two steps at a time. He looks back toward the barking dog and darts to the back of the apartment building, skirting a trash dumpster, and disappears.

Dara looks once more at the address on her palm, then glances up at the second floor apartment. "That dude just came out of Vadoma's apartment!"

From the back of the apartment building, a car door slams, tires squeal.

They dash up the stairs.

The apartment door hangs loose on one hinge.

Dara takes in the ransacked apartment. Overturned chairs. Toppled china cabinet, glass fragments strewn across the carpet. Tarot cards are scattered next to the couch.

A bloody kitchen knife lies on the carpet, and the scent of garlic wafts from the kitchen.

Vadoma staggers into the room, one hand pressed to her side.

"Vadoma!" Dara yells, rushing to her side.

"He was here," Vadoma whispers.

"Who?"

"Looking for you . . . the Jyotisha . . . and Mercy."

Too stunned to speak, Dara looks down at the blood on Vadoma's blouse.

Vadoma takes a step, stumbles, and Dara catches her arm, guides Vadoma over to the couch.

"I told him you were not here," Vadoma says, "but he tear things apart"—she glances about the room—"and when I went into kitchen to get knife, he grabbed it from my hand and cut me."

Dara looks down at the growing stain of blood on Vadoma's blouse and places her hand above it, circles her hand above the wound, waiting for the light to come. Her hand shakes from fear and tension—but there is no glow, no healing.

She remembers the words of Ayon, Vadoma's son: *It will not work on the dead or dying.* Or maybe, Dara thinks, the power's gone, used up.

"There's a land line," Diego says. "I'll call nine-one-one. What's the address?"

Dara checks her palm and shouts the address to Diego.

Vadoma leans back on the couch. "World is turned upside down," she says. "You are . . . Sanskaran bloodline and must put it back right side. Find, get back Jyoti—" She winces and tries to pull closer to Dara.

Vadoma's face is taut, strained. She coughs and shakes her head once, as though in pain, then closes her eyes.

Dara takes off her own hooded sweatshirt and presses the cloth onto the wound. She wants to stay by Vadoma's side, staunch the flow of blood. But once the paramedics arrive, she—the girl the world is looking for—will be found.

Dara thinks of the broken glass she'd once thrust into Gunarik's stomach and feels overcome by layers of helplessness—her mother, Ayon, Gunarik, Seb, and now Vadoma. There is a frightening echo to all of these, as though the same fatal wound keeps repeating itself, one after another.

Vadoma glances toward the street. "My two sons," she says, a slight smile playing about her lips, "are buried there."

Dara remembers the cemetery they'd passed.

"From my balcony," Vadoma says, "I can almost see their graves."

From the rear of the apartment, the sound of cabinets being opened.

"Go to Nuri," Vadoma says.

"Where is that?" Dara asks. Kicking aside a glass shard from the broken china cabinet, she kneels in front of Vadoma. Strokes the gray-white hair, now damp with perspiration.

"Is not place." Vadoma slowly spells the name. "Nuri's home"—her words are interrupted by coughing—"is not a home. I saw Nuri months ago—near freeway. Al-va-rado."

Blood drips from Vadoma's side onto the carpet. Vadoma winces, and her breath comes in sharp gasps. She's grown paler, shrinking further into herself. "Must tell you one thing," Vadoma says, her voice a tight whisper. "You did not let go of Jyotisha. It let go of *you*—to escape from someone else."

"Wh-who?" Dara thinks back to that moment when the Jyotisha had floated out above the crowd at the Old Zoo. "There was Diego, my dad"—her voice shakes—"you, the police."

The silver rings on Vadoma's fingers brush Dara's skin as she lifts a quivering hand to grasp Dara's arm.

"You were all looking up at the Jyotisha," Vadoma says. Her hand grips Dara's arm, and she pulls Dara closer. "You could not see the woman who was coming up from behind . . . but I was kneeling next to Gunarik's body—

and that is how I saw her . . . running toward you from the other direction. I know her."

The pounding of Dara's own heartbeat almost drowns out Vadoma's next words.

"The Jyotisha," Vadoma says, "was trying to get away—from *her*."

"Who—who was she?"

Time seems to slow for a moment and the bloody scene in Vadoma's apartment merges with the memory of the Lightband's radiant light over the picnic field at the Old Zoo. Vadoma's blood pulsates out, and Dara presses the sweatshirt harder into the wound. The cloth is turning red, and Vadoma gasps for air. Her body tilts to one side.

Dara moves nearer, cradles the back of Vadoma's head with one hand, and lowers her to a lying position. She places a throw pillow under Vadoma's head.

Dara waits for Vadoma to say more, but her body is motionless and her head settles into Dara's palm.

Dara uses a sleeve of her sweatshirt to wipe the blood from her trembling hand. Linc nudges her, and she pats the top of Linc's head, feels the bone at the base of one ear.

He nuzzles against her knee with the side of his face.

Dara caresses the feathers on her throat, hears Seb's voice in her head. *Feathers fly. Feathers fall. Be like the wind and let them go.* The gravity of her situation strikes her. She rises, takes several steps toward Diego, and buries her head in his chest as he puts an arm around her, holds her tight.

Anger surges through Dara—for Vadoma's death, for the unyielding loss of her own mother. She takes a hesitant step toward the window, uncertain where she should go. She stares at the bougainvillea-draped wall of the cemetery across the street, and when she speaks it's as if she is addressing someone on the other side of that wall. "By the power of my own"—Dara struggles for a moment to form the new word—"Sanskaran blood, I swear I will get the Jyotisha back." She turns to look at Vadoma's lifeless body. "And I will find the ones who did this to you . . ." The next word is a choked whisper: "Vadoma."

Sirens sound from down the street.

Something strokes the back of her neck. She turns her head. It's Diego's hand, and she falls into his arms.

"We gotta go," he says. "Here, found this in the closet."

She steps back, and he hands her an olive wool blanket, rolled tight and secured with two lengths of twine.

"I need something else to wear," Dara says. Her sweatshirt is still wadded against the wound in Vadoma's side. "It'll get cold out there, and this t-shirt won't be enough." She sees her reflection in the twilit window and makes out the mirrored backwards letters on the shirt.

Wolf

floW

Wild now, cut loose, a river runs.

Diego goes into the back of the apartment and returns with a knee-length sweater that looks like a quilt of beige and orange patches, a pointed elf hood on the top and wide, skirt-like hem at the bottom. He holds it up for Dara.

She nods, turns her back to him, and he holds it while she puts her arms through the sleeves. A bit tight, but it will keep her warm.

She secures the bedroll to the backpack, hoists it onto her shoulders, adjusts the straps. She pulls up the sweater hood, which smells of nutmeg.

Without a backward glance, they leave the apartment and head down the stairs. In the twilight, a green accent light illuminates the pink stucco. They dash to the back and follow an alley onto a side street as sirens stop on the street out front.

Without a word, Diego's hand grasps hers, and she tightens her own grip on Linc's leash. A cold, dry wind whips down the street.

CHAPTER 37

Dara and Diego walk several blocks before Diego finally breaks the silence. "Vadoma put up a fight in her apartment."

"I feel responsible for that," Dara says. "If it hadn't been for me . . ."

Diego stops and hugs her. "You did *not* kill Vadoma. Someone else did."

Her chin nudges the zipper of Diego's moto jacket, and they stand, silhouetted in front of a green neon store sign backgrounded by a flaming orange sunset.

"You have to get the Lightband," Diego says. "The way out is the way through."

Dara caresses the back of his neck with her hand and stands on tiptoes to kiss him.

Overhead, a streetlamp blinks on.

Linc, wanting to be a part of it, jumps up, front paws clawing at Dara's sweater.

They both reach down to touch him.

"We love you, too," Diego says. But his eyes are on Dara.

***

They stop to buy hot dogs from a street vendor.

"Four," Dara says. "And two with no bun." She turns to Diego. "Linc's gourmet dinner."

After a bite of his hot dog, Diego wipes his mouth, reaches into a pocket, and pulls out the store receipt Jasper had left behind. "Here's where we gotta go," he says. "Miranda Park."

""You think Mercy could actually be there?" Dara asks between bites. "Vadoma, though, said something about a woman named Nuri."

"Don't forget that someone guided you to find Mercy once before," Diego says, "and that didn't turn out real well. So be careful." He tosses the hot dog wrapper into a nearby trash can and thinks a moment before asking, "Did Gunarik ever say he actually killed your mother?"

"No, but he never denied it," Dara says. "What difference would that make now?"

"This guy we saw running from Vadoma's—could he somehow be connected to—to that?"

That.

The bare euphemism is not enough to stop the memory that once again cracks in her mind with sudden, whiplike force.

The loss strikes into her chest.

. . . *rose petals flung onto the polished surface of a white casket.*

That night, they eat trail mix from their backpacks and sleep, bundled against the cold, in the doorway of a windowless building.

***

Awakened at dawn by a loud street sweeper, Dara and Diego buy breakfast at a nearby McDonalds, where a young Mexican woman points them in the direction of Alvarado Street.

They follow Beverly Boulevard, parallel to the Hollywood Freeway, passing through graffiti-marked territory.

"I don't remember so many transients," Dara says.

"The closer you get to downtown,' Diego says, "the more you'll see."

"They're everywhere." She glances over at a brown hillside next to the freeway, dotted with homeless squatters. "Where did they all come from?"

"Homes," Diego says.

She continues to stare at the hillside encampments and thinks, we don't look a whole lot different than them. She surveys Diego and Linc, shifts the weight of her own backpack.

They reach Rampart Boulevard around noon, already tired from the long trek, and sit to rest in the shade of a covered bus bench next to Tommy's Burgers.

A man waiting for the bus tells them it's just a few more blocks to Alvarado.

On the last leg of their trek, they pass a house half-gutted by fire. One side is blackened, windows blown out. A chain metal fence has been erected in front of the house, red *Condemned—Keep Out* sign affixed to the front door.

They arrive at Alvarado sore and hungry from the hours-long trek. The freeway above the street resounds in a never-ending rush of displaced air, and Dara's shoulders ache from the backpack straps.

Beneath the freeway, an array of tarps, one-person tents, and large cardboard boxes cover the sidewalks, a colony of the down-and-out. Because the freeway overpass provides shade and shelter from the elements, Dara assumes the tents have been erected mainly to afford a measure of privacy.

Several transients are in wheelchairs, while another hobbles on crutches. From inside one tent, Dara hears the shrill wails of a child. A glazed-eyed young man mumbles incoherently as he lurches past. Old men with grizzled beards mill about, and one of them wields a battered broom to sweep the sidewalk in front of his tent.

Dara lowers her backpack, pulls out a protein bar.

A pickup truck pulls to the side and stops. A man gets out of the cab, climbs into the pickup bed, and proceeds to toss clothing and blankets onto the sidewalk. Homeless men and women scramble to retrieve what they can, clutching their bounty as they return to their own spaces.

Dara had expected to hear the freeway traffic overhead, but in the underpass it's the relentless street traffic noise that's deafening, a never-ending roar of engines and tires that pass by just yards from the homeless tents and tarps. *How is it possible to live like this?* she wonders.

A toothless woman limps by, eyes Dara, and mumbles something unintelligible.

"Ignore her," Diego says.

"Sweater," the woman says, louder this time. "I like."

Dara wraps Vadoma's sweater tighter around herself, and moves on.

"So, this is where we're supposed to find Nuri?" Diego asks. "Is she homeless, too, or is she living somewhere nearby? We really don't have a whole lot to go on."

The smell of stale urine beneath the overpass is overwhelming, and Dara feels the urge to move into more open air.

Near one end of the overpass, a Black man sits leaning against the concrete wall. He wears an army jacket, in his lap rolling papers and a pouch from which spill loose tobacco threads. By his side, a rib-thin dog lolls on the sidewalk, raising his head to gaze at the trio.

Linc barks and then tugs Diego to get closer to the other dog, but Dara hangs back.

"Nice dog," the man says. "What's his name?"

"Linc," Diego replies.

The man raises a hand to pet Linc and studies Diego and Dara. "Haven't seen you two before."

Dara hears a noise behind her and turns to see the woman who's taken an interest in the sweater. The woman flashes a toothless smile, and Dara retreats, stepping closer to Diego.

"We're not from here," Diego says. "Trying to find a friend."

"What's your friend's name?" the man says. "Maybe I know him."

"Her name's Nuri," Diego says.

"Nory?" He thinks for a moment and shakes his head. "Never heard of her." He proceeds to sprinkle tobacco onto a Zig Zag, rolls it, and wets the cigarette with his own spit. He lights it and blows out a stream of smoke. "My name's Isaac, by the way. And this is Rinny." He reaches over and scratches his dog's ear.

"I'm Diego. This is—" He looks back at Dara, pauses to let her offer a name.

She stands in Vadoma's long sweater, elf hood pulled over her head, the three feathers around her neck fluttering in a wind that blows through the tunnel. "Chloe," she says. It's then Dara notices a black flag hanging from a tent pole beside Isaac. "This yours?" she asks, moving closer to look at the flag.

"It's my home," Isaac says. "Most of us living here's vets."

"Vets?" Diego asks.

"'Nam, Eye-raq. I used to be on Skid Row, but had to crush cockroaches and beat the rats off with a stick just to clear a space for my bedroll. That's why I moved, first to Griffith Park and then here."

Dara looks around again. Hard to believe this is a step up in the world.

"Were you . . . injured," Dara asks, "in a war?" She lifts a tattered edge of the flag to see a golden armband emblazoned on the black cloth. She looks back to Isaac, trying to figure out where he might be maimed.

"Was," Isaac says. "*Was* injured. But not from no war."

Dara drops her hold on the flag and looks back at Isaac. "But you're okay now?"

"The healing girl," Isaac says, "and that"—he nods at the black flag—"that bracelet."

"I heard about her," Dara says.

"I was there in the picnic field. Me and Parking Lot was."

"What?"

"Parking Lot. He's in a tent down at the end, almost where the sun be shinin' on his bald head." The man guffaws and rolls another cigarette. "We call him Parking Lot because one time he got lost in one of those big underground garages, couldn't find his way out. Ended up having to sleep on Level Four." He chuckles.

"This flag," Dara says, "has something to do with—with a bracelet that healed you?"

"Are you for real? C'mon, girl." Isaac gives her a look like she'd claimed ignorance of the earth's rotation. "It's for the healing girl. There's a song this army buddy used to play all the time. 'Tie a yellow ribbon 'round the old oak tree'—you know, like 'til the soldier comes home. Well, I got a flag around my tent pole until that girl comes back. She ain't no soldier, but the healing girl sure did shoot off some bright tracers."

"Tracers?"

"Lights." He makes an arcing gesture with one arm. "I had these things covered my legs, open sores, had pus and stuff. A nice cop took me into the emergency room one time, but they couldn't do nothing. Just gave me some medicine and sent me home. Home, ha! See this leg now?" He pushes forward one leg and pulls up the hem of his dirty jeans. The skin is smooth ebony, dotted with faint pink blemishes. "Go on. Feel it."

Dara hesitates, but then holds out one hand to let it graze Isaac's calf. The skin is warm, glossy, and she withdraws her hand. She recalls the small patch of lush, verdant ground at the park where she'd healed Becca.

"Your hand tingles, you know that?" Isaac looks at her for a moment, as though trying to bring something into sharper focus.

"Must be some static electricity in the air," Dara says. But she'd felt it, too, a pins and needles sensation on her fingertips as she'd touched his skin.

"What'd you say your name was?" A note of suspicion has crept into Isaac's voice.

Dara draws the sweater hood more closely about her head. "Chloe."

"Chloe." An echo behind.

Dara turns and sees the old woman, hunched over, hands moving back and forth as though knitting an invisible garment. "Chloe," the woman repeats.

Unsettled by the old woman's behavior, Dara wants to get away, but at the same time is compelled to hear what Isaac might be able to tell her. She edges away from the woman and closer to Isaac.

Dara and Linc move protectively beside her.

Isaac stares at her for a moment, stubs out his cigarette on the sidewalk, and places the remnant next to him. "Well, maybe you're Chloe and maybe you ain't, and maybe you got a name you're trying to forget, but that's okay." He reaches over to pet Rinny. "I'll tell you what happened. Me and Parking Lot was camped out in Griffith Park, livin' there. Saw these cars streaming in, and somebody told us there was a girl could heal anybody with a bracelet. She'd been on a TV show—but we didn't know that at the time on account of we got no TV. Didn't believe it, but we was so close figured, what the hell. So we joined the crowd."

"What was it like?" She hangs on his words.

"Like nothin' I never seen and probably'll never see again. Girl steps out onto this cliff-like place, the top of an old animal den or something carved into the hillside next to the picnic field. I was near the back of the crowd so couldn't see real clear, but I could tell she wasn't nothing but a girl—smaller 'n you, dark hair. It looked like she let go of the bracelet or threw it. And the bracelet just drifted on its own, like deciding what it wanted to do, finally came out over the crowd. And then—boom!"

Dara could see it in her mind—the explosion of light as the Jyotisha showered everyone in its radiance. "What did it—how did it feel?"

"Like the first few seconds when you open your eyes and see the world, that bright light for the first time, or at least what I think that must be like. None of us can remember, but the light from the bracelet"—he stops, as though searching for the right words—"starting over new, fresh skin—" He reaches down, runs a weathered hand over his calf. "It was like . . . like being bathed in glory."

CHAPTER 38

"That woman you was looking for," Isaac says. "Nory? You can ask Parking Lot. He keeps his ears open, might of heard something. You'll find him down there." He nods toward the other side of the underpass.

"Thanks," Dara says. "Good to hear that you—you're better now."

Isaac picks up the cigarette butt he'd set down earlier, relights it, and reaches down a hand to pet Rinny. "I never expected a miracle," he says. "And certainly not in this messed-up life of mine—but I guess they do happen. Good luck finding your friend."

She and Diego both fist-bump Isaac, and Linc gives Rinny a gentle nose-nudge.

The three of them walk down the cluttered sidewalk, past a row of small nylon tents—blue, beige, camo—and sidewalk encampments.

Dara glances back and sees the old woman following them, her hands still engaged in a manic knitting motion.

Diego asks another man about Parking Lot, and they're directed farther down to where the passageway ends, next to a freeway off-ramp. A shopping cart piled high with bags sits near the exit ramp. Next to the cart, a wizened bald man with a stubbly beard lies on a bamboo beach mat. He wears a dirt-stained jacket and leans on one elbow, watching the traffic. One leg of his trousers looks like it's been splattered with mud.

"Parking Lot?" Dara asks.

The man looks up at her and Diego. "Fifty-seven red," he says.

"What?" Dara takes a step back.

"Hold on, now it's fifty-eight. Fifty-eight red, five hundred ninety-three black. It's like roulette. What are the odds? Watch, next one'll be black."

A black pickup truck pulls up to the stop sign at the end of the exit ramp.

"What'd I tell you. If I was in Vegas, I'd be a rich man." He laughs.

"Are you, um, Parking Lot?" Dara asks again.

"You musta been talking to that fool Isaac."

"So that's you?"

"If he says so," Parking Lot grunts.

Dara sees a piece of black cloth knotted to the handle of the shopping cart. It might have been the Lightband flag—or it could've been a rag. "Isaac told us you were with him at Griffith Park." Dara says. "Were you healed, too?"

Linc, kept in check by Diego, noses around the wheels of the shopping cart.

"You ever hear of Agent Orange?" Parking Lot asks. He sits up and looks at her.

"Who?"

"Ain't a person. It's this stuff they sprayed in 'Nam, called it a *defoliant*. Know what that means?"

Dara shakes her head.

"It stuff that kills the trees and bushes, supposed to expose the enemy. Our planes dosed it over there on the jungle. Trouble was it messed us up— worthless grunts ended up with cancer, diabetes, leukemia. That's what put me on the streets in the first place, I couldn't hold no job and state disability wasn't enough 'cept to live out here." He scans the desolate surroundings.

"Did a bracelet heal you, too, from the orange agent?" Dara asks. "Like it healed Isaac?"

"Sounds like Isaac's been telling you stories," he says. "I got bladder cancer. Or should I say, *had*. The VA didn't believe it was caused by Agent Orange, but they treated me. The cancer went away, but then come back. They told me it'd spread and . . . there wasn't much hope." Parking Lot shakes his head. "Up in Griffith Park, when that—that thing happened, I didn't know it cured me 'cause it's not like you can see the cancer. It's invisible, ain't a skin rash—but turns out it went away. That girl, the healing one, took it away is what I believe. Doctors at the VA tested me, says I was cured. They were happy, but they sure as hell didn't believe that bracelet done it."

"That's good you and Isaac both got healed," Dara says.

"Who said we both got healed?" Parking Lot shifts on the mat and looks at Dara.

"But I thought you just said—"

"I guess Isaac didn't tell you."

A rush of anxiety seizes Dara, and she stands up. "Tell us what?"

"Sure, Isaac's legs is healed," Parking Lot says. "And me, I got rid of the cancer. But last month, something strange happened."

"What?"

"Look." Parking Lot hikes up his pants leg to expose one leg.

The skin has erupted in several sores. Some are scabbed, while others bleed a bright red residue.

Dara cringes, reaches out a hand for Diego, and he clasps her fingers. "Do you see that?" she asks him.

Diego tightens his grip on her hand.

"It's not as bad as what Isaac had," Parking Lot says, "but they're on my leg just like his. It's getting worse, too—you see how some're bleeding a little? So if we both got healed, how do you explain this?" Parking Lot rolls his pants leg back down and resumes his car-counting vigil. "Sixty-one red," he mutters.

Linc pulls Diego over to some ice plant by the freeway sound wall so the dog can pee.

Dara follows, and they stop next to the noise barrier. "Heal one, wound another," she says. "It's almost like a cosmic equation that has to be balanced." Her voice softens. "Now Vadoma's gone, too. Is that because my life's been spared? Me for Vadoma? The Jyotisha protects and heals, but brings equal death and injury."

"You don't *have* the Lightband," Diego says. "I told you, there's no way you're responsible for that dude breaking into Vadoma's apartment and killing her."

"But the reason why that guy was there in the first place," Dara says, "is that he was looking for me and the Jyotisha. So if it wasn't for me, she'd still be alive." Dara shudders and wraps an arm around Diego's waist.

"Don't jump to conclusions," Diego says. "Those leg sores"—he glances over at Parking Lot—"could be a coincidence. People get all kinds of stuff out here on the streets. And that Agent Orange could have given Parking Lot a skin condition."

"How can you be sure? How do we know that for each person I healed with the Jyotisha—including up in Griffith Park—there's not someone else that got sick as a result." She looks down at Linc and shivers. "Maybe I messed up some other dog when I healed Linc."

Diego pulls Linc away from the sound wall. "Or maybe you've just got a crazy imagination," he says.

They return to Parking Lot.

"We're looking for somebody," Diego says.

"Someone named Nuri," Dara adds, still rattled by the sight of the sores on Parking Lot's leg. "Isaac thought you might—"

"Never heard anyone by that name," Parking Lot says, still fixated on cars coming down the exit ramp. "Five hundred ninety-nine black."

Someone tugs at her sweater, and she spins around to see the same toothless woman—hunched over, stringy gray hair falling about thin cheeks.

Dara pulls away. "Hey, let go."

The woman cackles, and her hands fret. Pinched thumb and forefinger weave rapid loops, stitching back and forth with unseen needles.

"Dog." She pauses her knitting long enough to reach out a hand toward Linc. "He is good doggie." Heavy Russian-sounding accent, voice coarse and frayed.

Linc takes a couple of steps toward the woman before Diego jerks back on the leash.

"Forget this," Diego says. "Let's go, Dar."

The woman returns to her imaginary knitting, and the compulsive gestures capture Dara's attention. She stands studying the woman: long black skirt under threadbare coat, laceless boot split at the sole exposing one side of a bare foot.

The woman again reaches out a hand to feel Dara's sweater. "Good," the woman says. "I make."

"What? You're making a sweater?" Unsettled by the woman's strangeness, Dara retreats a couple of steps and pulls the sweater tight, yet at the same time notes the woman's tattered coat. "Wish I could give this to you, but I need it myself."

"No need for me." The woman strokes one of her coat sleeves. "I am warm." She looks both ways down the street and leans toward Dara as if sharing a secret. "Nuri? Here." She resumes her weaving, but continues to eye Dara's sweater.

"You—you know Nuri?" Despite the disjointed ramblings, Dara clings to the chance that this unsettled woman might point them in the right direction.

Diego tugs Dara's sleeve. "Come on, let's go." He rolls his eyes. "She's like a little kid, repeating whatever we say. First, she heard you talking to Parking Lot about Nuri, and then it was the sweater."

"But she says Nuri is here. Maybe—"

"Do you see any other women around?" asks Diego, a note of exasperation in his voice.

"Make sweater." The woman once again eyes Dara's sweater and flashes a toothless grin. "This one different." She holds up her hands as though showing off her handwork. "I am making for baby."

Diego's right, Dara thought—this is a waste of time.

Yet something in the woman's eyes keeps Dara from turning away and she glances down at her own garment—Vadoma's knee-length sweater. "I got this from . . . a friend," she says. "Maybe you had a sweater that looked like this one?"

"I wore, before I came to this country." The woman stares back at Dara and resumes the ghostly knitting. "I must return home now," she says. "Aishe will be hungry."

"Who is Aishe?"

"My baby."

The idea that this woman might be caring for a baby seems mad, delusional. "We've gotta go," Dara says. "Diego? Can we give her a couple dollars?"

Diego swings his backpack around, digs out two crumpled bills, and hands them to Dara.

She takes a couple of steps toward the woman. "Here."

The woman holds out a gnarled hand.

Dara enfolds the woman's knotted fingers between her own hands and presses the bills into her palm. The woman's hand is hard, rough, and thin, the fingers tight and knobby. Dara can sense bones, tendons taut on the back of the hand.

The woman closes her eyes, and Dara feels the hard fingers tremble and radiate heat within her grasp. When the woman opens her eyes, Dara continues to be struck by something in the woman's manner. Perhaps it's the smile that crosses her face, or the eyes at once unsettling yet familiar.

The woman's hand tenses, pulls away, and she pockets the money. She squints and cocks her head to one side. "Child with sweater—what is your name? So I can thank with name. Someday make scarv for you."

Surely, Dara thought, the woman never watches the news, knows nothing about a healing girl—but there's no way to know for sure. Dara lowers her voice. "My name is Chloe." She's used her fake name enough times now—could it be out there, too?

Dara searches the woman's face, but there's no glimmer of recognition. And yet, Dara saw something in the woman's eyes a moment ago, and she needs to test it. "There's a—a piece of jewelry I'm looking for, too, not just a woman named Nuri. I once had—an arm bracelet—that was taken from me, and I need to find it." She thinks of the Lightband's healing rays, its light, its vibration in her hands. "So that I can use it again."

"Ah!" Something sparkles in the woman's eyes.

Dara's heart skips a beat.

The old woman looks around at the bleak landscape of freeway support columns, dirt, small tents, and rusted shopping carts. The never-ending rush of traffic. "Much trouble for a bracelet. Surely you can buy another."

"This one's special," Dara says. "You see my dog over there? I used the armband to heal him. And when my friend was shot"—Dara pauses, considers her words for a moment, and lowers her voice—"the Jyotisha, the arm bracelet, healed him, too."

The woman stops her knitting, hands held in place. She stares at Dara and blinks once. "Jyotisha?"

Dara freezes. "You've heard of it?" She watches the woman closely, detects a flicker in the eyes.

The woman shakes her head, as though to rid it of a troubling idea, and goes back to her invisible knitting. "Aishe cold and hungry. I must go to her."

"Stop." Dara puts out a hand and holds the woman's thin forearm. "Who is Aishe?"

"Maybe you cannot hear. I have told you. My baby girl. She needs me."

"What are you going to feed her? You have no food." Dara withdraws her hand.

"I have *baxtalo*. Warm soup. And I make for her this sweater." The woman's hands knit more furiously. "Much like yours. I do not have much time before they come."

"Before who comes?"

"I will give her away in new sweater after I feed *baxtalo*."

"Wait." Dara's heart pounds. "Your baby—you're giving her away?" None of it is true, cannot possibly be true. It's clear there is no sweater. No baby. No soup.

"They are coming for her." The woman's eyes flick to the left, then to the right. "I must finish." Knitting faster. "Must finish. Must finish."

"I think you . . ." Something catches in Dara's throat, and she realizes she's trembling. ". . . you are not making sense—"

"Must finish," the woman says. "Come." The woman leans toward Dara, and whispers, as though taking part in some conspiracy. "I will take you to Nuri." She turns and walks down the sidewalk with faltering yet determined steps, away from the homeless tents under the freeway.

CHAPTER 39

Though uncertain about this woman and where she might be leading them, Dara follows with Diego and Linc close behind. The woman turns and beckons them a little farther down the street to a fenced hillside. They slip through an opening in the chain link fence and trudge up a barren slope.

At the top of the hill, a tarp has been slung over the lower branches of a leafless tree, and on the ground lies a grimy pink blanket. Off to the side is a shopping cart laden with bags stuffed with various blankets, clothing, empty bottles. A short, three-legged stool sits in the shade.

From the hill's crest, the downtown skyline is visible—gleaming high-rises huddled tight against the neighborhoods that spill around them.

"I hide here." The woman stares down at the sidewalk and traffic. "Watch for when they come."

"Who? You said you'd show me Nuri."

"If they find me, they will get Aishe. And they must never find Aishe."

Dara looks around the grim encampment. "The least we can do is get you some food." She sighs with disappointment. They've been led to a dead end. "It doesn't look like there's any soup here, *bostolo* or whatever it's called. Diego, can you see if you might score us some food?"

"That sounds good. We could all use some food." He takes Linc, makes his way down the slope to Alvarado Street, and melts into the distance.

Dara sits with the woman. For several moments neither of them speaks as they stare down at the street. Dara is reminded of another scene, where she'd once sat on the rocks by the ocean at Carlsbad State Beach. Sunset. Ocean surface the color of shimmering orchids.

"You remind me a little of my mother," Dara says. "At least your eyes do."

"Why would that be, child? Did she make sweaters, too? And . . . where is mother, child?"

"She's gone."

"Is that why you are here, without home?"

"Partly."

"And what was mother's name?"

"Julia—but everyone called her Julie. Julie Adengard." Dara looks over at the woman. "Did you ever hear of her?"

"Julie. Hmm, no. Name is warm, like summertime, but I do not know it. Why should I know mother? Was she famous person?"

Diego returns a short time later with El Pollo Loco take-out for the three of them, plus some chicken for Linc. The woman sits on her three-legged stool and eats with her hands. She grasps the food with pincer-like fingers, nibbling at it like a squirrel, eyes darting around the whole time as though watching out for someone. "You brought others," the woman says between mouthfuls. "I have seen them following that boy"—she nods at Diego—"by feet, in cars."

"There's nobody following him," Dara insists, but just to make sure, she looks down at the street and surveys it in both directions: small Mexican pushcarts and a beaten-down neighborhood on the other side. "No one else. Just us. We came alone."

The woman seems momentarily reassured, but as soon as she finishes eating she wipes her hands on her coat and casts a furtive glance down at the street.

Dara keeps staring at her, trying to place the woman in a story that makes sense. Vadoma told Dara she needed to find Nuri, but she's found instead a crazy, homeless woman who sits on a stool, muttering to herself in a language Dara can't understand.

Dara turns to Diego and speaks as though the woman is not there—which, in some ways, she isn't. "Where do we go from here?" Dara lowers her voice, and nods over at the woman. "She can't possibly be of any help to me. She says she'd lead us to Nuri—and yet all we have is . . . this. No Nuri."

Diego feeds Linc chicken out of his hand and wipes his palms on a napkin. "Maybe we can look around the area a little longer," he says, "but we've already wasted enough time here." He stuffs food wrappers into a take-out bag.

They both rise, hoist their backpacks, and take a few steps down the short hill to the street.

Dara turns and casts a last glance at the woman, who stops knitting to watch them.

"We're going," Dara says.

"Is sunshine now." The woman glances up at the sky. She removes her black coat and sets it aside, revealing a dirty, gray t-shirt and bony arms. "Wait," she says. "I give you." She stands and walks to the bag-laden shopping cart, roots through it, and moments later holds up a string of beads.

"What're those?" Dara asks.

"Is gift. Wear with feathers." Toothless grin.

Dara brings a hand to the feathers dangling from her neck and takes a couple of steps toward the woman. The necklace the woman has presented is worn and scratched, the colors faded. "Okay. Thank you."

As the woman hands the bead necklace to Dara, their fingers touch, and a tingling sensation flows through Dara's fingertips.

"You take. I must finish sweater now." She moves her wrists in rapid strokes.

Dara clutches the beads in one hand and puts her other hand—the one with the Lightband metal—onto the woman's bare forearm, feels the woman's muscles working. Beneath Dara's own hand, the woman's pulse beats under wrinkled skin.

"Your hand, child—it is warm." Her arm relaxes, and she lowers her head, as though allowing the warmth to seep within.

Dara senses it radiating, too. Her hand grows warmer as she holds it against the woman's arm. She strokes the skin, senses the prickling in her own wrist. The current moves into her palm, her fingers.

Dara remembers another time, another place, when her mother had reached down a hand to bandage a wounded elbow, and Dara had felt a slight vibration from her mother's finger tips. She'd dismissed it then as a moment of static electricity.

But now, as she holds the woman's arm, the ache of that memory—her mother's touch— fuses with the prickling vibration in her hand and wrist. She looks down: her hand has grown more translucent, as though a powerful light is shining through it.

The wind picks up, rustling through the weeds on the hillside.

Dara's hand quivers, and she tightens her grip on the woman's arm to steady it. The current surges through Dara's hand. It glows, and the fingertips radiate white light. After a few moments, the effulgent light subsides, Dara's hand stops tingling, and she releases the woman's arm.

Diego steps close beside her, puts an arm around Dara's shoulder.

The old woman remains still, unmoving, at last slowly lifts her head to fix Dara with an intense stare.

In the woman's eyes is the same luminescence Dara had glimpsed earlier, the shimmer of deep well water catching the light. But this time the light stays, does not waver and die.

The woman takes a step back. "What did you say was name?" she asks.

"Dara Adengard." A gust of wind blows, carrying her name as though it, too, had some newfound power.

The woman looks down at her arm, at the place where Dara's hand had been. "My father—he had metal." She looks up at Dara and wraps one hand around her upper arm to indicate an armband. "Used for healing."

"It was called a Jyotisha, wasn't it?"

"Yah."

"And . . . who—who did he heal?"

The woman pauses, and it seems as though she is searching Dara's face for the answer. "Aishe."

"Why? What happened to Aishe that she had to be healed?"

"Was stabbed—by my brother."

Dara freezes, takes a step forward, stumbles.

Diego's strong arms are around her.

"Nuri." Dara chokes as she says the word.

"Yah, child. That is my name."

CHAPTER 40

The truth strikes Dara with full force. She stares at Nuri—the woman who, until moments ago, seemed little more than an aging transient with a fragile hold on reality. "You—you said Aishe was healed." Dara holds her breath, clenches and unclenches her fingers, feels them tingling. "Tell me—did she survive?" She already knows the answer.

"Yah, but I had to give away," Nuri says, "to keep safe because Shandor want to kill us all." She stops her knitting and gazes down at her hands. "Was not able to finish sweater when I gave away."

"She—Aishe—" Dara stumbles over the name and whispers, "she was my mother."

"But you said mother was gone."

"She was ki—" Dara catches the word in her mouth. She can't bear to bring the full weight of reality crashing down onto Nuri and feels compelled to soften the blow. "I mean, she passed away earlier this year."

Nuri looks intently at Dara. "Is true?" she asks. Her eyes flick over Dara's face and she brings a crooked finger to Dara's cheekbone. "I think maybe you have . . . Aishe here," she whispers. "I see in face."

"People said we looked alike."

Nuri slumps down onto the three-legged stool under the tree. "Your mother, my own Aishe? Then—you are—" She shakes her head as though to clear it and looks hard at Dara. "She had illness?" With faltering hands, Nuri resumes her knitting, but the weaving gestures have slowed, and she lets her hands fall into her lap.

Dara shakes her head, averts her eyes.

Diego's hand slips into hers.

"Then . . . was killed?" asks Nuri.

"I'm sorry." The words seem empty, inadequate.

There is a long silence, and when Nuri at last speaks, a sadness has come into her voice. "We both lose someone." She closes her eyes. "Me—a child." She opens her eyes and looks at Dara. "And you—a mother. World not always kind." She looks around the encampment, brushes a hand over her eyes, and makes a gesture as though putting aside the invisible knitting needles.

"I miss her, too." Tears stream down Dara's face. "I miss her bad sometimes."

"Come, child." Nuri motions with her hand.

Dara lets go of Diego and kneels beside Nuri, who puts an arm around her shoulder. Nuri pulls Dara close and enfolds her in two thin arms until Dara's head is pressed against Nuri's damp cheek. Dara closes her eyes and takes in the unexpected fragrance of nighttime flowers.

"You survive much," Nuri whispers, "for such young girl."

Dara pushes aside the ache and swallows a sob, raises her head, looks at Nuri's weathered face. "I have more to do," she says. "I must find the Jyotisha, and maybe you can help lead me there."

"I am old woman. All I have are memories and"—Nuri looks around the hillside, which seems to have grown greener—"and this place. Nothing more."

"Maybe your memories will lead me," Dara says. With a sleeve of the sweater, she dries her cheeks. "A woman named Vadoma sent me, told me to find you. Said she met you?"

"Name is familiar. But no one finds me. Until you."

"Vadoma did Tarot cards," Dara says. "It's how she knew the truth about me before I knew it myself. Maybe she read the cards and found her way to you."

Nuri shrugs. "I know mothing about those things."

"At any rate, you've come a long way and survived."

Nuri smiles. "One thing, in summer was not brown grass like this." She looks around. "But how strange, yah? Is green now, and tree has new—how you call?—buds. Much like old country where land was beautiful and there was lake with deep water where geese would come. Necks were long." She smiles at the memory. "White necks, blue sky."

"In the place where you used to live?"

The woman gives a slow nod. Ever since Dara touched Nuri's arm and sensed the power flow between them, something has changed in Nuri. She seems more focused, alert, and her words have greater clarity.

Nuri's eyes settle on a spot in the distance. "But was not summer when it happened, was winter. I never forget."

Diego sits cross-legged near Dara on the grass, leaning forward to listen while gently stroking Linc's head.

Nuri's words come slow at first, then more quickly as the story unfolds. "We—husband Nikolai, baby girls, and me—lived in Russian village of Turinsk, in Ural Mountains. It was winter, and snow was on road. On cold night, Nikolai drove us in sleigh with horse to visit my father—his name, Peshov. Girls was sleep, both in my arms."

Dara tenses. "Wait. You said *girls*. You had another besides Aishe?"

"Two daughters. Aishe and Luminitska."

She must have seen the puzzlement in Dara's face.

"How you say?" Nuri struggles for the right word. "The same. Twins, yah?"

Dara stares at Nuri, at the walnut face, chapped lips, wrinkled brown skin below her throat. Twins. A door to the past has just swung open. "What happened to the other twin?" Dara asks.

"Luminitska? I had to give away, same as Aishe."

"But you don't know what happened to her after that?"

Nuri shakes her head. "Luminitska more calm, quiet baby. I made for both sweaters, but Aishe's not done and always she cry for food." She looked about, as though searching for a pot of soup.

Is this why I'm here? Dara wonders—not just to get back the Jyotisha, but to trace the journey of an abandoned child? Had the Lightband meant to lead her there all along, to a girl who'd been given away? Was that its purpose? And perhaps that was why the Jyotisha had come to her in the first place—her destiny tied to a healing armband and a lost child.

Nuri continues with her story and tells how her brother Shandor killed Nikolai and tried to kill the two babies, but stabbed only Aishe before Nuri escaped to her father's. Dara knows the outlines of the story but listens intently as Nuri explains how her father had used the Jyotisha to heal Aishe's wound.

Thousands of miles away, Dara thinks, and almost fifty years removed from a small Russian village—yet *someone* had still managed to find her mother on the streets of Southern California.

"What happened to your father?" Dara asks.

"Shandor kill him with knife. Take Jyotisha."

A memory surges through Dara—her own father's stab wounds Dara had once healed with the Jyotisha. She wonders where he is at that moment, if he's okay, and imagines her dad's hand on her shoulder. She sits a little straighter.

"Shandor would have killed me, too," Nuri says, "but I escape, take both my daughters and run." She explains that when she'd cast a last backward glance at her brother Shandor, he was staring into his own bloody hands, entranced by the precious object he'd taken from his father.

"How did you get . . . here?" Dara looks around at the hillside.

Nuri explains that, fearing for their lives, she'd taken her daughters on a dangerous trek to one of the Russian coastal port cities that lay to the north.

Through the kindness of a stevedore, they'd stowed away on a cargo ship bound for Alaska, finally making their way down to California.

"I give away both girls for adopting—to protect."

And in that word "protect" Dara detects a plea for understanding—or, perhaps, forgiveness.

"Then I disappear," Nuri says, "hide on streets. Sometimes I find shelter in old houses where no one lives."

Dara nods. She and Diego had done that, too.

Although Nuri has never risen above a homeless and destitute life on the streets, she tells Dara it also kept her concealed. Without an address, no one could find her—until now.

There is one more unanswered question. "Who made the metal into an armband," Dara asks, "that became the Jyotisha?"

"My grandfather was blacksmith, found metal in rock from sky—how you call?"

"A meteorite?"

"Yah. My grandfather Yuri find metal in that rock, make into arm bracelet." She looks up at the overhead sky and lowers her voice. "Came to Earth from distant world."

"So you, my mother and—and . . . Luminitska—made it out alive?"

Nuri nods. "Luminitska wore tiny bracelet with her name when I gave away."

"You survived a long time like this," Dara says.

"I am strong blood. This"—she points at her head—"not so strong. But I think maybe you have helped make better."

"It wasn't just being on the streets that affected you." Dara glances around at the encampment. "You had to give up your children. But Shandor's dead now, and so are both his sons. Your brother can't harm you anymore." Dara thinks of the man who'd killed Vadoma. "There are others who can, though, and we must make sure you are safe. This is not a good place for you."

Nuri looks at Dara, and her expression seems to grow darker. "You, too, have survived much danger. I can see in eyes, they show pain. But you are like last leaf on tree that will not fall. I hope you can make through another *burya*. Because when you tell me about Aishe killed, I know—it is here." She looks out, as though dark rainclouds are even now driving toward them.

Dara shakes her head to rid it of the image that has just materialized: the last remaining foliage of a twisted tree above an ocean cliff as the wind howls and tries to tear it loose by the stem.

She brushes the feathers around her neck. "So many who've come into contact with the Jyotisha are dead. Ayon was Shandor's son, and he told me the armband would protect me. Maybe it did, but now the Jyotisha's not in my hands anymore—hasn't been for months—yet I've survived." She goes on to tell Nuri about Gunarik and Mercy.

"Perhaps Jyotisha still needs you," Nuri says. "That is why you are alive, to do something it wants, or maybe find it and help finish—." She pauses, searching for the word, and finally says, "—thing it must do."

"It's like the Jyotisha is programmed with some mission?" Dara asks.

Nuri nods. "Sansakran bloodline is split. The Jyotisha takes on the power of the user, for good or evil. Its power connects to"—she thinks for a moment—"code of our bloodline, put into us by some mysterious power when it was found." She stops and looks at Dara. "Have you felt somethings now, without Jyotisha in hands?"

"Like what?"

"Something strong, sudden thing, like what make light to shine. I felt in your hand."

"A part of the Jyotisha is here," she whispers, holding up her hand. "In my wrist, near the palm."

Nuri rises and there is a kind of majesty in her bearing. No longer does she appear the homeless vagrant, but instead seems to stand taller. "Come, my child." A breeze blows through her gray hair, and she holds out her arms to embrace Dara. The arms are thin, but strong. "You will take back what is ours, what was taken from us."

Dara steps back, and Nuri looks past her with worn and weathered eyes.

Linc rubs up against Nuri, and she leans down to stroke his sides with both hands.

"We need to get you some place safe," Dara says, "off the street."

"There are homeless shelters downtown where you can stay," Diego offers. He stands, puts on his backpack, and looks toward the tightly clustered skyline a mile away.

"No! The ones who killed Aishe try to find me. Not safe." Nuri surveys the barren hillside. "Here is safe."

Dara turns to Diego. "Remember that house we passed a few blocks away? Fire-damaged, red-tagged, looked totally abandoned?"

"She deserves better than that, don't you think?" Diego says.

Dara thinks for a moment. "If only we could get in touch with Brooke Park—"

"We'd have to find a cell phone—or rent one—and we don't have Brooke's direct line anymore."

"You got past the station operator once before," Dara says.

Diego nods. "Let me handle it," he says. "Wait here with Nuri and Linc."

***

Diego returns an hour later. "Found a dude in MacArthur Park," he says, "and gave him some beer money in exchange for using his cell. When I told the studio switchboard I was calling Brooke Park with info about Dara, they put me through to her. One of her assistants will come pick up Nuri at nine o'clock—after dark. Brooke said she'd take very special care of her."

"That's risky," Dara says. "Brooke's calls are being traced, and an assistant could be followed."

"If someone does trace the call, it'll just lead there"—Diego nods in the direction of MacArthur Park—"to a bunch of homeless people."

"Where is Nuri being picked up?"

"In front of El Pollo Loco."

Dara takes Nuri's hand and leads her down the slope. "You'll be taken care of, and I swear I'll come back for you—with the Jyotisha."

***

Dara hides with Linc in a Dollar Tree parking lot across the street, a short distance from El Pollo Loco. She watches Diego as he makes sure Nuri is seated on a bus bench. He hands her some money, dashes across the street, and ducks into the Dollar Tree. After several minutes, a compact car slides up to the bus stop. A young woman gets out and helps Nuri into the front seat. The car takes off, merging into traffic on Alvarado and fades out of sight.

Moments later, a black sedan with tinted windows cruises past the bus bench, brakes, slows, and continues on.

***

Dara and Diego sit on a low retaining wall that runs along one side of MacArthur Park, a block-long urban lake surrounded by dirt, brown grass, and cement. Groups of scruffy men lounge beneath dusty autumn leaves, and several drink from shared paper bags.

Dara stares out into the dark, and lowers her voice. "Nuri said that even though I don't have the Jyotisha, its power is still protecting me for a reason." She reaches out and to take Diego's hand. His fingers are rough, warm, and he slides closer.

"Your hand's shaking," he says. "Are you cold?"

"I'm thinking of Vadoma." She stops and looks away. "I'm here, still alive
. . . but others are not."

"*You* did not kill her."

"But if I find Mercy, will Mercy have to die—just so I can live? And my
dad—how much longer will he survive? Who's next? Who . . . ?" Her voice
trails off, and she looks into Diego's face.

A helicopter circles overhead, its spotlight illuminating a crime scene
several blocks away.

Diego casts an anxious glance toward the helicopter, then turns back to
Dara. "Look, you came back to get the Lightband. That's what you need to
do. Forget about everything else." He pulls out the receipt Jasper left
behind. "This address"—pointing at the payment slip—"I think it's south of
the Marina. We could catch the Metro downtown, take it in that direction."

Diego strokes her eyebrow with his thumb, and she leans into him, feels
his lips on hers. "Yeah, that sounds good," she whispers.

They get up and walk out of MacArthur Park through a graffiti-covered
pedestrian tunnel. Under the cover of darkness, Diego walks ahead while
Dara stays back, keeps her head down and holds onto Linc. They walk past
Langer's Deli and a surplus store, then cut over to a side street. She
remembers Seb's words: *Look ahead. But see everywhere, and feel what is
around you three-sixty.* They hike downtown, find the Metro station
entrance on Seventh Street. The platform's deep underground, and they
have to take three escalator flights to reach it.

Dara keeps hearing the echo of foot treads behind them on the cavernous
subway platform. When she glances around, there are dozens of footsteps—
high heels, flip-flops, sneakers—but none that seem to be concerned with
her. No one watching. No one following.

They stand waiting for the subway, and she leans down to scratch
between Linc's ears.

THE DIRECT BLOODLINE OF THE SANSKARAN

(may also be viewed on the author's website, www.philipbrownauthor.com)

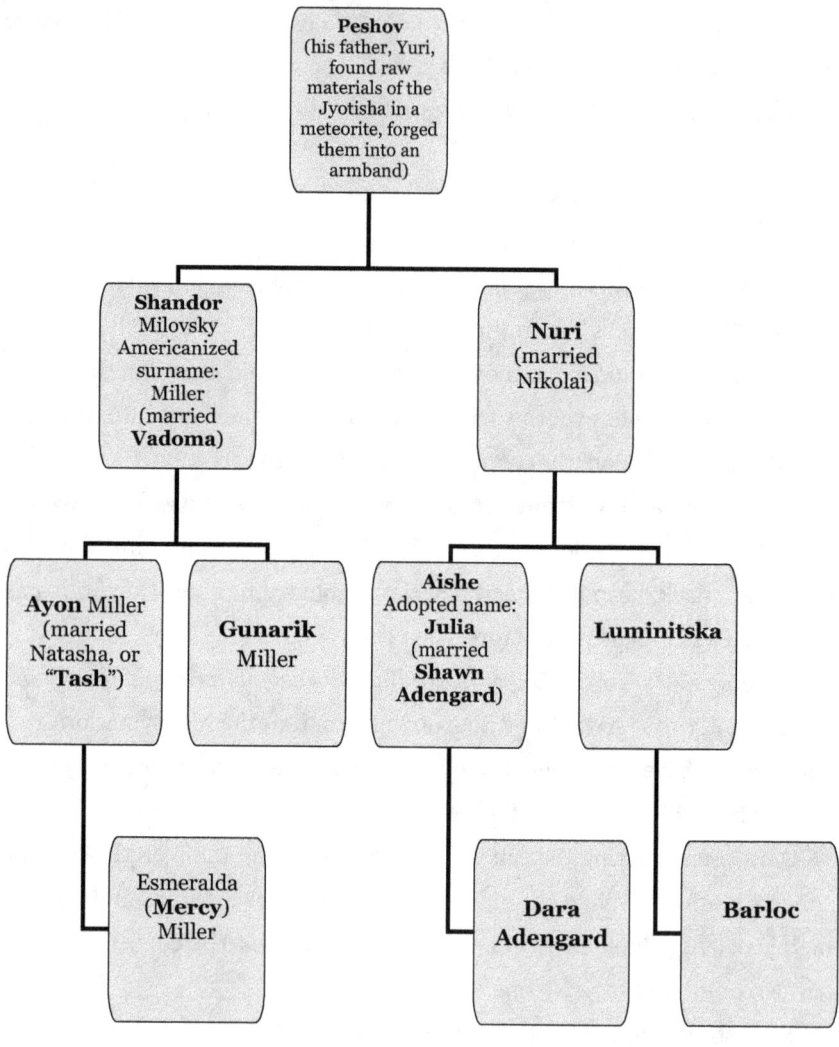

CHAPTER 41

What the—!" Santee slams a fist down on the desk so hard it causes the computer monitor to bounce. He stands, circles the office chair, and kicks it with a black military boot, which sends it spinning. "They've disappeared. Like they just became invisible, stepped into thin air." He glances over at Barr, who works a computer next to him. "What's at Seventh and Flower?"

Behind Santee, the small, windowless room hums with activity. Several people sit in front of large, double-screen computer monitors, studying maps, running cell phone data sets, monitoring closed circuit TV cameras.

"Hold on." Barr gestures at his own computer screen. "I've got the map right here. Metro station at Seventh, right where they disappeared. Underground." He has a high-pitched voice.

"But I thought that was a light rail," Santee says. "Goes on a street, no?"

"Most of the way, it does. But it starts as a subway, underground for the first part of the route." Barr peers at the screen and tugs his bow tie.

"So we've got a problem," Santee says, pacing behind Barr. "They could get off at one of the underground stops and we wouldn't know. At least, not immediately. Assuming that they're even in the Metro station right now."

"No big deal," Barr says. "We'll pick up the trail once they surface. It's just that the damn chip's out of range for the moment."

"Do we have anyone in the area can get down there and see what's happening?" Santee asks.

"It'll take us fifteen, twenty minutes."

"Maybe she suspects," Santee says, "and that's why they went down there in the first place, to get out of GPS range. It must be about the deepest place you can get in L.A. without digging a coal mine."

A man in a dark suit, plastic ID card strung around his neck, walks up to Santee. His shoes click on the linoleum. "Someone near the Gower site's asking what we do next."

"About?"

"The Tarot card reader, subject's prior contact, whole neighborhood's swarming with cops."

"Back off it. We do nothing." Santee swears under his breath. "I need everyone on this!" he yells, "Expo Line! Route, map, destinations!"

The room buzzes with activity.

Santee presses an earpiece, listens, and turns to Barr. "That kid, Diego Mendez, called into the TV studio."

"How can you be sure?" Barr asks.

"Oswalt's coordinating with NSA wireless tracking. Langley's got a recording of the call, but can't locate the actual phone. Seems the Mendez kid was arranging a pickup at an El Pollo Loco on Alvarado."

"And?"

"We were able to get an op to check it out, subject's gone."

"What if they just leave the mutt behind in the underground Metro?" Barr asks.

"Don't remind me what a dumbass you are. You think she'd do that? Dara Adengard's whip smart, but one thing she'll never do is leave that dog—which is the whole point, isn't it?"

"She left it once before," Barr says.

"She didn't have a choice. The Miller girl—"

"You mean Mercy?"

"Right. Esmeralda Miller, a-k-a Mercy—she secures element 120-X, Dara goes over the edge of that precipice at the old Griffith Park Zoo, and the dog—well, the dog was on national TV, an instant celebrity."

"We all saw that mutt," Barr says. "Big reunion with the fire crew."

Santee, noticing that several other people in the room have turned to listen, elaborates. He keeps one eye on the screen, but Dara can wait a minute. He has a captive audience to absorb the story of his genius. "The Adengard girl found the injured dog when it got separated from a fire crew fighting a blaze—that big one in the Ventura foothills last spring. After the dog was recovered following the Griffith Park incident, the fire department made sure it got tagged—just so he doesn't get lost again."

"But a barcode chip's good only if the dog gets found," Barr fills in.

"Right. So we made sure it wasn't just a barcode chip that got surgically implanted, but a full-blown GPS locator, sending out a constant positioning signal. No one knows that little detail but us."

"And you suggested the firefighters give the dog back to the Mendez kid," Barr says, "after they saw how much the two had bonded."

"That Diego kid's clueless. Trust me. Has no idea there's a tracking device in the dog. Now we just need Dara to lead us to the Miller girl—and element 120-X—with the mutt as our guide." Santee swings his chair back to his desk. "Wait, there it is—moving again." He follows a green dot on his own computer screen. "The Metro must've pulled up above ground now, near USC. They're moving fast, right along the Expo Line track." He snaps one of his red suspenders. "We're up and running, people!"

"Any guesses where they're headed?" Barr asks. "Does she know anyone in West L.A?"

"South Central's doubtful, and the line ends at, let me see . . . Santa Monica." Santee chuckles. "They gonna ride the Ferris wheel or something?" He leans back, keeps his eyes on the screen, and shouts over his shoulder. "Gimme an ETA to SanMo."

"Thirty-five minutes," someone calls from a desk across the room. "ETA ten forty-nine."

CHAPTER 42

Linc lies curled up under the Metro seat while Dara stares out the window at the passing city. They zip by sooty apartment buildings. Clotheslines strung from balcony railings. Auto repair shops. Streets that dead-end into the rail line. They whiz past an old man on a bicycle carrying a Chihuahua in one arm. Dara catches a glimpse of a black flag waving from a handlebar of the bicycle, flash of golden armlet on the fabric. The subway whooshes on quiet rails past shabby backyards.

They step off at Bergamot Station and trudge along Venice Boulevard toward the ocean. Although her own steps have slowed, Diego keeps moving ahead in the darkness. Other pedestrians are few and far between.

CHAPTER 43

"Barr, check out the picture." Santee taps the screen and a grainy photograph appears. "Taken five hours ago, on Alvarado." It shows the front view of a girl wearing a knee-length hooded sweater or cloak. Under the light-colored hood, short strands of blonde hair poke out, and three feathers dangle from a leather cord about her neck. She stands on a sidewalk, facing the traffic. "We sent in a surveillance op, who took this picture. He says the girl talked to several transients in the area, but none of them fit Mercy Miller's profile. We're pretty sure that's who she's looking for, though."

"Why not move, take her in," Barr says, "get a fingerprint ID. Just to make sure it's her."

"We gotta stay back until she leads us to Mercy—and the 120-X. Otherwise, the whole op's blown. We need both girls to help us figure out the 120-X." Santee zooms in on a section of the photo on the screen. "See part of that homeless tent in the background? Another black flag. "

"Damn things are all over," Barr says.

"But not for long, right?" Santee snaps a red suspender with one hand. "Let me take another look at that picture you got earlier. Compare."

"Right here," Barr says. He opens a photo icon on his large desktop screen. "Boy and his dog." A photo of Diego and Linc on Hollywood Boulevard, in a press of tourists near the Dolby Theater. Dara stands a little distance behind them in the picture, almost lost in the crowd, and Barr zooms in on her. Harley-Davidson cap, faded t-shirt with some words on it, eyes narrowed as she glares back at the camera. "Good as I could get," Barr says.

"Same girl," Santee says. He rolls his chair close to Barr and tucks his thumbs into the pair of suspenders.

"I tried to get as close as I could," Barr says, lowering his voice. "She was real gun-shy—and of course the girl didn't want anything to do with some dude with a camera. Snapped a picture anyway. Got to pet the dog, too, felt the chip hidden behind his ear, but buried deep—you gotta press in with a finger to feel it. That's when the mutt growled."

Santee opens a message on his phone. "Now the lab's saying it's a hundred percent positive ID. The girl's appearance is real different—but it's her."

Barr zooms in on her face.

"Facial recognition software," Santee explains, "analyzed skin texture, used an algorithm to match features—shape of mouth, eyes. No doubt about it. She's dyed her hair, chopped it."

"Tough chick," Barr says, "even without element 120-X. To tell you the truth, I didn't know if it was the dog or her that was growling."

A man wearing a plastic ID badge walks up, holds out a red phone for Santee.

"Santee here." He listens for a moment to the person on the other end of the line, sits up straighter in his chair. ""We're on it, sir," Santee says. "Almost there . . . I—right, but we just need— . . . Yes, sir, we'll do our best . . . That would be a disaster if anyone else—. . . We'll destroy the chip . . . yes, sir."

Santee hands the phone back to the man wearing the plastic ID badge and utters a profanity.

"What was that about?" Barr asks.

"Langley," Santee says. His face is red. "The Russians hacked into one of our servers. They're tracking the dog, too, knowing it'll lead to element 120-X. Oswalt wants us to either finish this now or abort the mission—and kill the dog."

"I've got her on aerial!" someone yells from another desk.

Santee swings his chair around to face his own computer and clicks on another icon in the sys-tray. It expands to fill the screen, showing a grainy, twilit aerial view of several people walking along a sidewalk. The drone's livestream appears to keep pace with two individuals, one wearing a hoodie and the other—a young man next to a dog—walking at a similar pace half a block ahead.

"Good work." Santee adjusts a headset. "We'd lost eyeballs on her there for a while."

"They had to swap out a battery in the drone," Barr says.

"Can't they hear it?" Santee turns and looks toward a man in the back of the room.

"No way. It's a couple hundred feet above their heads."

Santee holds one finger to his earpiece, listening, and then speaks into a wireless clip-on mike. "Get the drone a little lower."

"Where you think they're headed?" Barr asks.

"Wherever it is, looks like they've got some destination in mind."

"Is it possible they could be going to Miranda Island?" Barr opens a Google map on the monitor.

"That would be crazy. We've had the whole place sealed off for the past several days to run environmental tests. Why would she want to go there? Besides, we've already combed that whole area looking for the Miller girl." Santee presses one finger to his earpiece, turns to Barr. "Get rid of the drone. Now."

"Check."

"And get the vehicles into position," Santee says. "If she's contacting the Miller girl, we gotta be ready to move in." He turns to someone who's been standing in the shadows against the wall. "You're gonna want to see this," he says.

The woman—dark hair, tall, thin—steps forward into the bright glare of the fluorescent lights.

CHAPTER 44

"Look at Linc," Dara calls. "His tail's dragging—and I don't know how much longer I can go."

Diego drops back to walk beside her. "Just a little bit further."

At a gas station, they step to the rear, behind the closed car repair bays. Diego unzips his backpack and removes an empty Cheerios single-serve cup, goes into the restroom, and returns with water. While Linc laps it up, Diego studies a map taped to the window.

"Miranda's way south of Venice Beach," he says. "We're gonna need to rest, get some sleep."

Dara's stomach growls. "I'm hungry." She lowers her backpack and pulls out the last of the trail mix. It hasn't taken long to exhaust Diego's emergency food prep.

They're startled by a commotion of loud barking, and Linc strains against the leash. Another dog, in the back of a pickup truck parked at one of the gas pumps, has spotted Linc and the two dogs bark wildly at each other.

"Buddy!" A woman's voice calls from the other side of the truck.

Buddy, tethered in the truck bed, stops barking and wags his tail as Diego approaches with Linc, who jumps with his front paws on the rear fender.

"Nice dog you've got," Diego says. "This one"—he jerks back on the leash—"can take a little time to make up his mind deciding whether it's friend or foe. But I think maybe he's decided he found a friend."

Dara hangs back in the shadows.

The woman tops off the gas tank, clunks the nozzle into the pump, and comes around to the other side of the truck. "Mind if I pet him?"

Diego nods.

She leans down to pet Linc, who nuzzles her leg with his head. "I was noticing how you guys took care of your little beast. You got no car?"

"We took the Expo line."

"How much farther you got to go?" the woman asks.

***

It's warm inside the pickup truck. Soft country music plays on the radio, and Dara wishes she could stay here. She keeps her head averted, sweater hood pulled over her brow.

The woman slows and pulls the truck into a small, deserted parking lot. "Hope this helps y'all."

"Thanks for the lift," Diego says. The three of them tumble out of the extra cab seat in the pickup.

"Just a few blocks that way." The woman points out the open truck window. "But I sure don't know why you'd want to go there."

Dara reaches into the bed to pet Buddy, and the truck takes off.

After walking several more blocks, they reach a shabby area of shipyards with dinghies up on jack stand supports, a water reclamation plant, liquor stores with neon window signs,.

They pass a shuttered boardwalk and a short distance after that is the "island," a small park at the end of a jetty. When Dara and Diego arrive at the entrance, a cooling fog has rolled in. A closed metal gate faces them, topped with barbed wire. *Miranda Island*, a sign reads. *Government Property. Keep Out.* The fence extends out along the jetty a short distance into the water, making it virtually impossible to get onto the island without swimming.

"Guess this means we won't find Mercy here," Diego says.

Dara slumps against the fence. "We came all this way—for nothing."

"I'm wiped out and I'm hungry," Diego says. His voice has grown tired.

He rattles the chain link fence with both hands, and Dara shares his frustration.

They buy tacos from a catering truck around the corner and sit cross-legged on a bench next to a row of docks bordered by streetlights. Linc gulps down *carnitas* and lies down at Dara's feet.

A homeless man dozes near them in the dark, while another rummages through trash barrels, pulling out plastic bottles.

Dara and Diego take some clothes from their backpacks and use them to make a thin ground cover on a nearby patch of grass. They open bedroll blankets, and Dara settles into a restless sleep.

She's awakened sometime in the early morning darkness by the sound of a boat chugging out of its slip. She lies there, thinking about all that's happened., starting with the horror of Vadoma's death. And how it had felt when she'd touched Nuri's thin arm—the translucent glow of Dara's hand, a tingling vibration, an electric current surging from skin to skin.

She's startled out of her thoughts by the sound of a glass bottle breaking, followed by distant sirens, the loud screech of a bird.

The streetlights along the boat slips cast a misty radiance.

"You hear that, Diego?"

"What?" A sleepy murmur.

"Cars. Like somebody's stopping just over there. Backing up. Then another car."

"Fishermen coming to work."

"I thought I heard a police radio."

Diego doesn't answer, and she hears the sound of his even breathing.

Dara hears the screech again and as she peers into the haze, catches sight of a large bird flapping in descent. The bird's neck is long and graceful, and she hears the beat of its wings pounding in the quiet early morning air. It hovers for a moment, reaches down its long neck to grab some morsel in its beak, and ascends.

It's a goose—and for just that one moment in the misty glow of a streetlamp, it is wrapped in golden light.

CHAPTER 45

Mercy spits out a piece of gristle, crumples the tin foil taco wrapper, and tosses it in front of her. It bounces into the gutter.

Next to her, Jasper opens one eye, twists a short dreadlock between two fingers, and closes his eye again.

If only she could sleep, bundled in the doorway of a tackle shop next to the boat slips. She'd been angered by Jasper's failure to get Dara, and sleep eludes her. But what troubles her even more than Jasper's failure was her own reluctance—or was it inability?—to punish him with the Lightband. At the time, anger had welled up inside—and yet something stopped her from hurting him. It certainly wasn't love. Ever since her father's death, her heart had sealed up tight. So what was it?

The mist rolls in, and Mercy pulls the blanket tighter about her. Within the neck pouch, the armband vibrates, and she reaches a questioning hand. It stills.

The sound of breaking glass startles her, and she tenses, hears sirens. But the sirens fade into the distance, and it's quiet except for the sound of waves breaking on the distant rocks. A derelict in an overcoat walks past, checking out discarded cigarette butts, muttering under his breath. A bird with a long neck lands several yards away, the streetlamp casting it in a yellow color that reminds Mercy of her *bunica's* bead necklace.

A vehicle stops nearby, close enough to hear the ticking of the engine as it cools. Another car halts where she'd heard the first, followed by a short squawk—police radio static or a bird?

Jasper stirs next to her.

Thoughts race through Mercy's mind, and in those thoughts she hears voices. A father who is dead speaks to her of locked doors and of discovery—*Someone else has been found*—and puts a cool hand on the back of her neck. A mother who is alive whispers of an armband, of time and opportunity.

And there is another voice, a girl's, the one who has been found, and this one stands on a precipice where she speaks of healing a wound.

The voices come and the fog rolls in and Mercy pulls the blanket tight over her head to shut out the voices in the mist.

CHAPTER 46

Dara shivers in the early morning light. Although warmth radiates from Linc's body next to her, she pulls the blanket tighter. The fog hangs thick over the docks, and when she reaches over to pet Linc, his fur is damp.

Diego stirs, fumbles with his backpack, the sound of bills being counted. He gets up, walks to a nearby public restroom.

"I'll get us some food," he mumbles when he returns. He takes Linc, walks to the end of the boat slips, and disappears into a large, empty parking lot.

He comes back carrying a plastic bag. "Gas station mini-mart," he says, and pulls out muffins, breakfast burritos, Gatorade, and a couple of hot dogs he feeds to Linc.

"C'm here, boy," Dara says.

Linc trots up to Dara and she sets down her burrito to nuzzle the side of her head against Linc's. She plays with his ears and works her fingers into the space below, massaging behind his jaw. Without warning, Linc yelps and pulls back.

"What's the matter, boy?" Dara asks. She felt something in the instant before he'd yanked away. Something hard, buried under the fur. "Hey, Diego, put your finger here—but be careful, he's sensitive."

Diego presses the spot, and Linc once again lets out a sharp bark, jerks away, tosses his head. "I know exactly what that is," Diego says. "I've felt it before."

""What is it?" Dara asks.

"The fire department put in a chip in case he gets lost or goes missing again."

"Do you get what you're saying? They might consider him to be lost *now*, trying to find him with that chip."

"It's not like that," Diego says. "Not for tracking. It's just in case he's lost and found, like a stray, they can scan him."

"Are you sure?"

"Yeah, stop worrying."

Breaking off an end piece of the burrito, she chews and thinks for a moment. "I want to take another look at the entrance to Miranda Island. It was dark when we got here, and I couldn't see it that well."

"I don't think it'll lead you to Mercy." Diego pauses, takes a swig of orange Gatorade, and stares at Dara. "And what do you plan on doing when you find her? Beat her up and take the Lightband?"

She stands and faces the ocean, stares into the haze. A man had killed her mother, stabbed Vadoma. The Lightband meant death, wounds that healed but also wounds that didn't. Others surely wanted the Lightband—and would easily kill a teenage girl for a chance to hold it. The only problem was, they couldn't use it, which made *her*—and Mercy— all the more valuable. She turns back to Diego. "I'll do whatever I need to get it back. It's mine—and Nuri's. I made a promise."

Diego crumples up a burrito wrapper and swooshes it into a nearby trash can. "Okay, let's say for the sake of argument that you get the Lightband back—somehow—what then? Are you just going to carry it around for the rest of your life? Go around healing people in secret?"

"It was given to me for a reason," Dara says, "not just for safekeeping. Ayon told me it was connected to my destiny. Nuri told me the same thing— that the reason I've survived is to do something the Jyotisha wants, to help it finish whatever it is supposed to do." She thinks of her mother's twin, Luminitska, and once again wonders if she's somehow tied to the Lightband's journey.

"But you still don't know," Diego says.

"Remember Parking Lot and how he claimed that Isaac's skin condition somehow never really went away, just got passed on to him? What if that's true, and the Lightband has some power we don't know about?" She considers some more. "And remember the place where I healed Becca, how the grass oozed out chlorophyll? Can there be too much of a good thing?"

"What do you mean?"

"Too much healing," Dara says. "to the point where it turns into something bad. Should someone with a skin lesion get healed the same as a person with cancer? I once met a girl on the streets who wanted me to heal a fever blister—but is the Lightband just supposed to be like some magic Blistex?"

"It also healed a bullet wound," Diego says. He puts a hand to his stomach. "You—and it—saved me, and the world got to see that YouTube miracle video." As though it never happened in real life, but existed only in an alternate virtual reality. "Sometimes, there can never be too much of a good thing."

She feels warm and easy in her chest and leans in to kiss him. His mouth is cool and tastes like Gatorade.

***

In the daylight, the entrance to Miranda Island —a misnomer since it's attached to the shore by a jetty—is actually two gates, constructed of metal wire and secured with a heavy chain and lock. The visible side of the island is ringed by boulders and a quartet of palm trees. Except for the seagulls and a few barking sea lions, it appears deserted.

The only color comes from several faded orange, blue, and yellow paddleboats stacked on a splintered wooden pier to one side of the park. Everything else is brown dirt, withered grass. Even the palm trees are dead.

"What happened?" Diego asks. "I thought this was a park. The sign even says—"

"Ssh." Dara raises a hand to silence him and holds her breath. "The Lightband's close." She looks around. Several hundred yards up the coast, she can make out a Ferris wheel poking above the mist.

"How do you know?"

"My blood's tingling. I can just—feel it."

CHAPTER 47

Mercy is shaken into wakefulness by Jasper's hand on her shoulder.

"When I went to pee," he says, "I saw a bunch of black SUV's parked on a side street. We gotta get out of here. It ain't safe."

He drags her up, helps gather their meager belongings—blankets, knapsack, worn leather tote bag.

A slight vibration. Mercy touches the pouch around her neck.

Jasper tries to pull her into a run, but she holds back. "Slow down. Running will just attract attention."

They make their way to a shallow pedestrian tunnel that passes beneath the Coast Highway, connecting the beach to a cluster of bungalows on the other side. Jasper holds Mercy's hand as they pick their way down the beach and into the safety of the tunnel, its walls tagged with artistic graffiti. Once inside the tunnel, Mercy turns to look back and sees the jetty leading to Miranda Island in the near distance, bathed in morning haze.

Jasper crouches next to Mercy and works sand out of a flip-flop strap.

"How many SUV's?" Mercy asks.

"Five or six." Jasper brushes sand from one foot, puts on the flip-flop, and takes several steps to peer out the tunnel entrance. "Can't see much through that mist."

Mercy's heart pounds from the panicked awakening, and inside her something sickens. The dark tunnel is too much like the cave where Gunarik had once imprisoned her.

Jasper sits next to Mercy, both of them leaning against the side of the tunnel. Jasper takes her hand, runs a finger over her soft knuckles. "I'm sorry. Sorry I didn't get Dara." He looks at her with dark hazel eyes and twists a short dreadlock between two fingers.

Mercy pauses, remembering how she'd almost killed Jasper in anger when he came back without Dara, yet something held her in check then. She stares at her bare feet and the filthy edges of her hemp pants. "Don't fail me again. I need you to be by my side, to watch out for me—like you just did." She squeezes his hand and leans over to plant a kiss on his cheek.

Mercy rises, steps to the end of the tunnel, and stares out at the island. It had been a big risk to stay here, but the area was close to what had once been her home—and besides, who would think to look for her near the place she's destroyed?

Jasper steps beside her, and from the protection of the tunnel they both survey the beach. The fog has started to lift and sunlight is breaking through. She can make out brown fronds hanging from Miranda Park's palm trees. The vegetation is lifeless, and she experiences a sense of triumph. "It's done, no going back," she whispers to herself. In the distance, near the jetty, she spots an object in the sky. It looks like a large bird—but it doesn't swoop, instead remaining stationary as though caught in a headwind.

"Didn't you tell me that Dara had a dog?" Jasper asks.

"Why?"

"Do you see that couple with a dog, walking away from the locked gate?"

"People walk dogs on the beach." The Lightband vibrates within the pouch, this time with greater intensity.

"It looks like the same dog from the news," Jasper says. "And . . . I think it's him—Diego!"

"Impossible," Mercy says.

Jasper steps out of the tunnel "You didn't need to find Dara—she found you!" He looks back at Mercy. "This time, I'll get her. I won't fail you." He pulls out the switchblade and bolts onto the beach.

"No, Jass, wait!" Mercy takes several hesitant steps out from the tunnel, and cold sand presses between her toes. "Jasper!"

CHAPTER 48

Dara hears a girl's yell, muffled by the fog. Linc growls, strains at his leash, and pulls away from the metal gate in the direction of the voice.

Footsteps pound toward Dara in the sand, and through the wisps of thinning mist a young man races in her direction.

"It's Jasper!" Diego says.

Behind Jasper, a girl stands framed in a tunnel entrance. The girl breaks into a forward run . . . Mercy?

Jasper—short matted dreadlocks—is already on them, and Diego steps up to intercept him while keeping Linc in check.

Jasper's piercing dark eyes settle on Diego, and he takes a menacing step forward. "Get out of the way. This time, Dara's coming with me."

Linc growls and lunges against the restraining leash.

Dara tenses her hands into tight fists, digs a sneakered foot into the sand.

"Jasper!" Mercy emerges from the sunlit mist, hair long and unkempt. She runs up beside Jasper and grabs his hand. She gasps for breath, and her eyes light on Dara. "Take her, Jass, and let's get out of here." Mercy's voice is hoarse, her face sunburned.

Jasper presses a button on the switchblade handle, and it flips open. He menaces Diego with the knife, and Diego steps back.

Jasper grabs Dara's arm, and she smashes an elbow into his side. He winces, drops the knife, and lunges at her.

Dara jams a palm straight up into Jasper's jaw.

Stunned, he falls back, blood dripping from his mouth.

Linc, in a mad frenzy of protection and fury, barks and leaps at Jasper, but the leash has become entangled in Diego's legs and the dog is unable to free himself.

Mercy seizes the fallen knife, draws it back to thrust at Diego's back. Linc, now unrestrained, snarls and springs at Mercy. Before the knife strikes Diego, the dog's teeth clamp down on Mercy's hand. She screams as Linc growls and tears at her wrist, forcing her to drop the switchblade.

"Linc!" Dara picks up the knife and grabs Linc's leash. She pulls on the leash, but he refuses to let go of Mercy's hand.

There's a whirring sound above their heads.

"What the hell—?" Jasper says.

Diego raises his head.

Dara looks up to see a drone. She's momentarily confused and thinks of the Jyotisha—lifted, suspended above the Griffith Park picnic field.

Linc lets go of Mercy's hand, snarls, and the drone descends until it's just twenty feet above their heads.

A loud, disembodied voice comes from the drone: "Lie face down on the ground!"

A commotion draws Dara's attention past the boat slips to the parking lot. Sun shines through the haze, casting the fog wisps in a sparkling radiance. A swarm of SUV's careen to a halt at the near edge of the parking lot. Men rush out and position themselves behind open car doors, shotguns aimed. Several other men wearing street clothes—flannel shirts, blue jeans— cautiously step toward Dara over the sand, guns drawn and pointed.

Behind the advancing men strides a heavyset man wearing red suspenders and carrying a rifle. Dara knows him from somewhere, but she's in too much shock to have more than a faint recognition.

A black helicopter swoops in and circles overhead, the whup-whup of its blades stirring up the sand.

Dara and Mercy look at one another, and in Mercy's eyes, Dara sees the same confusion she feels inside.

And then all four of them—Dara, Diego, Jasper, and Mercy—are lying face down on the sand. Dara turns her head, and sees one of the men grab Linc's leash. Linc bares his teeth, snarls and strains to get at the man—but the dog is lassoed and kept in check using a pole device with a hoop at the end.

Dara has one side of her face in the sand, arms spread. Diego's hand is inches from her own, and she stretches her arm until one finger nudges his.

"You've been a very good boy," she hears someone say, southern accent over the noise of the helicopter.

Are they talking to Jasper?

"Scalpel, quick." The man with the southern accent calls out an order. "We need to cut the chip out of this dog—now!"

"No!" Dara and Diego scream in unison.

"Take no chances." A man's voice standing over Dara.

Mercy shrieks.

Something jolts Dara's side, and everything goes black.

CHAPTER 49

When Dara comes to, she's strapped to a gurney in the back of an SUV, rear seats removed. Two men, one on each side, cradle rifles, barrels pointed down. No windows in the back, but she can tell they're racing fast. A dull pain throbs in her side.

"Where's Diego?" she asks.

One of the men looks at her. No answer. The other one cocks his head to one side, as though to indicate another vehicle next to them.

"What happened? Where are you taking me?" Her heart pounds.

"We had to tase you," one of the men says. "Stun gun. Sorry. You probably passed out from the pain or maybe the shock." He doesn't tell her where they are going.

***

After what seems a long ride, the vehicle stops and the back doors open. Dara is lifted, gurney's wheels dropped, and she's trundled onto a sidewalk. She turns her head to one side and, although surrounded by a cordon of men, catches a glimpse of the black SUV she's just come out of, plus several other SUV's.

No cop cars. No Mercy. And no Diego—or Linc.

She's trembling.

A metal door to a building bangs open, and her gurney's pushed through a double set of doors. Industrial interior—exposed air ducts, cement support posts. Divided into rooms with modular partitions, some transparent and some fabric-covered. The building smells of cleaning solution. She's hustled over polished concrete into a room separated from an adjoining space by a Plexiglas divider. A woman dressed in white comes in and pokes a sharp object into her arm. It pricks, and Dara tries to pull back, but her arm is restrained. A wave of fear overwhelms her.

"Don't worry," the woman in white says. "It's just an electrolyte drip. You're dehydrated." She rolls up Dara's pants leg and attaches a Velcro cuff to her calf.

A series of beeps sounds from a machine behind Dara's head.

"Heart's racing," the woman in white says. "Blood pressure's high, trembling like a leaf. Neurological overload, stress—I'd say stage one shock." She turns to someone standing nearby. "Alprazolam, three milligrams."

A heavy-set man lifts Dara's head and places a pillow under it. As her head is raised, she catches a glimpse of a logo mounted above the door—two snakes and a pair of wings, words written underneath.

"I need her to be in her right mind." Man with a Southern drawl. "No drugs."

An orderly wheels a cart into the room, preps a blood draw needle, and wraps Dara's arm in a rubber strap above the elbow.

"Little pinch," the orderly says.

Dara turns her head away and finds herself looking into the room next to hers, separated by thick glass. Startled, she sees Mercy on the other side, eyes closed, also strapped to a gurney. Dara can see the sheet over Mercy's chest rise and fall with shallow, even breaths, as though she's sleeping. One of her hands is wrapped in thick bandages. Two men stand over Mercy, one of them writing on a clipboard.

"Where am I?" Dara asks.

The needle is withdrawn, piece of gauze taped to her arm.

"Where we're going to get some answers." A voice from the doorway.

Dara pulls her head up, then drops back onto the pillow. She'd seen him on the beach with the other men who took her. Up close, though, he looks friendly. Big dude, white shirt, red suspenders, salt-and-pepper beard, topped with a head of bristly gray hair. She knows him from somewhere else, too, but can't place it.

He lets out a pleasant laugh, and takes a couple of steps into the room.

"Griffith Park," she says, wincing at the pain in her side where the Taser had hit. "You were there and tried to get me away from the paramedics. Who are you?"

"Just a guy who wants what's best for you. Name's Rudy Santee, but most folks just call me Santee."

"Where's Diego? And my dog?"

"That dog was a big ol' help." Sidestepping her question.

"What do you mean?"

"Diego can fill you in."

"Diego?!" She tries to wriggle out of the wrist restraints, but they're tight.

"Bless your heart, child, he had nothing to do with it." Santee settles into an easy drawl. "It's a long story, but let's just say that Linc led us straight to Mercy." He nods at the adjacent room.

Dara closes her eyes. Of course. A tracking chip. She's been followed ever since they left Diego's. She tenses as another thought strikes her: Nuri. Have they found Nuri, too?

Santee steps to the head of the gurney, and his belly looms over her. "We were looking for the missing element 120-X —what you call the Jyotisha, or Lightband." There's a note of dismissive disdain in his voice. He pauses and seems to be studying the monitor placed behind her bed. "Your heart's still gallopin' like a quarter horse. Here's the thing, Dara—since the rest of the world seems to think you're so important, I'm glad we've taken you out of circulation. You know, sweetheart, we almost nailed you earlier—months ago, back at the government hospital. We were about to take you, but somehow you got away."

"What good is the Jyotisha if you can't make it do anything?" Dara asks.

"That is a dilemma, isn't it?" He steps back and appraises her.

"Do you have Diego? My dad?"

"It's element 120-X we're after. That, and you two girls. Such a nice bonus to have you. And"—nodding toward the adjacent room—"the Miller girl. Together, you'll help us figure out how to use it, won't you, darlin'?"

"And if I don't?" Her gaze drifts up, and she sees a convex camera lens embedded in the ceiling.

Santee sits on the edge of the bed and smiles. "I think you'll help us."

He's too close, and the bed sags from his weight. She senses the pressure from his thigh and edges her hip away. Her throat is dry. "Where—where am I?"

"Let's just say that everyone who's taken the least bit of interest in your Lightband—the military, FBI, CIA, you name it—goes through us now." He sweeps out an arm to indicate the building. "And I'm the top dog. So if you want to be a good little puppy, don't make me bark. 'Cause I will bite." He chortles at his own joke.

"How am I supposed to help you? You took Mercy—" She shifts her head, glances at the room next door—"so you've got the armband. You could just let us all go."

"We want answers," he says, "and you're going to give 'em to us. Understand?" Santee rises from the bed and taps on the glass wall. On the other side, Mercy still remains asleep—or unconscious—but one of the men attending her glances over at Santee and walks briskly over to Dara's room.

"Sir?" The man wears a white lab coat.

"Tell this young lady why she's here."

The man hesitates and gives Santee a questioning look.

"Tell her," Santee commands.

The man looks at Santee as he answers. "We're going to run a series of tests—brain scans, blood counts— to see how she interacts with element

120-X during various types of interface, find out how she makes it work. Similar to your plan for the Miller girl. After that, we're planning to—"

"Good enough." Santee cuts him off. "Thank you. You can go."

The man returns to Mercy's room on the other side of the glass wall.

"Pick your head up," Santee says.

Dara lifts up from the pillow and once again sees the emblem mounted above the door to her room.

THE CADUCEUS
BE THE CURE

"That's who we are," Santee says. "We're a private contractor for the CIA, an org called The Caduceus, although that probably doesn't mean anything to you. If you wanted to locate a line item on the federal budget for us, you'd never find it. We don't exist, and nobody in Congress wants to know anything about us. Plausible deniability, they call it." He laughs. "But we're good people. We want to find the cure."

"For what? Cancer?"

"Everything. There's a whole team of scientists who've studied those tapes of yours from YouTube and Brooke Park's TV show. And here you are, in the flesh." His laughter shakes the bed, and his belly moves under the too-tight buttons of the white shirt which exposes his navel.

"You still haven't answered my question about my dad and Diego. Where are they—and Linc?"

Santee ignores her question, gets up and looks at Mercy through the
transparent wall. "This—this armband you once had—contains an isotope, a
variation of a chemical element with some radioactivity—which simply
means it's deteriorating."

"Deteriorating?"

"Slowly, might keep going for millions of years. And you, uh, found it?
That Lightband?" Santee turns and shoots her a quizzical look, as though
wanting to explore those questions further.

Dara is silent. Why isn't he answering *her* questions about her dad,
Diego, and Linc?

"At any rate," he continues, "there are different types of elements. One
known type doesn't occur naturally here on earth, but comes from other
planets—or maybe even star systems—in the form of meteorites. That
appears to be where element 120-X—your Lightband—originated. From a
meteorite."

"I already know that."

"The thing is," Santee continues, "we've never seen this element before.
And you can help us understand how it works." He steps to her side, puts a
hand on her immobilized arm.

She thinks he's trying to demonstrate comfort, but her arm tenses and
she feels angry.

"We need you very much," Santee says. "But first—I'd like you to see
something."

He nods at an orderly who stands just outside the door. The man comes
in and, at Santee's direction, wheels Dara—still strapped to the gurney— out
of the glass-walled room while Santee maneuvers the monitor stand so that
it follows her. She sees mobile medical equipment—monitors, empty
stretchers—and work tables covered with electronic components, tools, and

parts of what appear to be disassembled drones. People in white lab coats bustle about, but stop what they're doing to watch as she passes by.

The layout seems to be at least two or three times the size of a school gym, and she can make out various offices housed along the perimeter, one a large work space with several computer stations. Inside that room, she catches a passing glimpse of a man in a bow tie tapping at a keyboard. He looks familiar, too.

Sound of a key unlocking a door. Then a second lock. The gurney is pushed into a small, dimly lit room, fire extinguisher mounted on the wall near the door.

"Over there," Santee says, and he nods at one wall.

Dara turns her head to gaze at a Plexiglas wall case. A light inside the case illuminates the Lightband locked in a thick, clear plastic box.

The vital signs monitor beeps behind her head and the cuff automatically tightens around her calf.

Dara's fingertips tingle, and she longs to reach out, grasp the familiar metal bands.

"You're one of the very few"—Santee stands facing her, stares at her wrist, and seems to be measuring her reactions—"who seems to be able to connect with element 120-X. And we want to find out why."

"What are you going to do with the Lightband—I mean element 120-X?"

"You've been able to heal with it," Santee says. "Maybe if we can figure out what the mechanism is—how you're able to do that—we can heal millions. You're just one little munchkin. You did that thing at Griffith Park, but your reach was not global. You didn't have the—the range, ability to eradicate all disease. Think of it—Ebola, viruses, cancer." His voice takes on a glowing tone. "And we haven't even started to talk about the environment. What if all that could be cured? You can't do that by yourself—but we could."

Dara thinks for a moment and tries to clear her head, but it feels fuzzy.

"Are you going to help us or not?" Santee drops the friendly manner, and his tone hardens.

"Not until you tell me what you've done with my dad and Diego."

"In that case," Santee says, "there's one more thing you got to see."

Her head pounds, and she lies back on the pillow, closes her eyes and thinks of Diego, his touch on her hand, his kiss on her lips. After several moments, she's roused from her thoughts by a cool sensation in front of her face. She opens her eyes and finds herself staring at an iPad screen Santee holds in front of her.

On the screen, her dad sits in a chair, fastened down with leg and arm restraints. His face is bruised. Blank, drugged expression. He stares straight ahead, wordless, but tall and straight. The camera, set at the level of his face, shows part of an empty room behind him.

"What have they done to you?" Dara screams.

"He can't hear you," Santee says. "The bruises are from when we captured him in the desert. He tried to escape after he went on TV—thus the leg irons. Brought it on himself."

"Where is he?" she asks. But there's something familiar about the room on the iPad, and she peers at it . . . overhead camera aperture in the ceiling above her dad . . . modular wall partition. She glances upward. A lot like this room. "I want to see him in person."

Santee clicks off the picture.

Dara stares into the lingering afterimage of her dad as it morphs into the reflection of her own face, and she takes a deep breath.

Santee studies her. "You asked about Diego, too." He fiddles with the screen, again holds the tablet in front of her face.

And there she sees Diego, slumped on the floor of another room. Santee adjusts the sound, and Dara can hear barking in the background.

Santee keeps the screen in front of her face so she's forced to look at Diego. "So you'll help us, right?"

"And if I don't?"

Santee sets the tablet down next to her. "Your dad's been AWOL for five months," he says, tucking both thumbs into his suspenders. "He was picked up near Adelanto, squattin' in a power station control room he'd broken into. That's more than AWOL, it's desertion. You know what the punishment is for that in the Navy?"

Dara shakes her head.

"Five years in the brig. Plus he'll lose all his pay and allowances. If you want to make it worse, we'll go all the way back to his stealin' a government vehicle, accessory to homicide—"

Dara knows Santee's referring to the dead body in the Buena Gardens the night she'd found the Jyotisha floating in the swimming pool. "And he avoids all that by . . ." Her words trail off.

Santee nods. "Simple. You cooperate, help us. We promise not to hurt you, and in exchange for your co-operation, I give you my word—my sacred vow"—he places a beefy hand over his heart, covering part of one red suspender—"that no charges, either civil or military, will be filed against your daddy. And Diego and the dog will both be freed, too."

"Why should I trust you?"

"No reason at all—except that I'm your only hope, as well as the only chance for your dad, Diego, your dog. You got no choice but to trust me. Believe me, they'll be free as birds once you he'p us."

CHAPTER 50

"We're going to run a few experiments on you," Santee says. He stands beside Dara's bed and loosens the arm restraints.

"What kind of experiments?"

"See what you can do with element 120-X."

"You mean the Lightband, right?" She pulls her hand in close to her side.

"What else would I be referring to?"

Dara glances through the glass wall at the adjacent room, where Mercy had been. The bed's empty. "Are you going to run the same tests with Mercy?"

Santee ignores her question. "We've got all your baseline readings—blood counts, metabolic panel, DNA extraction, gene panel sequencing—and we'll do some comparisons when you use element 120-X."

Dara's heart pounds at the thought that she might hold the Lightband again, yet at the same time she knows she's a human guinea pig. Her breathing quickens.

"But first, we gotta get you cleaned up."

A woman helps Dara out of bed and escorts her down a long hallway to the bathroom.

"There's a shower," the woman explains, "and you'll need to take off all your clothes, be sure to wash off the beach sand. You'll find some special soap in the shower—it says Betadine on the label. A disinfectant. Use it." The woman waits while Dara disrobes and steps into an all-metal shower.

The soap tingles and leaves her skin pink, and when Dara gets out of the shower her clothes have been taken away, in their place fresh underwear and a long, white gown.

"My three feathers," she says. "What did you do with them?"

"Don't worry," the woman says. "They're safe."

Dara feels exposed and vulnerable. Alone without her dad, without Diego and Linc, she's overcome with intense aloneness. The air conditioning blows cold air on her, and she shivers, hugs herself. The woman escorts her to a large room she hasn't seen before, separated into two sections by a long glass window with a connecting door. One section's a lab with medical equipment, while the other part appears to be a partitioned viewing area containing several cameras mounted on tripods.

People move about the lab area in white suits, booties, scrub caps, and surgical masks. Someone sets up a TV monitor, while others make adjustments to a machine with wires that sits on a white, wheeled cart. Next to the machine is a raised leather seat, armrest on one side.

"We're going to bathe both your hands and arms in hydrogen peroxide," the woman who'd escorted her says.

Dara thinks of her dad, AWOL, five years behind bars. "Okay. But . . . why?"

"We want to remove as many variables as possible. That includes germs you've brought in from outside that could possibly, uh, affect the 120-X."

The peroxide fizzes on her skin and has a faint chemical odor. After the woman sponges and dries her arms and hands, she guides Dara to the leather chair.

"Wait—am I going to be hooked up to those wires?" She tries to pull back.

"You don't even know what we're doing, do you?" the woman says. She turns Dara around to face her in front of the chair.

Dara shakes her head. "Not exactly." A sudden jolt of fear.

"You're about to find out." It's Santee, standing over to one side. She doesn't recognize him at first because he wears a green scrub cap, surgical mask, and a lab coat over the red suspenders. His mask moves, indicating a smile, and his eyes crinkle. "Just have a seat and give us a few minutes, little peapod. We need to finish setting up the lighting and cameras."

The leather seat chills Dara. A woman wearing a surgical mask dabs clear jelly on her skin before attaching wires to arms, legs, and chest. The woman straps a metallic headband device around Dara's head, the electrodes and headband both connected to the machine next to the chair. The woman affixes a blood monitor cuff to Dara's right bicep, and sets Dara's other arm on the armrest to take another blood sample. The woman's glasses steam above her mask, and Dara thinks perhaps she's nervous or excited.

After her blood is drawn, Dara is light-headed, and the weight of wires, cuffs, and metal seem like restraining leashes. People in surgical gowns flit past her field of vision, and she hears the soft pad of feet in paper hospital booties.

"This is just the first in a series of tests," Santee explains. "After this is completed, we'll check your blood again. You'll repeat this several times under varying conditions with a chance to recuperate fully after each test. Although you're hooked up for testing, you're not strapped down to the chair, and we've got a good meal waitin' for you when this test's done."

Dara's trembling and her heart pounds. She casts an anxious glance at the equipment and thinks once more of her dad, Diego, and Linc. If these tests help free them, it will be worth it. She also wonders about Mercy, a prisoner like Dara—would she ever be freed, too?

Both rooms—the lab and the viewing area—are crowded with lab workers. Most have finished setting up the equipment and stand off to one side or behind the glass partition, watching Dara. Several have taken positions behind the cameras and appear to have begun filming. Everyone except Dara wears surgical masks, and from her seat she scans the upper half of people's faces: eyeglasses . . . mascara . . . heavy dark eyebrows . . . false eyelashes. Each pair of eyes stares back at her.

Santee nods at someone who leaves and returns moments later with the small, clear plastic box and a remote. These are handed to Santee, hands protected by latex gloves. Dara recognizes the box she'd seen earlier, and the armband shimmers through thick plastic. Santee keys in a code on the remote, points it at the box, and there is a soft click. The lid opens with a pneumatic wheeze, and he steps up to Dara, holds it out to show her.

There it is—the Jyotisha, silver and gold braids glistening in the bright fluorescent lights.

Dara grasps for it, and at the same time her hand vibrates.

Santee pulls the box back. "Not yet," he says. "First, let me explain. We'll watch you heal someone, a simple experiment—although maybe the bracelet is not so simple." He nods at the Lightband, nestled in the box in his hand. "We thought we'd start with just a little hand injury. Jerry?"

A man steps through the door from the other side of the glass partition.

"Jerry does equipment repairs, maintenance. Show the girl your hand, Jerry."

Jerry holds out his hand in front of Dara and turns it over so she can see his knuckles. The back of his hand has a lot of dark hair, and there's a cut on the back of his index finger.

"He cut it yesterday when he was repairing something," Santee says. "Ever heal anything that small?"

Dara shakes her head.

"I know it's just a little cut," Santee says, "but we'll be able to calibrate our measurements this way."

Dara can see his salt-and-pepper beard protruding below the mask.

She's aware of people watching her through the glass, as though it's a see-through cage. Several others, including Santee and Jerry stand inside the lab area. Next to Santee is someone who also wears a surgical mask and holds up an iPhone pointed at Dara as though recording or taking pictures. The hand that holds the iPhone has blood-red fingernails.

"Think you can do it, Dara?" Santee prods.

"I—I'll try." Her throat is dry and she doesn't know what else to say. If she somehow fails, would her dad, Diego, and Linc be kept with no hope of release? *I've got to do this for them,* she thinks.

"Let's see what you can do, darlin'." Santee's surgical mask lifts at the corners and his voice lightens.

Dara grabs for the Lightband, and this time Santee allows her to lift it from the box. She holds it, turns it over in her hands, feels its familiar warmth, and stares with a sense of renewed wonder at the gold and silver bands.

She cups her other hand over it as though protecting a baby bird. How long has it been since she'd held it? Three, four months? She closes her eyes, and it tingles in her grasp.

It radiates warmth, and she opens her eyes, sees it begin to glow through her fingers. She removes her top hand. The Lightband quivers and rises imperceptibly. Her wrist trembles and an electric current surges into her palm, which starts to glow.

She looks around, but everyone is intent on the armband itself, and her hand looks like it could be reflecting the Lightband's radiance, not generating its own.

She thinks once more of the Old Zoo, how the Jyotisha had detached from her grasp and soared slowly out over the crowd with a will of its own. At the time, she didn't know if she'd ever get it back again.

But now, here it is.

Afraid it's about to fly away too soon, Dara wraps her fingers around the armband as though holding onto a collar. *I don't ever want to let you go again.* The Lightband pulls away, and she tightens her grip, rising from the chair as the armband tries to tug free.

The taped wires yank at her skin, and she senses a couple of them tear loose. The blood pressure cuff slowly constricts against her arm, then loosens. Behind her, the clatter of the electrode cart being moved to keep pace.

"Wait!" someone yells from behind.

"Let her keep moving." Santee's voice. "We'll get as much as we can, but we have to let this play out." His voice has become tense. "Becky, try to keep the other electrodes attached. See if you can push the equipment a little closer."

The glowing Lightband pulls Dara and she stretches her arm, takes a step, the metallic headband pulling her hair, pinching her scalp.

Jerry inches closer to her, hand extended.

The armband tugs Dara. Why is it still pulling her? Jerry's hand is right in front of her.

The Lightband is so close to Jerry now that he has to pull his hand back, still holding it up for the cut to be healed.

But instead of going in the direction of his hand, the Lightband vibrates harder and pulls Dara away from Jerry, toward—someone else.

Dara turns and follows the Lightband's pull as it vibrates harder in her grasp. She finds herself facing the red fingernail woman with the iPhone, close enough now to see eye mascara, brown bangs protruding from a pink scrub cap.

The woman takes a step back.

"It's okay," Santee says. He stands near her and holds up his hand, as though telling the woman to stop retreating.

The woman halts, but Dara can see that she's quivering, and her eyes have widened.

"You said it would be a simple test," the woman says, her mouth moving under the mask.

"Maybe not," Santee says. "Just hold steady."

Dara stands in front of the woman, trying to reign in the Lightband as it pulsates and glows. The Jyotisha pulls, just as it had done at Griffith Park when it left her and she didn't know if she'd ever get it back. Now, it once again trembles and heaves in the hard clasp of her fingers. Dara's heart beats faster, and she holds on tighter. She can't lose it again. She can't.

There is total silence, and Dara senses everyone's eyes on her and the Lightband.

And in that moment—surrounded by medical staff in a glass room as equipment whirs, sticky electrode pads on her skin—she looks into the woman's eyes and thinks of her mother, the moment of birth in a hospital. Her own birth. Dara wants to say the words, to speak to the Jyotisha, to tell it that letting go doesn't mean forever, doesn't mean loss. She wants to cry, but instead her chest shudders something loose, and it goes into the Lightband which shakes as though possessed by wrenching sobs.

Dara spreads her fingers and lets go.

Light radiates from her palm, and she holds it up, pointed toward the armband. Bright beams spring from her palm, bathing the Lightband, which pulsates with a multi-hued aurora. The memory of her mother merges with the powerful current surging from her wrist into her palm.

There are gasps all around, and out of the corner of her eye she sees someone make the sign of the Cross.

The Lightband vibrates through the air toward the woman, who drops the iPhone and takes a couple of steps back until she's pressed against the glass wall. The Lightband stops in front of the woman's face and slowly descends over her chest until it's in front of her stomach. With a sudden blast of light, it vibrates and whipsaws, positioning itself in front of the woman's belly.

In the woman's eyes is a look of horror.

A wind blows through the room and there's the sweet fragrance of flowers, like a springtime garden.

Dara drops down on her knees in front of the woman and holds out an open palm directed toward the armband, flooding it with radiance. The light in her hand ebbs, the vibrational current in her wrist eases, and she holds both hands under the Jyotisha. Its light, too, subsides, and it drops gently into her outstretched palms.

Dara is aware of the silence.

The woman does not move, but stares dumbstruck at Dara and the Lightband.

Dara looks at the surrounding glass walls: people are around all sides, silent, unmoving, transfixed.

The woman's hands are shaking as she brings them to her stomach. "How did it know?" she whispers. "How could it possibly have known?"

CHAPTER 51

Santee strokes his beard and looks down at Dara. "Welcome back," he says. "You were out for nearly an hour."

Dara glances around the room, the same one she'd been in when she arrived. "What happened?" She tugs at her arms, buckled down in belt restraints.

"You went a little crazy in there, and we had to sedate you, put you to sleep." He nods toward another part of the building. "I didn't want that to happen, but you left us no choice. You started demanding to know what happened to Doctor Reynolds—the woman you healed—telling us to let your dad go, screaming for Diego, Linc . . . had to get you under control."

Dara remembers the woman in the surgical mask, blood red fingernails. "What happened to her?" she asks. "I thought the Jyotisha was just going to heal that other dude's finger."

Santee considers Dara carefully before replying. "Doctor Reynolds is almost four months pregnant, although it didn't show yet, especially under her lab coat. None of us knew. And"—Santee takes a deep breath—"it seems she contracted a bad virus while in Brazil doing medical research. Went to a clinic here in the States to have some pregnancy tests done—and found out the baby was carrying the virus."

"That doesn't sound good," Dara says.

"It causes an irreversible birth defect," Santee says. "You see that up there?" He points at the symbol on the wall.

THE CADUCEUS
BE THE CURE

"In Greek myth," Santee explains, "the caduceus was the golden wand of medicine. Two snakes, intertwined. Mercury, the gods' messenger, carried the staff to protect him on his journey as he guided the dead to the underworld." He casts a quick glance at Dara. "It's a symbol of light and dark. That's why you belong here, you can bring light into the darkness."

Dara thinks of the Jyotisha, her and Mercy, healing and wounding. Opposites, two snakes wrapped around a wand.

"So what happened to Doctor Reynold's baby?" she asks.

"According to a serum test we just ran on both mother and fetus, the virus has, um, gone away. And an ultrasound showed that her baby is"—he pauses, looking at Dara—"normal. Normal in all respects. Healed."

"But I didn't think it could be reversed. I mean, a birth defect . . ."

"It can't. In fact"—Santee sucks in a breath, wrinkles his brow in thought—"that kind of thing never happens. I'd say it's impossible. But the baby's . . . cured. Totally." He sits on the edge of the bed and looks hard at Dara. "Let me see your hand. There was some kind of light came out of it when you healed Doctor Reynolds' baby."

"The Lightband's strong," Dara says.

""I'm gonna do an x-ray of your hand and wrist, find out what you got in there." He eyes her suspiciously. "Remember how I agreed to let your daddy and Diego go if you cooperated? Well, you ain't been cooperatin' and that's why we had to sedate you." He pats her arm. "You got to try a little harder next time."

***

There were more tests, more blood draws, and Dara relished the snacks and meals she was fed to help her regain strength—omelets, steak, chicken, yogurt parfaits, bananas, cakes and pies. She couldn't remember the last time she'd eaten this well.

Santee orders an x-ray, but it doesn't show anything. "Guess you were right," he says. "Just hardware in your wrist."

Relieved, Dara assumes the Jyotisha fragment must have blended with the "hardware." Thank you, Doctor Havens, she thinks.

The lab staff devises ways to allow Dara more mobility while still keeping her fixed to the electrodes. Smoother polyurethane wheels are attached to the monitor carts, and they roll easily if Dara moves about during the tests.

Blood enzymes are measured, before and after. She heals a cut, a scrape, the flu—and in one patient who's brought in, skin cancer. Each time, she's careful to keep a tight grip on the Jyotisha so it looks like the light is coming from it and not her hand, too.

She loses track of time, but guesses she's been here about ten days.

One morning, she's taken to the lab early.

"Here's what's gonna happen," Santee explains. "That poor little peapod—Mercy— was injured when we grabbed the element 120-X from her, back there at the beach. She fought for it, wouldn't give it up. One of her fingers was torn, plus your dog gnawed on her hand pretty good. We had to put in a few stitches, but it hasn't healed. Got infected."

Dara understands. They want to see what the Lightband would do with another Sanskaran.

Where did this stop? Santee promised Dara that her dad and Diego would be freed, but the testing went on and it seemed they were no closer to freedom than before.

"After Mercy, who's next?" Dara asks.

"We got just about everything we need now."

"So that means my dad and Diego will be freed? My dog, too?"

"All in due time."

"Can't you just give Mercy antibiotics?"

"We could do that," Santee says, "but we'd much rather see what you can do. Mercy's DNA is coded a bit differently, to where she does just the opposite with the 120-X—wounds instead of heals. Could it be redirected, reprogrammed? We'd like to find out. We've isolated a few possible genetic variables. It seems you and the Miller gal probably both started off with the same genetic switch, but it traveled a different path in her than you. What triggered the difference? Some mix of nature and nurture."

"I've done everything you wanted," Dara says, "and you've done nothing except put me through more tests." A surge of anger courses through her, and she has to restrain herself from aiming a well-placed kick a little below Santee's protruding belly.

"Tell you what," Santee says. "Do this for me, and I'll let you see your dog. A token of good faith. How about it? But first—let's see how you both, uh, perform."

***

Mercy is wheeled into the lab room, strapped to a gurney. Belt ties have been secured over her torso and legs, as well as her wrists.

She must have resisted, Dara thinks.

Mercy's injured finger and hand lie immobilized, swollen and red on a white cloth. She's hooked up to electrodes, blood samples taken, vital signs monitor set up.

The cameras begins to record, and Santee hands Dara the Lightband.

She stands next to Mercy's bed and looks down at her, turns the armband over and over in one hand, caressing its smooth metal braids.

Mercy looks back up at Dara, and for the first time, they have no choice but to study each other. Mercy's face is still reddened from the sun and wind, her lips chapped. Mercy's hair is chopped short. Her eyes are deep-set and dark, in permanent retreat from the world, and she stares back at Dara as though also reading the nuances of a familiar face.

"They want me to heal your hand," Dara says. As though to say: *If it was up to me, I'd never do it. But I'm being forced into this, into healing you like we're both part of some lab experiment. Please forgive me.*

Dara thinks for a moment, weighs the Lightband in her hand, and sets it down on the bed.

Mercy continues to stare up at Dara, blinks once, and Dara can see the hardness and calculation in Mercy's eyes.

"How ironic," Mercy says, her voice raspy. "You healing me—since you killed my father. But no Lightband?" She raises her head, and her eyes flick down to the armband laying by her side. "How do you expect to do anything?"

Dara is about to once again explain that she did not kill Ayon—but holds her tongue. She's repeated her innocence before, on the precipice at the Old Zoo, to no avail. "You tried to kill me," Dara says.

"Yes, I tried," Mercy says. "But trying is not doing. Someone else pushed you over the edge of the cliff onto the picnic field. It wasn't me."

"Who?"

Mercy clamps her lips shut, and Dara remembers how Vadoma had said the Jyotisha was trying to escape from someone—the person who'd pushed Dara over the precipice.

"It doesn't matter anymore," Dara says. "We're both here." She reaches down and unbuckles the arm restraint that binds Mercy's injured hand.

Mercy glances at Dara, and in Mercy's eyes is a flash of gratitude. The look is fleeting, but it's there. Their eyes lock. Mercy is a part of her, she realizes, sharing her bloodstream, and beyond that, they are also bonded by death and loss—a father gone, a mother buried.

Dara raises her empty hand over Mercy's chest without touching it. The nerves tingle in her hand, like it's fallen asleep and is just waking up.

The sheet that's been drawn over Mercy flutters. Mercy closes her eyes as her face grows tight, and her whole body tenses and shudders

Dara's hand lights up with an effulgent glow, the veins on the back of her hand tiny blue rivulets barely visible through the bright glow of her skin.

She hears a sharp intake of breath from the nearby R.N.: "She's doing it without the X!"

"It's in her hand." Santee says in a low voice. "Just like I suspected."

Mercy's body shakes, and the light from Dara's hand pours out. But around the surface of Mercy's body is an invisible shield the light will not penetrate.

Dara holds her hand over Mercy's injured finger—the angry, reddened skin where Mercy held on to the Lightband and refused to let it go.

Yet still the shield around Mercy repels the light, will not let it in. Mercy clenches her fist, tightens her arm. Sweat has broken out on her face and her body trembles beneath the sheets.

"Mercy's pulse is racing," Becky says. "BP's 180 over 140. We need to stop."

"One sec." Santee holds up a hand for quiet and motions the camera to zoom in closer.

Dara reaches nearer to Mercy's hand, trying to thrust the light through the invisible barrier, but an unseen force pushes her away. Dara strains with every ounce of strength to push her hand closer to Mercy. As though pulled by a hidden magnet, Dara's hand glides above the surface of Mercy's arm to her shoulder.

Mercy's shoulder jerks as though it's been punched.

Now Dara's hand is above Mercy's eyes, and the shield seems to lessen. Light pours from Dara's hand around Mercy's face.

Etched in Mercy's drawn features, Dara sees . . . Ayon's face—his dying moments when she'd cradled his head in her hands.

Dara, you cannot escape your destiny. It is here, right where you are.

And what about Mercy? Is this her destiny, to be strapped to a gurney in a sterile room while experiments are performed on her like some kind of lab mouse?

Dara looks down at Mercy, takes the back of Mercy's head in her hand, and leans down to whisper in her ear, "Your father brought us together. There must have been a reason. I know what it's like to lose a parent. I still know, and I'd never wish that on anyone. I *never* asked for any of this."

And from Dara's hand, cradling the back of Mercy's head, light streams out and around Mercy's head, enveloping her hair.

Mercy's body no longer tenses but has relaxed, and her eyes remain closed.

Dara lays Mercy's head on the pillow and passes her hand over Mercy's face as light continues to flow from her palm.

When the radiance subsides, Mercy's face is clear—no longer sunburned—the skin beautiful, pure porcelain framed by short dark hair, lips soft and smooth.

Mercy opens her eyes. "My head. No pain."

"It was hurting?" Dara asks.

Mercy nods, and her eyes glisten under the bright fluorescent lights.

"I never killed him," Dara whispers. "Your father saved my life, and I—I tried to save him with the Jyotisha—I'd only healed Linc, so I didn't even know—but I couldn't make it work." The words catch in her throat and she stops.

Mercy's hand wraps around the armband on the bed, gripping it tight. She raises her arm and hands the Lightband to Dara.

CHAPTER 52

Robert Reed, a large man with a puffy, unshaven face, sits at his work station re-reading the encrypted order from Rodolfo Santee, interagency head of The Caduceus, Ltd. It's clear that this is a Level Five covert op and should anyone show up at Alto Communications this morning, Reed would just be completing a test on a rush project. He moves the joy stick and the DJI Phantom 2 drone lifts off from the roof of a small warehouse by the train tracks two hundred miles away.

Twenty feet in the air, Reed's monitor shows a concrete river bank, a slag heap, flat one-story rooftops. The Phantom is run though a short set of in-flight checks, and when the drone reports a "green board," it's fully operational.

Fifty feet up, the view broadens. One hundred feet: a pair of churches, water tower, and business district. Still higher, flat field grids are visible beyond the edges of the small town. Two thousand feet in the air, the drone hovers and parks itself in a holding pattern as instructed by Reed.

A hazy, low cloud blows past the drone, momentarily obscuring the view. When the view clears, the drone steadies, and below lies the small town of Cutler, busy starting its day. Cars drop off kids at a school. A truck pulls out of a loading dock. A tractor churns soil in a steady cloud of dust. Anywhere, U.S.A., Reed thinks, as he pushes his drone control keyboard.

The drone responds, and green vapor is released, a mist that drifts downward into the town. The deadly spores hang for a moment in slow descent, and a light wind begins to scatter them.

CHAPTER 53

Santee guides Dara through an exit door into an outdoor pen, enclosed by a concrete wall, topped with barbed wire.

She breathes in fresh air, feels warm sunshine for the first time in days.

Linc is chained to the outside of an open metal shed and looks well-fed—Dara catches sight of two plastic dog dishes. The instant Linc sees Dara, his tail goes into a wagging frenzy, and he celebrates with high-pitched barks.

She leans down to hug him, the dog's wet tongue on her cheek. There's a patch of dried blood behind Linc's ear, and Dara hopes he didn't suffer when they cut out the tracking chip.

Santee stands a short distance away from her—beyond reach of the dog's chain. "You see?" he says. "I keep my promises."

"I missed you so much, boy," she whispers in Linc's ear, both hands stroking deep into his fur.

Santee grins, as though pleased to have effected this reunion.

Dara sits down cross-legged and pets Linc while she looks up at Santee. "Are you done testing me?" she asks.

"We're done," Santee says. "Now we're going to operate and extract the element I know you've got in your wrist. And after that"—he makes a flicking gesture with his fingers like something is being released—"we've got everything we need." He laughs, and his stomach bounces, the shirt buttons pulled taut, belly skin exposed.

"What happens to my dad and Diego?" Her heart is pounding.

Santee strokes his beard and shrugs. "Right now, we're setting up a test to see if we can operate element 120-X without either of you two girls, and then we can—." He stops short. "We've got work to do."

Dara ceases stroking Linc's neck and looks up at Santee. Her voice quivers. "What do you mean, without us?"

"I—we want to tap element 120-X's power—ourselves." He smiles and tucks one thumb under a suspender. "That's all I meant."

Dara tries to swallow, but her throat is dry. "What exactly . . . are you going to do with the element—I mean, Jyotisha?" she asks.

"That's classified. Time to say good-bye to your dog."

"Good-bye? I thought—" Her hand trembles against Linc's fur as the realization dawns on her. "No!"

"Don't you worry your little pea-pickin' head. Why, he's not even your dog." He laughs, and his stomach bounces.

Santee pries Dara's arms from around Linc's neck and pushes her through a door.

Dara looks back over her shoulder. Linc's eyes shine in the sunlight, staying fixed on her until the door closes, and his fierce barks echo long after she's gone inside.

CHAPTER 54

Dara falls asleep early and awakens to the sound of a freight train in the distance. The light in her room is dimmed, the building hushed—nighttime, she thinks. The faraway train rolls over the tracks, slow, rhythmic, endless . . . metal wheels scraping on iron tracks.

From somewhere outside the building, mingled with the freight train, comes the familiar barking of a dog, followed by a whine or a whimper. Her heart stops.

The freight train fades into the distance, and in its quiet wake is another sound—branches shaking against the outside walls. A strong wind has come up.

The door to her room opens, and someone whisks in—white lab coat, nurse or doctor, so many who come and go, poke and prod. This one's a woman who sets down a plastic bag, fiddles with the monitor behind Dara's bed, unties the wrist restraints, lifts one of Dara's hands and attaches a fingertip pulse reader.

The woman bends close to Dara's ear, and Dara catches the fragrance of body wash, feels warm breath on her cheek.

"Listen carefully," the woman says.

Dara turns to look at a tuft of brown hair which hangs over the woman's brow. Dara recognizes the eyes.

"You saved my unborn baby," the woman whispers. "Now I'm here to save you."

"Doctor Reynolds? What about—"

"Shh. None of you will live through the night. They've already taken Mercy. You must listen and do exactly as I say. Pretend I'm taking your vitals." Doctor Reynolds takes Dara's hand, unclips the pulse reader. Her hair is a thick, wavy bob, and her eyes have a permanent squint as though she's forgotten her glasses.

Dara grips Reynolds' hand, and turns her head to look at Mercy's room through the glass partition. It's empty. Anger wells up inside Dara, and she turns back to Reynolds. "I'm not leaving without my dad, Diego—and my dog."

"Here. Put these on." Reynolds reaches into the plastic bag, withdraws some clothes, and hands them to Dara.

Dara glances at the ceiling camera.

"Those are friendly eyes watching the monitor—for the moment," Reynolds says. "A guy who's on your side."

Doctor Reynolds blocks the camera with one hand while Dara slips on jeans, t-shirt, sneakers—and over those a white lab coat, surgical mask, scrub cap.

"I brought you these." Reynolds hands her the three feathers, still on a leather cord.

"Thank you." Dara loops them over her head, and they fall around her neck. Her heart pounds.

"The guard who was posted by your door," Reynolds says, "isn't going to be doing much guarding." She holds up a syringe.

"What's that?" Dara asks.

"Neuromuscular blocking agent. Deadly if given in large enough doses, although the guard should recover." Reynolds squints at the aperture in the ceiling. "Someone monitors the cameras throughout the night—but they're on break, replaced by one of ours. There are quite a few in here who've come to secretly admire you." She checks her watch. "We have a six minute window before the one on break gets back to his post." Reynolds takes a deep breath. "—I'm coming with you, I'll help get you out of here, and besides— She pats her stomach. "—I've got someone else I need to protect."

"Then let's go," Dara says.

Reynolds pushes open the door, and they move out into a dimly lit hallway, stepping over the unconscious body of a man in a white lab coat. Outside, Dara can hear the wind blow so hard it seems to rock the building.

CHAPTER 55

The seconds tick by. Five minutes now, maybe less, before somebody else looks at the monitor, sees her empty room.

The corridor is empty, the only sounds their footsteps and the outside wind. Doctor Reynolds walks ahead, leading the way.

Dara buttons the lab coat and pauses to tighten and adjust the surgical mask so it covers as much of her lower face as possible. She tilts the scrub cap over her brow.

Footsteps approach from up ahead, but she and Reynolds keep pace down the hallway. Someone draws near and nods as he passes. "The test's a go," he says. "They're starting up the machine now. Get to the viewing room."

Dara nods back.

They round a corner, walk down another corridor, come to a door with a small, square window, light streaming from within. Reynolds halts, gestures at the door, and Dara stands on tiptoes to look through the glass.

Inside the room, Mercy lies strapped to a gurney, eyes wide open as she looks at Santee. He's positioned at the foot of the gurney, wearing his usual suspenders.

A woman stands next to Santee.

On Mercy's face is a look of fear.

It's the same room where Santee showed Dara the Lightband, and through the window she glimpses it encased in Plexiglas. A fire extinguisher hangs nearby.

Reynolds steps in front of Dara, squints through the window, takes a deep breath, inserts a key. Click. Then a second lock. Click. The door swings open, and Santee turns to look at Dara and Doctor Reynolds.

"You're just in time," Santee says. "Give us a hand here."

Dara nods and steps into the room behind Reynolds, who shields the syringe behind her back in a trembling hand.

The woman next to Mercy's gurney takes a step back.

Behind the Plexiglas, the Lightband glows with a faint iridescence.

"I'm tryin' to get this little sweetheart to"—Santee, breathless, presses on Mercy's shoulder—"keep her arm steady. She won't hold still enough."

Dara hangs back by the door, notices that both Mercy's arms are strapped down.

"I said, we could use your help," Santee commands. "Don't just stand there like a couple of dumb fools. We're about to test the machine, and I need one more blood sample."

"What are you giving me?" Mercy asks. Her voice shakes.

"Just a little sedation," Santee replies. "It'll make you feel good."

Dara remembers Reynolds' words: *None of you will live through the night.*

Dara takes two more steps and looks more closely at the woman standing next to Mercy. She has a thin mouth twisted into a smile. A perfect, aquiline nose.

"Honest, sweetie," the woman says to Mercy. "You're way too tense. This'll help."

"One of you pull her wrist," Santee says, looking at Dara and Reynolds, "so I can get a needle in there. Tash, hold her shoulder."

Tash?

Dara remembers the name, from when she'd been questioned by Rachel at the hospital.

Her blood runs cold.

Mercy's mother. What is she doing here?

"It's okay, hon," Tash says to Mercy. "Mr. Santee just has to do this so you can sleep."

Santee looks at Reynolds. "You might need to fetch another dose of Ativan."

"I brought some right here." Reynolds holds up the loaded syringe.

"Perfect," Santee says. "but that's a huge dosage."

Mercy struggles against the restraints.

Santee leans over the gurney, his belly creased against the edge, and pulls one of Mercy's arms to straighten it on the gurney. One finger taps a vein to juice it up. He glances back at Dara. "C'm here. Hold her arm down." But something else catches his eye, and he lets go of Mercy, straightens, scrutinizes Dara more closely.

Dara takes a step back.

"Wait," Santee says. He advances on Dara and tears the scrub cap from her head. "You? How did you ever—" He turns, yanks open a drawer, pulls out a scalpel, and turns to Reynolds. "I can't believe you let this little chickadee hoodwink you."

"What makes you think I did?" Reynolds says.

Santee glances from Reynolds to Dara, and back to Reynolds. "So you're both in on this?"

Dara lowers the mask so that it hangs below her chin. She notes the scalpel, the way Santee holds it in his hand—like a surgical utensil, not a weapon. She squares her feet. "I forced Doctor Reynolds into it," Dara says. *Stall for time.*

"Too late, darlin'," Santee says. "We've already got what we need from you. Just need this last blood draw from Mercy."

Santee jabs at Dara with the scalpel, and she steps back.

Howling wind. Tree branches lash the outside walls.

Dara's eyes flick from Tash to Santee and back again. "The wind—it's from the Jyotisha machine, isn't it?"

"That's correct," Santee says. "We've managed to engineer element 120-X —make it ourselves—and it's being tested now. We just needed one more, uh, sample." His eyes glance to where Mercy lies on the gurney.

"You sent the man who killed Vadoma, didn't you?" Dara asks.

"She resisted," Santee says, "and paid the price."

He takes a couple of steps, nimble for a man so large, and thrusts the scalpel at Dara.

She parries his arm with a swift upward kick.

He grips the scalpel as though he's about to cut into a cadaver, and lunges again.

She sidesteps him, grabs his wrist and pulls hard. She drives from her legs, punching her other hand into his face, fist crunching against his flesh.

Santee is rocked back on his feet.

At that moment, a deafening explosion from somewhere close sends a blast wave through the room, and Dara is blown back by the detonation. Painful pressure in her ears. Ceiling tiles drop, and the Plexiglas shatters. The heavy metal door to the room is torn from its hinges, propelled right at Dara. She sees it coming, raises an arm to block it, and the edge of the steel door hits her wrist, gashing it deep.

The air fills with dust, and Mercy coughs. A klaxon blares. Ceiling sprinklers spray water, turning the gray dust into paste.

Reynolds brings the syringe out from behind her back, and drives the needle into Santee's side. She presses her thumb hard on the plunger, the liquid level drops to zero, and she yanks out the needle.

Santee takes one lurching step toward Dara and tumbles to the floor.

Blood pours from Dara's wound, and she presses the element 120-X wrist with her other hand.

Tash picks up the fallen scalpel and menaces Doctor Reynolds with it, keeping her in check.

Dara stands on unsteady feet, dripping wet from the sprinklers, and looks from Mercy to Tash.

"What the hell just happened?" Tash asks, raising her voice above the sound of the alarm.

"The explosion came from the direction of Santee's new 120-X machine," Reynolds says. "Something must have gone wrong during the test."

"Untie me, mother!"

"Of course, my sweet," Tash says, still keeping the scalpel pointed at Reynolds. "You just need to promise me one thing."

"What?"

"That you'll help me use the Lightband—for your father, for Ayon. You have the power, and we can do so much together."

"You just tried to help Santee," Mercy says.

"I'm the only chance you've got right now. If I leave you strapped to that thing, you'll be killed, burned alive."

A strong odor of smoke comes from outside the room, and the alarm continues to shriek.

The heat grows more intense.

"Yes!" Mercy struggles against the restraints. "Whatever you want—just undo these!"

Tash releases the belts. "Quick, Mercy hon. We need to move fast."

Mercy sits up, swings her legs over the side of the gurney, and stands.

Weakened, Dara falls down on her knees next to Santee's body. Blood continues to flow from her wrist. She hears footsteps, and Tash stands over her.

"I tried to kill you once before," Tash says.

"When?" Dara whispers, feeling dizzy. She looks down at Tash's shoes, a pair of pointy-toed, sparkly silver flats.

"I'm the one who pushed you over the cliff," Tash says.

"You?"

"This time I'll make sure you don't survive."

Dara, still on her knees, light-headed, puts a bloody hand on the floor to brace herself.

Tash turns to Mercy. "Hurry, my love. I'm going to finish this"—she raises the scalpel—"and then we leave. Together."

"Wait," Mercy says. "Give it to me first." Mercy forcefully grabs the slim scalpel from her mother's hand.

"What are you doing?" Tash asks.

"Getting the Lightband—for us."

Dara sees Mercy lean down next to a thin piece of shattered Plexiglas. She jabs the acrylic with the scalpel until pieces fall away, and she pulls something loose.

In a daze, Dara watches blood flow from her wrist onto the linoleum.

"Good for you," Tash says. "Now give me back the knife. Let me finish Dara off, and—what are you doing? I told you to give me the knife."

Mercy—robin's egg blue nightgown, face strewn with dust and water—backs away from her mother. "You—you were going to help kill me," Mercy says. "Just like you tried to have me stabbed when I was a child." The words sound far away, and Dara thinks she sees Mercy point a nozzle, something red, a cylinder, at Tash.

"You're crazy," Tash says. "Why would I ever—no, it was going to be ours. Our Lightband, to honor Ayon. I was just—".

There's a hissing noise, and the air fills with white powder.

"Don't!" Tash's voice, far off, muffled, coughing. "Turn it off!"

Dara feels as though she's drifting off to a pleasant sleep and collapses the rest of the way onto the cold floor as warm powder sprays over her skin.

But there is something else . . . at her wrist . . . also warm. It must be the blood, she thinks. She manages to open one eye partway. Someone kneels next to her—a pale blue figure. Dara's vision dims, but there's a light, or something that glows. Maybe this is death, she thinks, the light that illuminates the way to the next world.

The wind, though. There is still the wind. Is she outdoors now? Dara has a sensation of flying above the building, carried by the wind, and she breathes in sweet jasmine.

CHAPTER 56

Dara becomes aware of the room. The wind has stopped blowing, and Mercy kneels next to her. Beside them lies a bloody scalpel and a fire extinguisher, the floor covered in chemical powder. In Mercy's hand, the Lightband still glows as she lifts it away from Dara's wrist.

"Quick," Mercy says. "We have to get you out of here." She sets the armband in Dara's palm.

When Dara encircles the armband with her hand, her fingers glow through encrusted blood. She slides the Lightband up her arm until it nestles against her bicep.

Mercy helps her to stand.

Out of the corner of her eye, she sees Tash approach.

Mercy turns. "Keep away from Dara, mother."

"But our plan—"

"The Lightband belongs to Dara," Mercy says. "Stay back, don't touch her." She picks up the bloody scalpel and points it at her mother.

"What happened?" Tash asks. "You just healed her, but that was—"

"It's different now," Mercy says.

"We have to get the others," Dara says. She crawls over to Santee's body, reaches a hand into his pocket, and pulls out a set of keys.

"I know where to find them," Reynolds says. "Quick."

Reynolds motions Dara and Mercy out into the hallway. Running footsteps echo toward them from another part of the building, and Dara stumbles after Mercy and Reynolds, away from the footsteps.

Tash does not follow, and Mercy tosses the scalpel aside.

All three of them—Dara, Mercy, and Doctor Reynolds—pick their way through a debris-strewn hallway, sidestepping shattered glass and overturned carts. The overhead fire sprinklers have stopped.

A distant, muffled shout reaches them.

"That's my dad's voice!" Dara says. She hears crackling flames nearby. "He could be trapped. Same with Diego and Linc."

"This way," Reynolds says.

"Dad!" Dara yells.

There is an answering shout, and they proceed a little further as several burning embers shower down from the ceiling. It grows hotter, and sweat trickles down Dara's face.

A man runs past them, gasping for air. "Wrong way!" he shouts. "Get out!" He disappears behind them.

"Here, this door," Reynolds says, coughing. "We don't have much time. You get your dad— Mercy and I will get Diego. I've got another set of keys."

Inside the room, Dara's dad sits chained on the floor. Dara tries several small keys until she finds one that unlocks the manacles that bind him. He struggles to stand, and Dara helps to pull him up.

"How did you escape—?" he starts to asks.

"I'll explain later."

"Where's Santee?"

"Dead."

Mercy and Reynolds burst into the room with Diego, their faces stained with soot.

"Diego!" Dara says. "Thank God you're safe."

Diego reaches out a hand to Dara, but before his fingers find hers, a cloud of dark smoke billows into the room. Dara coughs, has difficulty getting her breath.

"Everyone down on the floor!" Dad yells. "Follow me. And stay low!"

Dara lies flat, her nose pressed to the floor, struggling to breathe.

"Now!" Dad commands. "Go!"

They crawl out into the hallway, edging beneath the smoke as flames encroach from behind. Dara follows Diego's feet in front of her, and in the narrow space between floor and smoke can make out her dad and the corridor ahead.

All around them—crackling heat. The ceiling burns above their heads.

"The exit door," Reynolds shouts, "just to your left!"

Dad stands, shoves it open, and they stumble outside, coughing violently.

Dara gulps fresh air into her lungs.

Dad, wheezing, puts an arm around her. "Okay?" he asks.

"I'm still breathing," she says.

Loud barking in the distance.

"Linc!" Diego says.

"The dog's over there, on the other side of the building," Reynolds says.

They keep down to avoid the smoke that erupts through blown-out windows and make their way around the building. Fire shoots up from the roof, and burning embers shower all around them.

Up ahead is a metal storage shed.

Desperate barking.

Flames lick toward the shed, and the heat intensifies.

Diego runs ahead through patches of fire, unlatches the door, and throws it open. He gathers Linc in his arms and dashes back, dodging flames in his path.

Reynolds leads them to a large metal gate, and they all rush through it into the street. The building erupts skywards in flames, and muffled explosions sound from within the burning walls.

Safe across the street, Diego sets Linc down and brushes back his own ash-strewn hair. Linc leaps up on Dara and she lets him lick her face, smells the smoke in his fur.

A cacophony of sirens converges from all directions. Fire trucks, lights flashing. Large hoses deploy, and firefighters yell above the noise of the inferno. The street shines with water runoff.

"Can't stick around," Dad says. "Gotta get out of here."

Down the street, people congregate on a corner, drawn by the sight of leaping flames. A pair of police cars pulls up and blocks the street near the gathering crowd.

"They'll figure we're employees," Diego says. "Dara's wearing that lab coat, looks like she's a fire victim. If we try to run, they'll suspect we set the fire."

Dara looks at Mercy, her dad, Diego, their faces covered with soot, ash, and sweat rivulets. Blood trickles from a cut on her dad's head. She thinks of the Jyotisha, feels for it on her upper arm, and her hand seeks Diego's.

"You're right," she says. "No more running."

A firefighter emerges from the building. He supports another, both gasping for air, and the Lightband vibrates on Dara's arm.

"Jack's been hit by a falling beam!" the firefighter yells. "Oxygen tank—and we need an ambulance." Both firefighters collapse on the sidewalk across the street from where Dara stands.

Another firefighter stumbles out of the burning inferno. Others emerge—doctors, nurses, lab workers, some of whom Dara recognizes. Dazed and hurt, they stagger out gasping for air. Several scream, calling for help with injuries.

"Upgrade, priority five!" a firefighter yells. "We need more EMT's!"

One of the injured look over, sees Dara, and points in her direction.

The Jyotisha vibrates harder, and Dara drops her lab coat to the sidewalk. She slides the Lightband down over her forearm, into her palm, feels its warmth. It glows, quivers, and when she opens her hand to let go, the Lightband moves through the air—but not toward the injured firefighter.

Instead, Mercy steps forward, and the Lightband flutters into her outstretched palm.

Some of the injured—burned, gasping for air— now have their eyes fixed on the glowing armband across the street. Several of the firefighters, torn between the fire and the Lightband, cast quick glances over their shoulders.

Yellow and blue triage tarps are laid on the sidewalk, and firefighters position the injured.

Mercy holds the Lightband before her where it shines with a golden splendor. She holds out her other hand for Dara.

Dara takes Mercy's hand in her own, and the two girls cross the street toward the triage area. While Mercy wields the Lightband, Dara kneels next to a fallen firefighter. Energy surges into her palm. Dara holds it turned toward the fallen firefighter, and her hand glows, dried blood thick on her wrist. She holds her hand over his burns, and streams of light bathe him in radiance.

Dara looks up for a moment and sees Tash emerge from the burning building. She limps away, dragging one foot, and brushes ash from her clothes.

Bright smoke billows into the dark sky. Large hoses writhe, and the remaining firefighters struggle to subdue the conflagration, all the while casting glances toward Dara and Mercy.

Dara takes note of the crowd on the opposite side—passers-by drawn at first by the flames and smoke and then by the Lightband's fireworks, the rays from Dara's healing palm. Many now hold phone cameras, recording or live streaming. Others stand silent, transfixed.

A Channel 7 satellite truck pulls up down the street, and a news helicopter circles overhead.

Mist from one of the water hoses hits Dara in the face, and she turns her attention back to the triage area. The Lightband hangs in midair over the wounded while a strong wind gusts, fanning the flames, and water runoff glistens in the armband's light.

CHAPTER 57

Dara leans back into the rear seat of a white stretch limo, her dad and Diego next to her, Linc on the floor.

"Why's the driver slowing down?" Dara asks. "We're not there yet. I thought the studio was in the Valley." She glances behind at the black limo which trails them.

"This whole ride was pre-mapped in the news," her dad says.

Along Sunset Boulevard, clusters of people line the streets. A woman with a walker lifts a thin arm and waves as the limo passes. Many wave black flags imprinted with a golden armband.

Diego leans down, ruffles the back of Linc's head, holds up one ear, and says softly, "You're in a parade, boy."

Through the tinted windows, Dara senses a yearning in people's eyes, and her fingers tremble. She presses a palm against the tinted window, and a cheer goes up from the crowd. Her palm glows against the smoky glass.

Several emulate Dara by holding up one hand with palm turned outward, as though bearing witness to the moment, connecting.

The limo makes its way over Barham into the last rays of a setting sun and then down Cahuenga. The limo turns, drives up to a guard shack. The guard salutes and waves them through, the other black limo close behind. Both limousines pull up to a pair of studio entrances.

Dara gets out and, feeling nervous, raises a hand to stroke the three feathers that dangle from her neck.

Mercy and Nuri disembark from the other limo.

Mercy takes Nuri's hand as the two of them are surrounded by men and women in suits and earpieces who escort Mercy and Nuri inside a separate entrance to the building.

Studio workers have gathered outside to watch the arrival of the two limos, and several applaud when they recognize Dara.

She hears whispers: "Dara . . . Diego! . . . the Missing Soldier . . . who was that old lady in the sweater? . . . Here, boy. What's his name? Linc? Belonged to a fire station, didn't he?"

Dara speaks with a security guard before the group is rushed through a heavy door, down a hallway, and into a small room with plush chairs and a leather couch.

Dara looks around the room, tries to take it all in. It seems unreal, to be here with Diego and her dad, both of whom stay close by her side. Mercy— black sheath dress, purple cape, emerald green headband—is ushered with Nuri into the same room, and both stand silent against the wall, Nuri's weathered hand clutching Mercy's wrist.

Fruit and finger foods, as well as numerous beverages, are set out on a table.

Linc has been given a camouflage collar and glittering silver chain leash, which Diego grips tight. The dog sits on the floor, alert, ears tweaking with every movement about him.

Dara holds Diego tight and kisses him on the cheek, kneels down to embrace Linc.

"This must be Linc," a production assistant says. "Okay if I pet him, too?"

Dara nods and walks over to Mercy's side. Mercy leans a head against Dara's shoulder. Dara puts an arm around her, and all three—the two girls and Nuri—speak softly amongst themselves.

"I am glad this survived fire," Nuri says, indicating the sweater she wears. "I never want to lose."

Diego's father—an 805 tat on the back of his neck, wearing an orange and black Harley shirt—has come into the room and stands next to his son.

Diego's sister, Jenny, is also there, as well as several production assistants wearing plastic ID cards.

Dara keeps glancing around the room, as though trying to spot someone else.

A young man in a Hawaiian shirt strides in. "Everyone who's going to be on the show, follow me to makeup," he says. "The rest need to wait here."

Dara, her dad, Mercy, Nuri, and Diego—who holds onto Linc—follow the man down a corridor to a large makeup room. Rows of swivel chairs face long wall mirrors framed with lights. Dara is shown to a chair.

Linc sits by her knee, ever alert.

"My cat Sophie's still chasing mice"—a voice behind Dara—"like she'd never been sick."

Dara raises her head and sees a familiar face reflected in the mirror. "Lauren?"

Lauren smiles. "Brooke asked me to take special care of you."

"I'll never forget," Dara says, "how I healed your cat Sophie on live TV."

"You were amazing."

Within less than fifteen minutes, Lauren has feathered Dara's short hair into layered blonde tufts. She continues working with scissors, brush, and a curling iron until at last Dara's hair is worked into a messy, windblown chicness.

A makeup artist touches up Dara's face and when Dara stares at her own reflection, the face that gazes back at her is one she hardly recognizes, the eyes no longer young and carefree but more settled and deep. Her mouth has become fuller, cheekbones more defined.

"You know you're beautiful, right?" Lauren says.

"Thanks," Dara says, "but you wouldn't have said that if you'd seen me in the desert."

"Here, I think you should wear this. Go change." Lauren hands Dara a package tied with string.

***

The man in the Hawaiian shirt escorts the six of them—he calls them "the Light Guardians"— to the sound stage, where they are told to wait behind a side curtain.

Mercy finds Dara and takes her hand. "You look incredible," Mercy says. "Where'd you get that outfit?"

"Brooke's hair dresser."

The two girls stand side by side in the wings, one wearing a black sheath dress and emerald headband, the other a flowing, white, floor-length gown cinched at the waist with a white belt.

When the Light Guardians are ushered onto the stage, the audience rises, stands in silence. A lone pair of hands begins a slow clap. Other hands join, then others, until there is a crescendo of applause. Dara casts a glance around, looking for someone, notices raised TV monitors at either edge of the stage.

The group is directed to sit in chairs that have been arranged in an angle, with a large overstuffed beige chair—Brooke's seat, Dara assumes—at the apex. Production assistants attach lapel microphones. Lauren comes onto the stage, uses a small-touch-up brush on Dara's hair, and calls out "Spraying!" She holds a towel over Dara's eyes and spritzes hairspray. Dara glances around, notes that others are also getting last-minute makeup and hair adjustments.

At last, Brooke comes onto the stage, surrounded by production assistants. She nods at Dara and her father, takes her seat in the stuffed armchair facing the others, and waits motionless while a mike is affixed to her blue satin blouse. Someone places notecards in her lap, and Lauren steps up to retouch Brooke's makeup and hair. A man wearing a plastic badge comes up to her, leans down, and whispers in the star's ear. Brooke nods.

Cameras are wheeled into position on the stage, the audience lights go off, stage lights dim, and . . . 3-2-1 . . . they are live.

An announcer's deep voice intones, "Welcome to a special *live* primetime edition of *YOLO with Brooke*. Featuring the Light Girl who came in from the desert, Dara Adengard, and special guests—the Light Guardians. Now, ladies and gentlemen, please welcome . . . Brooke Park."

A single spotlight illuminates Brooke Park, and she looks at the audience. "You are witnessing a very special event. You know Dara Adengard. You've met her father, Shawn. Now they're here, with us, along with several others. Please welcome"—she pauses, her voice subdued, restrained— "the Light Guardians."

Someone coughs once in the audience, but other than that it's quiet, hushed.

The lights slowly come up on the rest of the stage.

CHAPTER 58

One by one, Brooke draws out from Dara, Diego, and Dara's father their stories of survival and heroism. Even Linc gets his moment in the spotlight when Diego points out where the dog's fur was singed in the Caduceus fire.

"Here's the scar," Diego adds, showing the spot behind Linc's ear, "where the tracking chip was planted."

Brooke is not the inquisitor she'd been in the past, but instead seems to reflect the muted awe and reverence of the audience.

"Donations, large and small, have continued to pour in for Dara," she says. "The studio has set up a trust account, the Lightband Fund. When we went on the air, the fund exceeded half a million dollars. Dara?"

Dara glances at her father, then at Diego. "The money's not mine," she says. "We'll be okay." She thinks of Isaac, Parking Lot—and Nuri. All the hillsides dotted with those who had no other place to live. "I'd like it if the homeless had homes. Could the money be used for that?"

"That's a noble sentiment," Brooke says, "but I don't know if that's quite what people had in mind when they sent in money—often just small bills—in response to your last interview. But it's something I'm sure can be worked out."

She turns her attention to Nuri. "I've had an opportunity to get to know you over the past weeks, Nuri, and you've quite a story of persisting against the odds. How long did you live on the streets?"

"Many year," Nuri replies.

"I think you told me forty?"

Nuri dips her head.

"And something special brought you here to America," Brooke says. "What was it?"

"To protect daughters."

"How many?"

"Two girls," Nuri says. "Twins."

"And what were you protecting them from?"

"From family—my own brother—who want to kill them. I gave for adoption, to protect. One daughter became mother of Dara—although I never knew."

Dara glances at the monitor, and sees that the camera has moved in for a close-up of her own face. She reaches up a hand and strokes the downy feather necklace. *Feathers fly*, she thinks. *Feathers fall. Be like the wind and let them go.*

"You say one daughter survived," Brooke says. "What about your other daughter?"

"Was also disappeared, into adoption, so I do not know what became."

Brooke glances down at the notecards in her lap. "I'd like to turn our attention," she says, looking up, "to Esmeralda Miller—Mercy."

The camera moves in for a close-up of Mercy, her face framed by short dark hair secured with the bright green headband.

"Mercy, you've surfaced, disappeared, and surfaced again," Brooke says. "With the sole exception of Dara, I can't think of anyone in my experience who's become such a social media obsession. You and Dara both survived that fire, and the world got to see you using the Lightband. Where did that power come from?"

Mercy sits up straight in the chair, her Aunt Nuri close beside. Nuri slips a weathered hand around Mercy's forearm and holds it tight in a protective grasp.

"Although Dara is in reality my cousin," Mercy says, "she feels like my sister. I share with her the Sanskaran bloodline, our DNA altered by a force that came from somewhere out there" —she gestures overhead—"and gave us special power. I thought it was my power to wound, like my uncle, to give others pain just as I had received."

"Pain you received?" Brook asks. "From where?"

Dara is once again impressed with how Brooke penetrates the surface and drills down into the made-for-TV emotions.

"I've had to walk through a different kind of fire to burn away the past," Mercy replies, "and come out the other side. The only love I ever had was from my father. He and I fled when I was eleven to escape from my mother, who tried to kill me. She was going to have someone stab me. I used the Lightband to destroy the place where it happened, thinking that might somehow erase the past, the rocky shoreline where it all began."

Dara stares at Mercy and takes in this new information.

"Do you still have that same power—to hurt?" Brooke asks.

"I might be able to reach for it, but I found a greater power." She considers for a moment. "I told you the only love I got was from my father? That was not quite true. There was someone else. Her name was Vadoma— my *bunica*."

"*Bunica?*"

"In the language of her family, it means grandmother. She wasn't part of the bloodline, so the only power she had was love." For the first time, Dara sees Mercy smile. The camera zooms in for a close-up, and Dara studies the monitor. A silver filling glints in Mercy's uneven teeth, and the smile lights up her face.

"We know of Vadoma," Brooke says, "from Dara's past appearance on this show."

"I remember her, too," Nuri says. "She found me, explained me how she used Tarot card spread—I think that is what she named—for finding location, but I cannot remember so much the details."

"There's something you need to know," Dara says, looking at Mercy. She can't bear to speak the words she's about to say and looks around as though seeking a way out. "So much was happening—Santee, the fire—there was no time to tell you before."

"Tell her what?" Brooke asks.

Dara takes a deep breath. "Vadoma died trying to protect me," she says. "Diego and I did everything we could to save her."

Mercy's smile fades, replaced by a look of horror.

"She was stabbed," Dara says, "by a man who was after the Jyotisha. Diego was there with me right after it happened. We were too late. I'm . . . I'm sorry."

Mercy stifles a gasp. "Oh—!" All the blood seems to drain from her face. "No, it can't be—stabbed, like my father."

A feeling of déjà vu sweeps over Dara. She's been here before, in Gunarik's cave, telling Mercy that her father had been stabbed to death. "The wound keeps repeating," Dara says. "You said when you were a child, Mercy, someone tried to stab *you*. My mother was stabbed, my dad, Ayon, Vadoma—where does it end?!" She rises partway from her chair as though seeking escape from the fatal chain.

Mercy buries her face in her hands and Dara sees on the monitor the cruelty of the camera, moving in for another close-up. "Move that camera away!" Dara yells. She goes to Mercy, kneels beside her, and hugs her. Dara feels Mercy's breath on her cheek, Mercy's sobs on her shoulder.

Linc trots up to Dara, nudges her arm, and she reaches down to pet him. Dara soothes Mercy's hair and goes back to her seat, glaring at one of the camera operators.

"Parts of my family," Mercy says, stifling a sob, "—not my father, but others—triggered hatred in me. Yes, I hated the world. It's only when I chose love over hate that I learned to heal."

"There was a reason," Dara adds, "why the Lightband brought Mercy and me together."

"And what might that be?" Brooke asks.

"I lost my mother," Dara says, "and pain cries out."

"When it cries loud enough," Mercy added, "love appears." She clenches Nuri's hand and reaches out to Dara.

Dara rises once more and stands by Mercy, holding her hand. "Our superpower is heartache," she says. "Mercy kept the armband safe and guarded it with her life."

"Dara, you've told us about how you finally took back the Lightband," Brooke says, her voice soft and gentle. "Can you show it to us?"

Dara lets go of Mercy's hand and raises the sleeve of her gown to reveal the braided, gold and silver bands, worn smooth by time and touch. She glances at the TV monitor, which shows a close-up of the armband. It begins to glow. A slight vibration of the metal bands is visible on the monitor, and the Lightband quivers against her arm.

A hushed murmur sweeps over the audience.

Why is it vibrating now? Dara wonders. She raises a hand to the Jyotisha and notes its warmth. Her hand, too, pulses with energy, and she looks around, trying to fathom the cause. Is someone on the stage sick? In the audience?

There's a stir from the studio audience. As Dara's eyes search, she spots two figures making their way down the aisle toward the stage—a boy and a girl. As they draw closer, she sees that the boy is a teenager with floppy blonde hair and a puka shell necklace. The girl, smaller and younger, holds the boy's hand and clutches a teddy bear.

Dara breathes a sigh of relief. Security let them through. She stands and calls to them. "Tyler, Mia."

A spotlight picks them up and all eyes are fixed on the pair as they make their way onto the stage.

"We—we have more guests?" Brooke asks, taken aback.

Tyler and his younger sister step into the stage lights. Mia wears a simple light blue dress, and on her head is a blue sequin baseball cap. No hair peeks out from beneath the cap.

Dara senses her gown flowing about her as she rises to hug Tyler, then Mia. Mia's eyes are even more sunken and pale, her arms thinner than they'd been at the EAM Halloween meet-up.

Dara turns to look at Brooke. "I made a promise," she says. "This is Tyler and his sister, Mia. Tyler recognized me on the streets, but says he'd keep my secret if I would heal his sister. At the time, I couldn't do that."

"And that's—is that why they're here now?" Brooke asks, seeking to recover some semblance of control over her own show.

"It was thanks to Tyler," Dara says, "that I was able to reunite with Diego and Linc—and that's a big reason why I 'm here today. One thing I know for sure is that I can't do this on my own."

"Come here for a moment, Mia," Brooke says, softening her voice.

Mia clutches her teddy bear tight and approaches Brooke.

"How old are you?" Brooke stands, detaches the lapel mike from her blouse, and leans down, holding it toward Mia.

"Ten," Mia says.

"Can you tell me what Dara was going to heal for you?"

"Cancer." Mia's voice quavers. "It's called lymphoma."

Dara glances over at the TV monitor and sees a close-up of a woman in the audience, dabbing her eyes.

Brooke turns to Dara and steps aside.

But instead of walking up to Mia, Dara approaches Mercy and takes her hand.

Mercy rises, and Dara hands her the Jyotisha.

Dara is aware of the silence all around, except for the sound of her own heartbeat as Mercy stands. The Lightband glows brighter, and the fragrance—"Like lilies," a woman in the front row murmurs—wafts through the cold studio air. The Jyotisha's light grows brighter until its brilliance dazzles. It lifts from Mercy's hand and floats through the air to station above Mia's head where it shakes with radiant power.

At the same time, a current of energy surges from Dara's wrist into her palm. Her hand shimmers, translucent, and when she turns her palm toward Mia, a beam of light streams forth.

Mia is bathed in radiance, the light sparkling off her sequined hat, the pale blue dress lit.

Dara thinks she catches a whisper behind her, and for a moment mistakes it for her mother's voice. But it's just the soft breeze of the Jyotisha blowing through the stage curtains.

CHAPTER 59

Escorted by a bevy of production assistants, Dara and Mercy walk together back to the green room. Dara looks behind her, but can't see her dad, Diego, Nuri, or Linc. She assumes they've been led separately.

A short, stout woman takes the lead and pushes open the door to the greenroom.

Inside, Dara is taken aback by the sight of half a dozen men, some in suits, others in blue jackets that say FBI on the front in yellow letters. They look like clones of each other—Bluetooth headsets, chiseled faces.

"What's going on?" Mercy asks.

"Hello, Dara." A woman's voice behind them.

Dara wheels around. To her astonishment, standing next to the door is Rachel, the woman from the hospital who'd made sure Dara had the Jyotisha fragment implanted in her wrist. Her hair is secured in a ponytail with a yellow ribbon, and she wears a blue suit jacket, tailored pants.

"You—you're here?" Dara says. "Last time I saw you, it was in the parking lot—I didn't even know if you'd made it. What are you doing here now?"

"I'll explain," Rachel says, "but first we need to get you and Mercy out of here."

She takes several steps toward Dara, walking with a slight limp.

Dara hugs her and feels a holster under Rachel's jacket. She holds on to Rachel for a moment, doesn't want to let go. "It's gotten pretty intense," Dara says, and something catches in her throat, "ever since you helped me to get away from the hospital."

"I'm glad you survived," Rachel says, stepping back to look at Dara. "I always knew you would. You're an amazing girl—but now we've got to get you and Mercy to safety."

Dara hears movement behind her and turns to see an FBI agent, taller than the others, move toward Dara and Mercy with rapid steps and an intense gaze.

"This is my partner," Rachel says. "His name's Jimmy, and his job is to do whatever is necessary to keep you both protected."

Jimmy is already directing them out the door and down a long hallway as he speaks into a lapel transmitter.

Rachel sticks close beside Dara and Mercy, turning her head to glance behind. The other agents form a tight phalanx around them. Jimmy opens a door and they step out into night darkness, illuminated by outdoor security lights.

"Stop," Mercy demands. "Tell us where we're going."

Jimmy, silhouetted in the light from the open door, turns and faces her. "A secure location," he says. "We're dealing with multiple attack vectors right now."

Dara grips Mercy's hand.

"There's no time," Jimmy says. "Let's move."

"Not without the others," Dara says.

Several agents step outside to form a surveillance circle around a black Ford Explorer.

Jimmy's face hardens and he bites off his words. "Your dad, boyfriend, and dog are being safeguarded," he says, "for their protection, as well as yours. This is a matter of utmost urgency and goes high up the command chain. High up. Do you understand? Now, no more questions until we're out of here."

Mercy presses Dara's back and they move toward the Explorer.

The ground shudders and Dara's hair blows. She looks up to see a helicopter descending into an open area of the studio back lot a short distance away. Its landing gear still a foot off the ground, two men in sunglasses jump out and sprint toward Dara and Mercy.

"They're after us!" Rachel says. "Hurry!" She pushes Dara into the rear of the Explorer. Mercy jumps in after her, and Rachel takes the front passenger seat. Jimmy leaps into the driver's seat.

The agents positioned around the vehicle open fire on the men who run toward them from the helicopter. One of the men falls to the ground and the other staggers, then collapses forward face down.

"Go!" Rachel says.

The Explorer jerks and takes off. With a quick squeal of tire rubber, it accelerates away from the helicopter and heads toward the studio exit.

Rachel, riding shotgun, stares out the heavily tinted window, one hand inside her jacket.

"Hold tight," Jimmy says, "we're not stopping."

The Explorer flashes by the guard shack and slides into the street, tires screeching. When the vehicle comes back under control, Dara exhales a deep breath, but holds her unanswered questions in check.

After several tense minutes, Dara leans forward toward Rachel. "You still haven't told us what this is about."

"Isn't it obvious?" Rachel asks. "Those men from the helicopter would have taken you if we hadn't got there in time."

"Who were they?" Mercy asks.

"Santee was so fixated on his own prize," Rachel says, turning around to look at Dara and Mercy, "grabbing element 120-X, that he didn't consider others might figure out how to track the dog, too. That's exactly what happened. The Russians, Chinese—and very likely others, too—hacked into the Caduceus server and were on the verge of getting the Lightband for themselves before Santee's team seized you. When you went on Brooke's show, you hung a target on your chest. We had no way to stop you."

"How come you know all this?" Mercy asks.

"We had an informant in Santee's lab," Rachel says. "Saving you two girls and the Lightband has become a national priority, and every resource was brought to bear on getting you out safely."

"If you knew all that," Mercy says, "why didn't you get us out of Santee's lab earlier?"

The Explorer speeds onto the freeway. On the curved freeway entry lane, Dara leans against Mercy, feels the Lightband under Mercy's dress sleeve. The metal bands are warm and quiver gently, as though in reassurance. At the same time, a tingling sensation travels from Dara's wrist to her fingers.

"We had to let things play out," Rachel says, "and preserve our informant's cover until the end."

They exit the freeway, get back on, double back. Dara sees Jimmy's eyes in the rear view mirror, searching for vehicles that could be following.

"We're clear," Jimmy says.

Rachel lets out a deep breath.

"But didn't you realize," Mercy asks, "that Santee was on the verge of killing us?"

"We got you out of there, didn't we?" Rachel asks. "Right now, we're headed for the Federal Building. Is that safe enough for you? You wanted to know what this is all about." Rachel pulls out her cell phone, enters a code, taps the screen a couple of times, and hands it back to Dara and Mercy.

Dara holds the phone so that both she and Mercy can see the small screen. Picture of a small lobby waiting area with three rows of blue plastic seats. A sign above a reception window—Dara reverse-pinches the picture so they can read the wording on the sign: *Please sign in. If you are experiencing difficulty breathing, advise the desk immediately.* In the photo, the room is packed with people, some on gurneys, many lying on the floor or stretched out on the seats. They are attended by medical personnel, all of whom wear personal protective suits, boots, hair coverings, 360 face shields.

"Where is this?" Mercy asks.

"A small Urgent Care up in northern California, near a rural community. Cutler."

"And?"

"The whole town's been struck with a deadly virus," Rachel says. "It came on suddenly and seems to have hit just about everyone in the area." Rachel looks at Dara and Mercy. "We think that Santee had a lot to do with it."

"What!?" Dara looks at the picture again before handing the phone back to Rachel.

"It appears this was merely the start," Rachel says. "There's more H2ND, or END Virus, timed to release through a series of self-activated, auto-piloted drones. The thing is" —she pauses, and appears to be assembling her thoughts—"we don't know when and we don't know where."

"You mean there's more to come?"

Rachel nods and tucks the cell phone back into her pocket.

"And Santee is behind it?" Dara asks.

"Disease has affected the course of history," Rachel says. "Think of the Black Plague, the 1918 flu pandemic, cholera, AIDS. Santee believed that if you can control disease, you control the future. And the key to that level of control was 120-X—the power of the Lightband."

"I can't believe anyone would purposely cause disease." Dara struggles to grasp the enormity of what is happening. "Just so . . . so he can heal it?"

"Who says he was going to cure it?"

"Huh? I thought you—"

"Having the cure and using it are two different things. Santee believed the sick need to pay a price—loyalty or money. Unfortunately, the fire and explosion wiped out his plans, except that the End Virus is still being released." Rachel pauses, looks from Dara to Mercy. "You two girls—and element 120-X—might be our only hope." She turns her attention to the road ahead.

Dara leans back in the seat as the Explorer drives down the freeway. To heal a pandemic, she thinks, would be Griffith Park and the Old Zoo multiplied by hundreds of thousands. Is she going to have to live with this burden forever? The Jyotisha had come to her, but is it so she can do the impossible—heal the world?

A better choice, it now seems, would be to destroy both the Lightband and the element in her wrist. Maybe then, the chain of destruction would be broken—a chain which stretches from its shimmering discovery in a swimming pool at the Buena Gardens to now bind the world in its tightening grasp.

"Chopper overhead," Jimmy says. "Not sure if it's following us."

"Get into an underground garage," Rachel says.

Jimmy races to the next freeway exit, executes a couple of turns, and tears into a garage beneath a Whole Foods. He pulls into an empty space, engine idling.

They wait in silence. Rachel casts nervous glances toward the entrance. Minutes tick by.

"I think we're in the clear," Jimmy says.

"One more thing." Rachel turns to look at Dara. "We've been in touch with Nuri, through Brooke Park."

Startled, Dara leans forward.

"The studio's been cooperative," Rachel continues, "although it goes without saying that Brooke's main aim was to protect you—as well as Nuri.

You might be interested to know that with Nuri's help, we managed to research your mother back to the adoption placement agency. And as a result, we've located a link to someone else."

"Who?" Dara's heart skips a beat, and she looks beside her to see Mercy tense her body as she also focuses on Rachel's words.

"Her name is Crystal," Rachel says. "At least, that's who she became when she was adopted. And we have something of hers."

"What is it?" Mercy asks.

Dara holds her breath.

"A baby bracelet imprinted with another name—her given name—in Russian. A beautiful name."

"Luminitska?" Dara whispers, and feels the rush of blood in her ears.

Rachel nods.

Luminitska.

"My mother's twin." Dara speaks the words softly as though they might break if spoken too loud.

"Our aunt," Mercy says, a note of wonder in her voice.

Rachel leans over the seat and hands Dara a small jewelry box.

Dara lifts the lid, stares at the contents of the black velvet-lined box.

A tiny bracelet lies nestled inside, connecting threads broken. Dara carefully lifts the pieces, arranges them in her palm just as they'd been laid out in the box. On each bead: Cyrillic lettering, the red enamel chipped and faded.

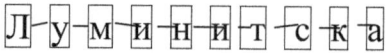

"For a baby's tiny ankle," Mercy says.

Dara senses the present moment shifting, like loose sand beneath her feet. Something about the time-eroded beads, the faded lettering in a language she doesn't know, strikes Dara. A connection sears through her. "How did you know," she asks, "that this anklet belonged to . . . my mom's twin sister? It could've been anybody. I mean, there's the name, which I assume is the same, but—"

"Babies like to put their feet in their mouths, and that means—"

"Saliva," Mercy says.

"Correct," Rachel says. "There was enough sputum residue preserved on the anklet for us to extract a DNA sample and effect a positive match."

"A 'match'?" Dara asks.

"Julia—your mother—was a crime victim, blood from the crime scene preserved for future evidence. Lo and behold—a familial match to the DNA on this baby's jewelry."

Rachel's police-procedural language—Mom "a crime victim"—reduces the loss, makes it seem cold and remote. But it never was. Dara fights back tears. The beaded anklet is more than a baby's identifying bauble—it's a link to her mother. She stares at the baby anklet in her palm.

Worn beads. Red enamel.

A distant time, faraway place.

"Okay, Jimmy, let's get out of here," Rachel says. "Take the streets."

"Where did you say you found this?" Dara asks, her insides a swirling mixture of discovery and apprehension.

Jimmy eases the SUV out of the garage and onto the street.

"From the baby's adoptive parents," Rachel says.

"They must have been hard to find," Mercy says.

"We traced back through the adoption path." Rachel's words are soft, kind. "The child ran away as a teenager over twenty years ago, disappeared, never found."

Dara weighs the past in the palm of her hand: a feather-light trinket that once encircled the flesh and infant bones of her aunt. A door is opening, but she has no idea what lurks on the other side.

She slides the beads back into the tiny jewelry box.

They ride in silence, the Explorer gliding down Coldwater Canyon through the palm-studded darkness.

If you enjoyed reading *Light Guardian*, please be so kind as to post a review on Amazon.

COMING SOON!

Light Conqueror, final book in the *Light Runner* series, follows Dara and Mercy as they join forces to stop a cataclysmic global pandemic.

For more information and to discover more about Phil's next book in the series, go to www.philipbrownauthor.com.

Acknowledgements

Special thanks to my wife, Karin, for her patience, ideas, and suggestions. Without her, this book could not have been written.

Big shout-out to my writing critique group: Shelba Robison, Judith Mathision, Richard Hulse, Charlotte Rossler, and Carol Malone. I keep learning from you and couldn't have done it without you.

Thank you to Larry Rice—friend, editor, reader—for his feedback and invaluable help in shaping this book.